Andy
Blackmore
Police Constable
Series

Going Home

Simpson Munro

This paperback edition published 2024 by Jasami Publishing Ltd
an imprint of Jasami Publishing Ltd
Glasgow, Scotland
https://jasamipublishingltd.com

ISBN 978-1-913798-43-7

Disclaimer
This book contains attitudes representative of the time period regarding language and cultural depiction. This is intended to reflect an accurate representation of the attitudes of the time, and is not meant to cause any offence, just accuracy relating to the time period.

Visit JasamiPublishingLtd.com to read more about all our books and to purchase them. You will also find features, author information and news of any events, also be the first to hear about our new releases.

Jasami Acknowledgements

The Jasami team is integral to the production of all of our titles. They are talented, creative and hardworking. Thank you!

Cover Designer

Holly Richards

Editors

Anton Trock Lundhal

Calum Clarke

David MacKenzie

Review Editor

Bailey Caughey

Special Assistance

Sofia Łobocka

Acknowledgements

I would like to thank Anton, Calum, and David, for all their hard work in editing this book, the third in the Andy Blackmore, Police Constable series.

I also want to thank Michèle Smith, Managing Director of Jasami Publishing Ltd for listening to my moans and groans, keeping me on the straight and narrow with the patience of a saint and for publishing Blackmore's trilogy.

To my small but loyal band of followers this is the one you have been waiting for, I hope the ending meets your expectations.

Shift finished, closing my locker and going home.

Dedication

This book is dedicated to my children and my children's children.

Table of Contents

Prologue	2
Chapter One	4
Chapter Two	17
Chapter Three	35
Chapter Four	47
Chapter Five	64
Chapter Six	81
Chapter Seven	91
Chapter Eight	104
Chapter Nine	119
Chapter Ten	134
Chapter Eleven	139
Chapter Twelve	142
Chapter Thirteen	147
Chapter Fourteen	151
Chapter Fifteen	158
Chapter Sixteen	163
Chapter Seventeen	167
Chapter Eighteen	173
Chapter Nineteen	179
Chapter Twenty	185
Chapter Twenty-One	191
Chapter Twenty-Two	202
Chapter Twenty-Three	209
Chapter Twenty-Four	213
Chapter Twenty-Five	218
Chapter Twenty-Six	227
Chapter Twenty-Seven	233
Chapter Twenty-Eight	238
Chapter Twenty-Nine	244
Epilogue	248
Ranking of Police Officers	253
Glaswegian	254
Japanese Phrases	255
About the Author	256

Prologue

When Acting Detective Constable Andrew Blackmore's secondment ended, little did he know that he had been watched from start to finish by senior officers at police headquarters who knew of his relationship with Susan Berger and her family. They also knew that with his style of policing, albeit a bit dubious at times, he was the one, with the right guidance, who could bring a new major inquiry to a successful conclusion. This despite his lack of experience.

As ADC Blackmore left the Criminal Investigation Department for the last time, he thanked his colleagues for their commitment to him and for passing on their knowledge to enhance his career. He was looking forward to going home to his shift at Bankvale Police Office and a life without his beloved Susan Berger.

Following the death of Susan, Andy decided that he would have a week away from everything and everyone, booking a holiday on his beloved island of Tenerife. The week he planned for peace and quiet did not go as expected when he met old flame Catherine Smith and her friends.

In just over two and a half short years in the job, he had made an impact on senior officers, but he had also become a major target for those within and outwith the police service who had secrets to conceal. Despite everything that had happened professionally and personally, Andy knew he was returning to work with colleagues and friends.

Part One

Andy's Return

Chapter One

It was at the start of July 1982 that Andy was rostered to return to Bankvale after his secondment to the Criminal Investigation Department. Following the biggest eye-opener about life in the service, Andy was going home to his shift. He had been out on the streets with these people since day one; these were the people he knew he could trust, but his experience with the CID proved to him that he couldn't trust anyone in this job where there was very sensitive information involved and the main players were of importance in various walks of life.

As he entered his flat, his telephone answering machine indicator was flashing, displaying a backlog of missed messages. That could wait until he was ready; it had already waited a week following his break in Tenerife, so a few hours more would not make a difference.

He threw his bag to the kitchen floor, as virtually everything in it needed washed. The one bag he did not throw down was the bag containing his allowance of duty-free brandy.

The washing machine churned around, his clothes being thrown from side to side, like his recent past, removing the black sand from the beach in Tenerife. He went to make a cup of tea. The milk in the fridge had turned sour in his absence, so he had to make do with tea sans milk. *Susan would have loved this, me drinking tea without milk,* he thought to himself, as he sauntered back into the living room.

"Okay," he sighed, going to the answering machine and pushing the play button.

The first three calls were from June, who sounded increasingly anxious with each call. Weirdly, there was also one from his brother.

"Andy, it's June. For Christ's sake, mate, call me!"

"Andy, this is Colin Berger. Call me please as a matter of urgency."

"Andy, it's Catherine. Can you call me please when you get home? I'm on night shift; I normally get up just after four o'clock, so any time then." *This was the call he was waiting on. Este es tu destino,* he thought, *this is your destiny.*

His first call was to June to find out what all the anxiety was about.

"Hi, this is June, I'm not here at the moment, so please leave your message and I'll get back to you as soon as possible," her answering machine responded.

"June, this is Andy. Call me back, please," was his short, sharp message, which was interrupted as June quickly picked up her phone.

"Andy, where the hell have you been?! I've been trying to contact you for a week!"

"I'm on annual leave, so I flew to Tenerife."

"You did what?" she exclaimed.

"I went to Tenerife, to Las Americas."

"Did you tell anyone you were going?"

"No, I just went away, June. What's this all about?"

"Can I come and see you, please?" she pleaded.

"Tonight?" His tone concerned.

"Yes, we have to talk and not on the phone."

"Yeah, sure, if it's that important." He hung up, then dialled Catherine's number.

"Hello Catherine."

"Hi Andy, I wasn't sure if you'd call or not after getting back."

"I believe we have a wedding to attend on Saturday together if the invite still stands?"

"Yes, of course it does. I'm on nights tonight; maybe tomorrow you would like to have dinner here and meet Barry again. I told him I met you in Tenerife and he's looking forward to seeing you."

"Yeah, that would be nice, and we can make arrangements for the wedding."

"There's something you should know about that before we go. It's not local."

"Okay, no problem. I'll see you tomorrow and you can fill me in with the details. Bye for now."

A broad smile crossed her face, happy that Andy had telephoned her.

Later that evening, the doorbell rang at Andy's flat.

Andy opened the door and June quickly brushed past him with an anxious look on her face.

"How was your holiday?"

"Fine thanks, but that's not the reason you're here, is it?"

"No, of course not. We, meaning you and I, are in bother – big bother."

5

"I'm listening." Andy sat at the table, June drawing back a chair and joining him.

"Andy, there is going to be a fatal accident inquiry into the deaths of the Bergers. Secondly, there will be an internal investigation into the inquiry you were on, what you know now and knew at the time. I have a friend who overheard a conversation with senior officers and outsiders, and they are desperate to know what you have on them, if anything. They were talking about suspensions, but no names were mentioned."

"Let me make a call, please." Andy began dialling a new number and putting it on speakerphone for June's sake. "Colin Berger? This is Andy Blackmore. I'm sorry I've not called sooner but I've been on holiday over the past week."

"Oh, no problem, Andy I thought that you should know that I had a visit from some of Brian's friends asking me about your relationship with Susan, Sandra, and Brian."

"Friends? What do you mean by friends, Colin?"

"They were senior police officers, Andy, not in uniform."

"Okay, and you said what?"

"That I didn't meet you until after their deaths and, telling the truth, I knew nothing."

"Did they say exactly why they were wanting to know this?"

"No, they didn't, but then they asked if I found anything in the house that could be considered sensitive. I knew what they meant, but I asked if it was anything to do with Brian's work, they just dropped the subject after that, but I think it's the stuff I gave you that they wanted."

"Colin, please never mention that to anyone."

"No, I won't, and if there's anything I can help you with, please say."

"Thank you, Colin."

"Goodbye Andy," Colin replied.

"Bye," Andy hung up the phone. "I take it you heard all that?"

"Yes," she replied. "Was your flat all in order when you got back earlier?"

Andy looked around. "Seems to be."

"I take it your hiding place is secure?"

Andy went into the bathroom; everything was where he left it.

"Yeah, all good, so, how do you know about the pending suspensions?"

"As I said, I have a friend who overheard senior officers talking, including Superintendent McGrory."

"When is all this going to end, June?" Andy sighed.

"When they get everything they want, and there's no evidence left for anyone to see." June shook her head in dismay. "Hey, you're looking good, big man, your break's done you well by the look of it."

"Thanks," Andy smiled. "And before it comes out; when I was in Tenerife, Catherine was there with a crowd of her friends."

"Did you—"

"No, before you say anything, we didn't."

"So, what next?"

"I'm going with her to a wedding on Saturday as a friend," Andy informed her.

"Yeah, right, a friend. Am I never gonna get a shot at you?" June commented laughing.

"You're top of my list, promise," Andy replied with a grin. "Oh, by the way, I have something to show you."

"Now you're talking, big man!" June winked.

"Behave," Andy laughed.

"Andy, I don't want this to sound wrong, or for you to take this the wrong way, but, you and Catherine, so soon after Susan has died, some people might see that as her getting you on the rebound or getting you at a weak moment in time, do you know what I'm saying?"

"Yes, I do."

Andy explained how they met up in Tenerife and that nothing was planned by either of them. He reassured June that they were friends, and nothing more was happening, and it would be that way for the foreseeable future.

"Okay, big man, I believe you."

Andy went into the bedroom and returned carrying the box that contained the Susan Berger Trophy. June looked at it and her eyes filled with tears, as she was so proud that it was going to the school.

"Would you like to come with me to hand this over? you were there when we met at the school."

"Yeah, I'd be proud to be there with you."

"Great, I'll make arrangements with the headteacher, now then, getting back to why you're here, what can we do about all this?"

"At the moment, nothing I suppose."

"Andy, why would they be asking about you and Sandra and Brian?"

"There was no love lost there between Brian and me. He knew that I knew everything about him."

"What about Sheena and Sandra, how much did you know about them?"

"Not a lot at the start, you were there when it all came out in the wash," he replied. "The bit you don't know is that he tried to set me up in a honey trap with his wife Sandra while he photographed us, and he was going to show the photos to Susan to split us up. Then, when that didn't work, he was going to take me to a game's night, again to split Susan and me up. He was determined that we would not get married - he'd all but organised the Games Night plan to be either with one of the girls from the home or with Sandra and Sheena."

"That's evil beyond belief!" She paused, "So where and when did it all come out that this was going to happen?"

"I was in their house when she, Sandra, came in wearing a long black coat - she opened it and she was wearing, er, let's say not a lot.She stood talking to me, telling me everything he had planned and to get out, which I did, then she told Brian I didn't want her, as she was too old."

"How did he react to that?"

"Sandra told me later he was raging." Something occurred to Andy. "Do you know, I've never told anyone about you and Sheena. Sorry, I did tell Susan because she thought that we were having an affair the night I let you stay here."

"Does anyone at work know?"

"Not from me," Andy replied.

"Does Catherine know anything about all of this?"

"A little, just a little. She knows about the deaths, as she heard about that at work."

"Okay," June nodded.

"What about you, have you told anyone?"

June shook her head.

June began to explain how she and Sheena met and how their relationship developed over a while. June had never imagined that she would end up in a relationship with a woman, as she had previously only ever gone out with guys. She said that Sheena was tender and caring, and eventually, she fell for her, and they became lovers. Sheena was different from guys, as she knew how to please her in every way, and through time June learned how to please Sheena. June said that she could not deny now that she was attracted to women, but she was seriously attracted to her "big man" and was desperate to have him back on the shift.

"So, Ms Brown, does that mean you're attracted to both men and women?"

"I'm attracted to women, yes, and I'm attracted to a man. That's all I'm saying."

"Do you miss her?"

"As much as you miss Susan," June replied. "What are your plans for the next few days, Andy?"

"Well, I'm going to Catherine's tomorrow night to see her brother Barry. There is a repair job to do between Barry and me. Then on Saturday, I'm going to a wedding, but I don't know where."

"So, you're going somewhere with your ex, but you don't know where?" June was laughing.

"Exactly," Andy replied. "Do you want to stay over and have a drink?"

"No thanks, that is not a great idea, but thank you for the offer. I have to get back to my place. Some of us have to work tomorrow," she replied, looking at him with her mind in turmoil.

"Geez, I forgot about that."

"We have some interesting times ahead, Andy."

"We sure do, June," he replied as she stood up and headed into the hallway.

"See, that's what makes us so good together," remarked June, opening the door to leave, looking and smiling at her friend. The sincerity in her voice struck Andy.

"Night, you," and Andy closed the door.

The following morning, Andy drove to Catherine's flat, the previous evening with June fresh in his mind, he knew that he had to separate June from Catherine, Andy rapped on Catherine's door with that familiar knock of his that she would recognise. However, it was not Catherine who opened the door.

"Hello Andy," Barry greeted him warily. "Come in. I knew it was you."

"How did you know that, Barry?"

"Because of the way you knocked on the door."

"So, you've not forgotten then."

"No," Barry replied.

"Hey," came a soft voice from nearby.

"Hi Catherine." Andy handed her a small bunch of flowers and kissing her cheek.

"Barry will keep you busy while I finish the carbonara."

"Nice,"

Barry was watching Andy interact with Catherine, and Andy could see that he was thinking. It was only a matter of time before Barry started to question Andy, so he decided he would tell the truth, within Barry's ability and capabilities to understand.

As Catherine sat down at the table with both, she asked Barry if he was glad to see Andy.

"Yes, but he might go away again."

"Barry, when I went away the last time … I never wanted to do that."

"So why did you?"

"Because I had to."

"I don't understand."

"Barry," Andy spoke softly, looking at him and pausing briefly, "sometimes people have a slight difference of opinion, or sometimes they just know or think other things are more important in their lives - these two people don't talk for a while, but eventually they do as friends all over again."

"Did we argue, Andy?" Barry sounded hurt.

"No, we didn't, Barry."

"So why didn't you come and see me?"

"I'm sorry, Barry, I should have," Andy placed his hand on Barry's and giving it a reassuring squeeze.

"It's okay. You're here now," replied Barry as he wrapped the pasta around his fork.

"Thank you."

"Are you going to see Catherine again?"

"Maybe."

"That's good. She's missed you."

"How do you know that, Barry?" glancing at Catherine with a smile.

"Because she tells everyone she misses you. She even tells me," Barry had that childlike innocence.

Catherine sat with her head bowed at the table, concentrating on her meal. She couldn't stop Barry talking about her, but at least he was saying the things to Andy that she couldn't say herself, Andy looked at Barry, "If, and I say if, your big sister and I get on okay, then I promise you shall be my best friend ever, how about that?"

"Catherine, Andy is going to be my best friend ever if you get on okay."

"Well, Barry, I'll just have to make sure that happens now, won't I?," Catherine replied, smiling at her brother.

"Right, so, the wedding tomorrow," turning to look at her, "where and when?"

"Dumfries Abbey, three o'clock in the afternoon. The other thing is, before Tenerife, I booked an overnight stay."

"Well, I'm sure as grown adults we can cope with that for one night, or I can sleep in the car and just bring a sleeping bag with me. So, shall I get you at about, what, noon?"

"Yes, please."

"Righty-ho," was a familiar casual reply she recalled from the past.

"I'll call ahead and let the hotel know that you'll be doubling up in my room, yeah?"

Andy nodded, looking down at his empty plate, "Yeah, why not?" thinking about the situation and what June had said about Catherine, but it was a wedding with far-travelled guests, and he doubted there would be a spare room.

After dinner, Andy went back to his flat and got his suit ready for the wedding. Considering what he had witnessed on the island, it should be interesting with some of the guests that would be there, and the mother of the bride having her extramarital sessions with the locals.

On Saturday morning, Andy arrived at Catherine's small flat and knocked on the door.

"Hiya, where's Barry?" surprised that Catherine had opened the door; usually, he was first to see who was calling.

"He's with a friend of his."

"Great, let's go if you're ready," lifting her bag from the hallway floor and putting it in the boot of his car.

As they headed south, Catherine explained that the groom was from the Borders and that it had always been his dream to get married in Dumfries Abbey, plus his forefathers had all gotten married there, so he felt it was only right to continue the family tradition.

Catherine got a feeling from Andy that he was miles away during the journey. She knew he was suffering from the loss of Susan but also had a feeling something was bothering him personally. Female intuition she would call it.

When they finally reached the hotel in Dumfries, the sound of the car tyres crushing the red stoned driveway leading to the car park announced their arrival.

As they stepped out of the car, they looked at the large grey stone building that was to host the wedding, the arched doorway that would lead to the reception, and the large stained-glass windows that would give the building that olde Scottish welcome to guests from far and wide.

Lifting their bags from the boot of the car, Andy and Catherine approached the entrance, then upon pushing the large mahogany glazed doors open, they saw the magnificent red and green tartan carpet leading to the reception desk.

"Hi, I have a reservation that was altered yesterday to include another person."

"Name, please," the uniformed receptionist requested.

"Catherine Smith."

"Catherine Smith and Andrew Blackmore, is that correct?"

"Yes."

"Welcome to Dumfries Abbey Hotel," the receptionist greeted them, looking at Andy fleetingly. "Here's your key, Miss Smith. You're in Room 101."

"Thank you," replied Catherine.

Catherine and Andy went upstairs to the first floor. She unlocked the door and pushed it open; they went in and surveyed the room.

"Oh, this isn't what I was expecting." Catherine stated staring at the double bed.

"Catherine Smith, you've brought me here to seduce me with your charms!" Andy laughed.

"No, I've not, Andrew Blackmore!" She playfully whacked him on the shoulder as they put their bags onto the bed. Now flustered, Catherine continued, "Andy, this was supposed to be a twin-bedded room.".

"Right, it is what it is, so let's just get on with it."

About two-thirty that afternoon, thirty minutes before the wedding, Catherine arrived in the lounge of the hotel where Andy was waiting for her, as he had left her in the room to get dressed after he did. Catherine appeared in a beautiful red dress, which hugged her tall, slim figure. A large-brimmed black hat sat atop her dark shoulder-length hair, which had grown longer since their first meeting, and she also wore a pair of black high-heeled shoes.

"Well, how do I look?" giving him a little twirl.

"Honestly? Stunning," he replied, looking into her blue eyes.

"Thank you."

"I mean it, you're stunning."

As other guests sat around waiting before being called into the bridal room, Catherine leaned forward and kissed Andy gently on his lips. Realising what she had just done, "I'm sorry, I didn't mean to do that," regretting her actions.

"Catherine, let's just enjoy the day and the weekend together, please,"

The congregation stood as the wedding couple took their vows and Andy felt a hand slip into his. He looked at Catherine and the years rolled back for him, as they did for her in Tenerife, but this was not where he wanted to be in terms of his feelings for her at this time.

After dinner, the reception got into full swing. While waiting at the bar, Andy bumped into Brenda.

"Hey, how are you, Brenda?"

"I'm good thanks, Andy," she replied.

"Did you enjoy the party in Tenerife?"

"Yeah, it was a good couple of days. Can I say something to you, Andy?"

"Yeah, sure."

"See, Catherine, she's a mate of ours. She loves you, big style."

"Thanks, Brenda." Brenda tottered off, drink in hand, Andy finally managed to order drinks at the bar, and when he turned around, he was face-to-face with Betty.

"Ah, hello Andy, you probably don't remember me, I'm Betty, I'm the mother of the bride."

"Oh, I remember you, alright," Andy chuckled at the memory.

"How do you remember me?" raising an eyebrow, forgetting that they had met while she was in a drunken stupor in Tenerife.

"You don't want to know," he replied with a smile, the beach scene playing in his head.

"Do you know something, Andy? See my pal Catherine, she's brilliant and she loves you."

"How do you know that, Betty?"

"We all know what happened between you two, and she's not been out with anyone since you."

"Really?"

"Aye, and every day since then she's missed you. Now, you go get her!"

"Cheers, Betty," as he brushed past her on his return to the table where Catherine was waiting.

Catherine watched as Andy went over to the DJ, having placed a vodka and orange in front of her and brandy for himself. He returned to the table and sat beside her, looking at the bride with her new husband, who had her final fling with a waiter near the pool.

"Ladies and gentlemen, the band will be back very shortly," the DJ announced as the next song faded in. "This is Elton John with Blue Eyes."

"Come on, Catherine." Andy, got to his feet and offering her his hand before joining the other guests on the dance floor.

"Are you kidding?"

"Nope.".

As Andy and Catherine took to the floor, there were cheers from the Tenerife Party; the men were at a loss as to why, but the girls knew what was happening, and it was a special moment for them, and Catherine, as she held herself close to Andy.

"Hey Catherine, you got your man back!" came a shout from a nearby table.

"Catherine, baby, keep him close this time, or he's mine!" came another shout.

"We love you, Catherine, hold on tight!" came from the bar area.

"This is out of order," laughed Catherine.

"I can tell you something," Andy was laughing. "Your hen 'doo will not be in Tenerife!"

"Oh, I know, you know too many people there," Catherine tinged with a smile. She rested her head on his chest. "Andy B, when I first saw you in the pool at the gym you made my heart pound. I loved you so much because you accepted Barry for being Barry. I hated myself for losing you." She looked into his eyes. "Can I ask you something? Are we back together, even if we have an age difference? Because I don't care about that, I just love you, Andy."

"Are we back together?" Andy echoed, as the song came to an end, and they let go of each other. "To be honest, I need a bit of time to reflect, but that doesn't mean no." Catherine nodded and went over to her friends.

"Well?" enquired Betty.

"We're getting there, but it's going to be a while, if at all." Betty gave her a tight hug.

"Good girl,"

As the night ended, Andy and Catherine held each other closely; it was as if they had not been apart for a day over the past two years. Their time in Tenerife confirmed something special between them and they knew now that they had both lost someone dear to them.

"Oh – my – God!" exclaimed Betty. "I've been watching you two all night, so has my man, and you both look amazing together!"

"Thank you, Betty,"

"Hey Catherine," Betty whispered to her. "I'd do him if he wasn't yours, I told my man that!"

"Oh, for god's sake, Betty!" Catherine laughed at her comment.

Andy just shook his head in wonderment as he looked at Catherine because Betty had a riveter's whisper.

"Ladies and gentlemen, the evening is coming to a close and the bride and groom have some, er, business to attend to, so we'd better finish up," the lead singer of the band announced. There were cries of "One more tune!" and the singer held up his hands to placate them. "Here's one last classic; Auld Lang Syne."

As everyone gathered on the floor, circling the bride and groom and their parents, Andy kept a tight grip on Catherine. The evening ended in true Scottish fashion, with everyone crashing into each other at the centre of the dance floor.

Afterwards, as calm descended on the proceedings, some of the guests sat in the lounge area, where a few of Catherine's workmates joined them with their husbands. They sat around tables that had been pulled together and a few innuendos were being thrown around over drinks.

"So, how was the girls weekend away, then?" asked Brenda's husband, Alan.

"Great!"

"Hey Andy, how'd you end up there?" Alan slurred.

"By sheer accident, I was there a few days before them."

"Right, Mr. B," Catherine whispered, "bedtime before the conversation becomes awkward."

"Nice to meet you all," Andy said, getting to his feet. "I've been summoned."

Inside the room, Catherine noticed a change in Andy's demeanour. He had become sullen all of a sudden and she sensed concern. *Was it him being there with her? Was it what people would think? Or was it work-related?* she thought to herself as she watched him remove his suit jacket and his tie, then sit on the end of the bed with his eyes closed, rubbing his face slowly with his hands.

"Hey, are you okay?" as she was going into the bathroom to change for bed.

"Yeah, nothing for you to worry about."

"Andy, something's bothering you; I'm here for you to share your thoughts."

"They say honesty is the best policy, so to be honest with you; is this not too soon after everything that's happened to both of us? Now, my head is wasted."

"As friends, we shall be just fine,"

"Yeah, I know that, and thank you," as he watched her closing the bathroom door.

Catherine did not know the extent of Andy's involvement in the Berger inquiry and Andy was worried that she would get drawn in by association. She was unaware of Andy's concerns about the internal investigation and the pending fatal accident inquiry. He didn't want to go into that with her at this time and potentially ruin their weekend together.

Chapter Two

The wedding finery had been packed away and replaced with casual clothing for breakfast.

As bleary-eyed guests surveyed the complimentary breakfast buffet some, if not most, were suffering from the effects of alcohol from the night before. Ignoring these effects, however, was Andy who ravenously tucked into his porridge before demolishing a full fry up, followed by tea and toast.

"Geez, Andy, how can you get through all that this morning?"

"Because I need to keep my strength up," Andy smiled "I have to drive us back to reality and working shifts again."

Goodbyes and thanks were shared by all - excluding the newlyweds, of course, who were still otherwise engaged and hadn't made it down for breakfast - before Andy and Catherine made their way back up the road towards home. A few hours later, they arrived at Andy's flat. As he opened the door, Catherine walked in, knowing that she was walking in the shadow of Susan and the ghost of her past there. She looked at the old couch that she was so familiar with from the past. Little had changed.

"Long time since I've been here."

"Yeah, a long while indeed," Andy agreed. "I just want to drop off these bags, then I'll get you home. Would you like tea or coffee or something?"

"No thank you, I have to go get Barry before I settle for the day," she replied, running her forefinger along the back of the old couch.

"You know that we have to sit down and talk,"

"Yes, I know, and you have to get over what's happened. I have been where you are now, Andy,"

"Do you know your shifts for this week?"

"I start tomorrow night and finish Friday morning,"

"That's handy, my last day's Thursday. So, do we both have the weekend off?"

"Looks that way,"

"Oh," Andy suddenly remembered, "I forgot to phone my brother before we went to the wedding."

"You'd better call him,"

"I'll do that after I get you home."

Andy drove Catherine to her flat, where she collected her car and then continued onto her friends' house to pick up Barry, Andy returned to his flat and called his brother. Alice answered the telephone and the first thing she asked was why they had not heard from him for over a week, so he filled her in on his travels, including the wedding in Dumfries, but he didn't divulge who he attended it with. Alice then handed the phone over to Ricky.

"Hey mate, how're things?"

"Fine thanks, and yourself, Ricky?"

"I'm good Andy, but we need to talk about Mum. I've put the house on the market."

"I'm starting back at work tomorrow, but if you stick the kettle on, I can be there soon."

"The sooner the better!"

Andy got into his car and drove to the East End of Glasgow. Truth be told, he wasn't in the mood for going anywhere right now, but he knew this was something that had to be addressed as soon as possible. Ricky's house would not be on the market long before it was snatched up, as its location was in high demand, so he had to act quickly. Given what had gone on in the past over the sale of their mother's house, a massive rift could occur between Ricky and himself again, and Andy was not sure if Ricky could cope with that in his current state of mind, Andy knew he had to tread carefully.

Alice opened the door, and he saw the stress written all over her face.

"Come in," Alice was overjoyed seeing Andy wrapping her arms around him in a short hug.

"Where's Ricky?"

"He's out for a walk at the moment."

"But he knew I was coming," Andy pointed out. "What's going on?"

"Look at that tan! Where've you been, Andy?" Alice avoided his question.

"In Tenerife; I needed to get away."

Coffee poured, they walked into the sprawling lounge and sat close together on the large leather settee. Alice opened up to Andy. She told him that an estate agent had appeared at the door to evaluate the property; that was the first time she knew anything about the house going up for sale. She was worried about "Mum" and what Ricky was planning for her, Andy asked if he had arranged this move and she confirmed that Ricky had. Alice also let him know that she understood that he was entitled to a share of their mother's house, but she didn't know what Ricky's thoughts were on that score.

Alice gazed into her cup before looking at Andy and telling him that she was leaving Ricky for the sake of their kids and her sanity, and likely to seek a divorce, but the big consideration was the kids. She had received a start date for a new job that would take her back to being a lawyer and getting an income for herself, plus she would be doing some private work on her own to help.

"Well, bro, where have you been hiding out?" Ricky asked as he walked into the lounge. At that moment, Alice chose to leave the brothers together without acknowledging Ricky's return.

"Tenerife," Andy replied curtly.

"You look well."

"Thanks. So, why have you brought me here, Ricky?"

"Oh, I have no doubt your good pal Alice will have filled you in," he replied in a snide tone.

"What does that mean?" Andy replied, looking at Ricky through narrowing eyes.

"It's obvious you two are close like a pair of conniving thieves," Ricky replied. "Anyway, the house is up for sale, and Alice is going to leave me, although she hasn't told me yet." After a brief pause, Ricky continued. "As for Mum, I'm going to look for a nursing home for her."

"And how do you intend to pay for that?"

"From the sale of this place," Ricky answered. "Oh, did you know that nothing came of your inquiry, as everyone walked away from the charges?" He was trying to wind Andy up.

"Ricky, slow down. From the sale of your family home, where are you going?" Andy was concerned about his brother's whole demeanour. "What you're saying is that you're kicking Alice and the kids and Mum out, right?"

"Yes, as a matter of fact, I am"

"After all the damage you've done to your family, this is the final insult," Andy fumed quietly. "Well, I want the first shout at this place!"

"What do you mean?"

"What are you asking for this place?"

"Offers over seventy thousand pounds."

"You're being an arse, so I want Mum's part of the house assessed apart from the main building."

"Are you windin' me up?" Ricky fumed.

"Nope," Andy replied, looking directly into his brother's eyes.

"You're as nasty as they say you are, brother."

"Oh? And who said that?"

"It doesn't matter now. Thankfully, Benny McLaughlin sorted everything out at the Crown Office in Edinburgh."

"Benny McLaughlin from school? He was years ahead of us."

"Yeah, that's him, the brain box. Works in the Crown Office now."

This was a major revelation. The fact that there was someone inside the Crown Office in Edinburgh watching for the reports arriving and having a major say as to whether the accused would face justice… This was something that Andy had to investigate quietly, then take it further, Andy appeared to let his brother's comment pass him by but, Andy being Andy, it was very much foremost in his mind.

"Bro, you'll never beat the system," Ricky continued, pointing his forefinger into Andy's face. "But I know the system can beat you now."

"Do you know something? There's a chance, that's what David was told before his fight with Goliath, tell me something, Ricky. How the hell do you know McLaughlin? He's much older than either of us."

"Think about it," that was the reply Andy was looking for.

As Andy left the lounge, he closed the door on Ricky and shrugged his shoulders looking at Alice. She whispered that she had heard everything that was said and thanked him with a soft kiss on the lips.

"Where's Mum?"

"In her flat," Alice answered.

"Let's go through, then."

Alice and Andy walked through the house, nothing was said between them.

"See before we go in here…" Alice had her hand on the doorknob. "Are you seeing anyone?"

"Now, why would you ask that, Alice?"

"Just a thought," she said, looking at him.

"Alice, this is dangerous ground," shaking his head.

"So what? I'm leaving him."

"Let's just see Mum," changing the subject, not making mention of Catherine.

The two of them went into the small flat, where they chatted for a while with his mother, and it became apparent to Andy that she was fading faster into her world than even he had realised, Andy gave his mum a warm hug as usual before leaving her in her small part of this large house. Ricky was nowhere to be seen, and Andy made no effort to find him as he made his way towards the door.

"Alice, where are the kids?"

"With my parents."

"Tell them I'm thinking of them."

"Yes, I will. Call me, please?" Alice, closed the door. As she turned, Ricky was standing, watching her "Call me, please?" Ricky mocked, before throwing a crystal glass the length of the hallway, causing it to shatter against the door frame showering Alice with fragments of glass. Alice was shocked and her mind was made up there and then, this was the last straw, before she left the house, and him with his alcohol.

As Andy sat in his flat, on the couch, thinking about everything that was going on in his life, he asked Susan for help from the grave to figure everything out and what her advice would be. About Benny MacLaughlin? Another ace card for him if the worst happens. Concerning his sister-in-law, Alice? She was playing a dangerous game, best left alone. With his mum? She had to be the priority. Catherine was his decision alone.

Uniform hanging up, white shirt ironed, the crease on his sleeves running from the shoulder to the cuff like a sharp razor blade - he was ready for the early shift the following morning for the first time in over six months.

As Andy drove to the office, there was a feeling of euphoria and that sense of going home.

There was a parking space out on the road as if it had been reserved for his return. As he entered the office, both the civilian staff and his shift welcomed him back with hugs and handshakes, and even a jovial bit of ribbing from his colleagues, despite being in and out of the office numerous times during his secondment.

"Hey big man, do I get a kiss to welcome you back?"

"Nope Joe, the only thing of mine that'll hit your lips is my right hand," he jested.

"Aw, that's not fair," laughed Joe as he shook Andy's hand.

"Hey, what about me?" June wrapped her arms around Andy. "Welcome home."

"So, you're Andy, then,"

"Yep," answered Andy. "And you are?"

"Your new probationer, Maggie McGill." She shook hands with him.

"Hello Maggie, muster time; welcome to hell," Andy joked with a cheeky smile.

"Andy, chuck it," laughed June. "She's been here a few weeks waiting for you."

"June, you've been here for years waiting for me."

"So have I!" shouted Joe.

The whole shift had a good laugh that morning.

"Andy Blackmore is back guys, fasten your seatbelts!" June announced.

Andy and the rest of the guys made their way to the muster room and waited for the morning briefing.

"June! June, come here! What is it about this guy Blackmore?"

June sensed some fun to be had at the expense of the new rookie on the shift.

"Maggie, if you're out with Andy on the night shift and you see him putting a mattress into the back of the van, it's game on!"

"Thanks, June, I'll watch out for that next week," Maggie commented innocently and looking a little concerned, which was noticed by Joe as Maggie entered the muster room.

June sat next to Joe at the early shift muster.

"What have you been telling Maggie June?"

"Oh, she wanted to know if she would be with Andy on the night shift or if she would be with me," she had a mischievous look on her face. Before Joe could ask anything further, Sergeant Black entered the room "Good morning, troops, and welcome back, Andy," looking at his young officer. Back in the old routine, he went through the briefing papers as the night shift made their way out of the building. "Same teams as before, Andy you can come with me, and we can go over what's been happening since you last graced us with your presence."

With morning teas downed without interruption and vehicles washed a gleaming white, the officers drove their cars out of the yard and headed for their areas, and more than likely their tea howffs - local shops or factories where they would get the local gossip and glean little bits of information from staff and customers to help them fight local crime.

"Come in, Andy," invited Sergeant Black. "Take a seat." Andy watched as the sergeant removed a sealed envelope from his top right-hand drawer marked "private and confidential" with the name "PC Andrew Blackmore" emblazoned on the front in red writing. Sergeant Black opened the envelope.

"This is the first time I've seen this, so give me a minute."

Slipping his right hand into his uniform jacket, Sergeant Black withdrew his Embassy cigarette packet. Without taking his eyes off the first page of the report, he fumbled in his other pockets, searching for his lighter. Lighter found and put to work, great palls of smoke rose towards the ceiling, Andy sat silently as he watched his sergeant go over the report of his secondment in detail, which was compiled over six months, with comments by everyone from his detective sergeant up through the Detective ranks, Andy never let on that he was aware of the reports by DS Anderson and DI O'Dowd, but beyond that, he knew nothing. Sergeant Black was not the sort of person to show much emotion, but as he read through the report, Andy sensed that he was pleased.

"Well, here we go, Andy," he paused. "From DS Anderson, it says simply; 'Thorough, efficient team member. Want him back ASAP.' Andy, he never says that! From DI O'Dowd, it says; 'Concur with the foregoing, the sooner the better. Recommended for a Chief Constable's Commendation concerning a successful conclusion of the wilful fire-raising inquiry.' So far so good, Andy."

Andy watched his sergeant's facial expression change; this was the part of the report Andy had not seen. He watched as his sergeant glanced from the report to him becoming more frequent.

"What have you done Andy, who've you upset?"

"Sergeant, I haven't a clue what you're talking about."

"Well, you've signed and acknowledged a damning report."

"Can I see it, please?" Andy looked. "Page one, yes, page two, yes, but after that, I've never seen this part of the report." He read it; the DCI wrote that he was not recommended for transfer to the Criminal Investigation Department, citing "reasons confidential." The Detective Superintendent wrote; "Having discussed the foregoing with ADC Blackmore's DCI, concur with comment." A Detective Chief Superintendent wrote; "Further inquiry into the conduct of this officer required."

"Sergeant, I've never seen this before," Andy protested.

"Well, you've bloody well signed it," was his terse reply as ash dripped from the tip of his cigarette.

"Sergeant, look at the signatures," pointing at the foot of pages one and two.

Sergeant Black looked at the signatures on those pages, then at the rest, which bore no comparison to the untrained eye and were obvious forgeries.

"I just don't understand what's going on with you, Andy," the sergeant complained.

"Can we go for a drive please down to the loch? There's a lot you don't know."

"Yeah, sure." The sergeant put out his cigarette, got to his feet, and went into the public office. "John, Andy and I are going out, if you need us," telling the station constable if he was required.

"No problem Sergeant."

At the loch, they got out of the vehicle and sat against the bonnet of the car, facing down the loch as the water rippled in the slight breeze. Sergeant Black remained silent as he lit another cigarette and waited on Andy to start the conversation, Andy poured his heart out about everything; the death of Susan; the Bergers; Sheena; the recordings on video; the diary; just about everything that had happened over the past six months with that inquiry and everything that had happened in his family and how it was all interconnected. He even went as far as disclosing the connection between the lodge and those within and the Crown Office.

"With you, having just over two and a half years' service and me heading for thirty years' service, I've never known anyone to create so many waves in this job," he took a long draw on his cigarette "You do know that when you get involved this deep, you're going nowhere in the future. Your promotion prospects died in the last six months for the rest of your career; this will be noted somewhere for the rest of time."

"Do you know something, Sergeant?" Andy took a few steps forward, then leaned against the safety rail separating him from the loch and facing his sergeant. "I honestly don't care. All this cost me Susan, who I was going to marry and spend the rest of my days with, so, really, promotion is the least of my concerns."

"What about the evidence you have, the diary, the videos?"

"Well, that's well covered. If anything happens to me, someone knows where it all is."

"And where's that?"

"That's my insurance. Only one person knows," replied Andy. "As you know, I was disillusioned before and ready to go; this time, if pushed, I'm going to take a lot of important people down with me. I would go back to the building trade gladly, knowing they would be going to jail for a long time. I need to get back to normality in life and on this shift, it's all I ask."

In the car, on the way back to the office, Sergeant Black indicated he was putting aside their difference in rank, and this was now something he felt Andy should know. Sergeant Black informed Andy he knew about his relationship with Susan from day one, his connection to the Bergers, Andy's trip to Tenerife and accompanying Catherine to the wedding in Dumfries, Andy's eyes narrowed as he looked at Sergeant Black.

"The only person who knew about that was June."

"Wrong, Andy,"

"You knew too?"

Sergeant Black smiled. "Andy, I like you; you remind me of me at your age."

"Who told you about Tenerife and Catherine? Was it June?"

"No, it was the Divisional Commander. You were being watched from start to finish; I'll always deny I told you that, though, so you didn't hear it from me. Your report from the secondment, I don't believe for a minute. My old head in this job tells me something is afoot."

"Can I ask something? Are they running scared of me?"

"Yes."

"Well, tell them I'm finished, I just want to go back to normal." Andy paused, turning towards his sergeant, then asking, "Are you spying on me also?"

"No, I'm looking after you, but be careful, Andy, the womanising leaves you wide open to being set up."

That reply was not expanded on, Andy did not question it; he had enough on his mind.

As the car came to a halt in the office's car park, Andy and Sergeant Black got out and leaned on the roof across the vehicle, looking at each other.

"Can I go walkabout for a while, please?" meaning that he wanted to go back on the beat in the community.

"Yeah, sure," the sergeant replied gently.

As Andy worked his beat, he was given a warm welcome back at some of his previous tea stops by old acquaintances, while some others, the local drunks, and petty criminals, were not so glad to see him back on the beat.

Over the next couple of days, Andy quietly got back into the swing of the shift. Although he was a dedicated officer, his mind was rarely far away from his tumultuous personal life.

"Control to Andy," John called over the radio.

"Go ahead,"

"Can you go see Big Barney Scullion? He wants to see you."

"John, I'm soaking wet, tired, and it's half one in the afternoon, can't the late shift take it?"

"Negative, he requested you," came the reply.

"Did he say what it was about?"

"He'll tell you when you get there."

"Aye, roger that, but I'm not gonna waste any time with him."

"That's a roger, Andy, see you tomorrow."

"That sounds ominous," but he got no reply. Barney Scullion was not the brightest guy in the world, so Andy knew this could prove difficult.

"Barney, I'm cold and wet, what can I do for you?" as the door opened to the Scullion household.

"Oh, come in, come in, great to see you."

Barney stood there in his long coat, flat cap, blue suit, shirt and tie, and his big takity army boots bulled to the point where he could see his reflection on the toe caps, Andy wondered if he wore them to bed!

Andy was led into the kitchen, where Barney offered him a cup of tea, but from previous experience, Andy knew to refuse. Barney would have none of it, however, and he poured out tea into two cups that did not look like they had been cleaned in weeks, Andy watched as the scum rose to the top. Barney made his usual offer to Andy to view his war wounds on his legs, and again Andy declined.

"How's your tea, Andy?"

"Great, Barney," pretending to drink it. Then he stood up and washed his cup.

"Barney, what did you want to see me about?"

"It's the wife, Andy."

"Aye, how is she?"

"Well, she's dead."

"I'm sorry to hear that," replied Andy solemnly. "I've been away for a while. When did she die?" trying to be polite despite only having one thought in his head; to get back to the office and finish for the day.

"During the night," replied Barney.

"Sorry, Barney, my condolences." Andy looked at his watch. "I need to go now."

"Aye, nae problem, Andy," replied Barney with a deep sigh.

As Andy was making his way down the narrow corridor to the front door, Barney coughed a little attracting Andy's attention. "Andy, do you want to see her before you go?"

"What do you mean?" Andy answered with his back to Barney.

"She's in here on the couch."

"What?" spluttered Andy.

Barney opened the living room door.

"See, Andy, there she is," Barney pointed into the living room as Andy got a feeling of impending doom.

There lay the body of the deceased Sadie Scullion, flat out on the couch, Andy went over and kneeled beside her. Sure, as fate, to cliché, she was as dead as a doornail and as stiff as a board; she had been dead for hours.

"Andy, look, she didnae eat her dinner last night; I got through the war eating my dinner, she didnae, now she's dead."

"Right, okay, so she didnae eat her dinner, but I don't think that's the cause of death, big man."

"Dae ye no think so, Andy?"

"Well, big man, I'm no pathologist, but I doubt it," replied Andy, trying to keep a straight face.

"Okay, Andy, if you say so," replied Barney, shrugging his shoulders.

"Barney, see when you phoned the office, did you tell John about this?"

"Oh, aye, ah told John that Sadie was pure dead."

"Okay, Barney, nae problem."

Andy contacted the control room and requested that a police casualty surgeon and the local undertaker attend at the house. While waiting on the doctor, Andy got all the details required for a sudden death report that would have to be completed before he went home. His immediate thought was that John knew exactly what he was sending him to, as that was his sense of humour.

"Long time no see, Andy," the police casualty surgeon remarked when he arrived at the house at the same time as the undertaker. He looked over Sadie's body, "Aye, she's dead, a post-mortem is recommended."

"Thanks, doctor."

"Right, Andy, let's get her down the road."

As they carried the coffin from the house, the undertaker decided that the shortest distance between the house and the hearse was a straight line up the grass embankment. Not the best idea for Andy, as he had on leather shoes and lost his footing halfway up the hill, crashing to the turf with the coffin underneath him and sliding back down the hill to the pathway, taking the undertaker with him.

"Use the path, mate, it's much easier!" shouted a local, who had seen the whole sorry escapade.

As Sadie was deposited into the refrigerator pending her post-mortem at the local mortuary, Andy felt a pang of sorrow for the big man sitting up in his house alone. Would he survive without her? They had been together for over fifty years.

When he got back to the office, soaked and muddy, Andy was not exactly pleased with the proceedings of the day, but professionally, he completed his report before heading for home, Andy chuckled as he reflected that nobody would believe him if he told them what had happened that afternoon.

The next day, Andy was on his final early shift before his days off.

"Good morning, Andy,"

"Aye John" grunted Andy.

"Was everything okay at the Scullion house yesterday?"

"I'm sure you knew how everything was before I even got there, John."

John laughed. "Well, you're CID trained now, so I could think of no one better to send."

"Aye, thanks for that, mate, I'll return the favour someday," Andy joked.

Once everyone had arrived, the sergeant announced, "Right, Andy, with Joe on his long weekend off, can you take Maggie out and show her everything?" That brought a giggle from June, which brought an inquisitive look from the sergeant. "Oh, and Maggie, if you get a sudden death call today when you're with Andy, make sure to stay on the path."

Andy knew then that the story of his slide down the hill was out and about and there was no going back.

"Come on, Maggie, have you met big Jessie yet?"

"Naw," came the reply from Maggie, in her broad Glaswegian accent.

"Right, you will once we get the car washed and cleaned."

Later, as they walked into the newsagent's, Andy did the introductions "Jessie, this is Maggie."

"Hey hen," as Jessie hugged Andy. "You should be so glad to be out with this guy."

"How are you, Jessie?"

"I missed you when I was off this beat."

"I missed you too, and that stupid grin of yours."

"Thanks."

Jessie's expression changed. "Andy, I'm so sorry, I heard what happened."

"Thanks, Jessie,"

"Right, come here, Maggie, I'll show you where the kettle is." He turned to Jessie. "Hey, where's the boss?"

"He's away home for a family funeral, so I'm the boss at the moment, Andy."

"Oh dear, I hope the business survives," joked Andy.

"It will," declared Jessie.

After a catch up of events since Andy went away, it was time for the officers to depart Andy's favourite howff.

"See ya, Jessie."

"Sure thing, big man and Maggie, nice to meet you. Good luck with him, you'll need it!" She paused, waiting for the perfect moment… Now. "Oh, Andy, by the way," shouted Jessie as he reached the door, "be careful if the grass is wet today!" She then burst into fits of laughter.

"Thanks for that piece of advice, Jessie," he left shaking his head.

Andy and Maggie drove around the streets, Andy quizzed her what cases she had been involved in since she arrived on the shift and how she was getting on with everyone. The good thing was that she was positive about everyone who had been helping her out since her arrival, Andy told her that he believed that they were getting paired up for night shift according to the rota hanging in the muster room.

"Yeah, we need tae talk aboot that."

"Talk about what?"

"Us on night shift. June has telt me…" Maggie looked sheepish.

"Told you what, Maggie?"

"This is awkward, erm… She telt me aboot your reputation wae the lassies, aboot taking a mattress in the back of the van."

"Oh really?"

"Andy, I have a man, ah've been wae him for years."

"What else did June say?"

"Nuthin. Well, er… She said you were hung like a horse."

"Maggie, listen to me, I love June to bits; she's my best mate here, but she's a massive wind-up merchant, and you being new here, she's winding you up big style."

"You're kidding me, Andy?" she exclaimed, putting her hand to her mouth.

"Nope. So, here's what you and I are going to do."

Andy and Maggie took their break, they went into the kitchen.

"June, can I have a word with you, please, before you go back out?" as she walked towards the ladies' toilets.

A few minutes later, June and Maggie came back into the kitchen together. June lifted her jacket off the back of her chair with a parting shout to Andy, "See ya, stud." Andy and Maggie gave each other a thumbs-up; part one of the plan was completed.

When they went back out, Andy told Maggie that he had something to do at half-past eleven, so they drove around for a while before going to the hospital mortuary.

"Whit are we dain here, Andy?"

"I had a sudden death yesterday, so I have to be here for the identification of the deceased."

"Ah've never seen anyone deid, Andy."

"Well, like I was told a few years ago, they don't bite."

"Who telt ye that?"

"The pathologist."

"Aw right, that's no funny."

"Come on, Maggie" arriving at the mortuary. "I'll introduce you to my friend Chic; he makes canoes."

"Hi Maggie,"

"Hi," Maggie looked at her surroundings "Whit dae you dae here?"

"I look after things."

"Andy said you make canoes, is that your hobby?"

"Did he now?" Chic glanced at Andy fleetingly. "You can stay and see for yourself later."

"Sounds great."

"Mr. Blackmore, so nice to see you again," Professor Murray swept into the mortuary. "And who is this lovely lady?"

"This is Maggie McClure, sir."

"Margaret, pleased to meet you. I'm Professor Murray, your host pathologist for today," with a hint of his mischievous nature reserved for all new police officers.

"Aw right, pleased to meet ya, pal."

"Andrew, I love her already Margaret, has Andrew told you of his first experience here?"

"Naw, he husnae."

"Sir, I expect you to offer her the same opportunity as you gave me a couple of years ago,"

"Certainly, Andrew" Professor Murray, knew exactly what Andy meant.

Andy told Maggie that they could not be here for this part of the proceedings and had to go back to the waiting room. As they sat there, in walked big Barney to identify his wife, Andy's heart went out to him, as he was on his own. Maggie watched as Barney sat opposite her and Andy; she could virtually see her reflection on his boots, they were so highly polished for the occasion.

"You okay, Barney?"

"Aye, Andy," Barney continued politely, "I'm telling you, if she'd ate her dinner, she wid have been okay."

"Possibly," humouring him. "But who knows, maybe it was just her time to go, Barney. Maggie, can you take Barney through to identify his wife, please?"

"Can you no' do it Andy?"

"No, I'm next."

Barney and Andy identified the deceased as Sadie Scullion before she was wheeled away.

"So, Andrew, before I start, what do you think was the cause of death?" asked Professor Murray.

"Well, sir, according to Barney she didn't eat her dinner."

"Right, we shall see," Professor Murray responded. "Margaret, do you wish to join us?"

"Yeah, okay," as the first incision was made.

"Come on, Maggie," helping her to her feet.

"Oh hell, what happened there?"

"You fainted. Maybe this is not your gig, Maggie. Perhaps we should leave the canoe making for another day."

"Yeah," Maggie agreed as they went outside for fresh air. "Gonnae dae me a favour, Andy, gonnae no say anythin'?"

"Nae problem."

When they got back to the office, Maggie, starting to recover from what just happened, went into the toilet. June had just locked up a guy on a warrant and saw Andy.

"Where's Maggie?"

"In the ladies,"

"You, me, outside," she said angrily. "Right, so she told me what happened."

"Eh, she told you what?"

"Andy, it was broad daylight, what if someone had seen you two shagging in the car?"

"June, it just happened, it was a spur of the moment thing."

"Jesus! See if anything goes tits up for you now, you're on your own, I'm gone."

"Alright," as June thundered back into the office, slamming the door open, before going down the corridor in the mother of all moods.

At two o'clock, the shift ended for the weekend, Andy said nothing about Maggie fainting; it was just one of those things. Everyone has their moments.

"Come on, you, hurry up."

Andy and Maggie were leaning against his car, arms folded, legs crossed, with smiles on their faces, staring at June as she left the office. June was marching across the road towards her car when she looked at them and realised that she had been conned big style.

"Constable Brown, never mess with one Eastender, far less two."

"You pair of absolute bar stewards!" as they all burst out laughing. "Welcome to the shift, Maggie."

"Thanks for today, Andy, I just wish I'd seen the end of the post-mortem."

Chuckling "There'll be plenty more, don't worry."

As June was about to pull away from the office in her car, Maggie put out her hand and stopped her.

Maggie leaned into the open window of June's car and spoke quietly, "Hey, if you're not married, June, would you like to go for a drink Saturday night?"

"Yeah, gimme a call, I could do with a night out," replied June.

"How about Annie's, off Bath Street, say eight o'clock? I have a lot of friends there."

June looked at Maggie and smiled. "Yeah, sure, why not?"

Annie's Bar was not unfamiliar with June, as she had been a frequent visitor there with Sheena.

Andy's joy of getting one over on June would be short-lived as news from the East End filtered towards him in the west, and he still had to have a heart-to-heart conversation with Catherine.

Meanwhile, inside the office, as he finished his shift, Sergeant Black put on his jacket, getting ready to leave for home. He was then handed a list of transfers and promotions by the station constable, a copy of which was left on the sub divisional officer's desk.

Sergeant Black sat back on his desk, flicking through the pages, shaking his head in disbelief at what he was reading. This was the beginning of the end, and the transfers were effective from late shift Wednesday; after the night shift, it would be the last time they were all together. Seven more days together with possibly the best shift he had ever had in his service.

As Andy stepped into his flat, he could hear the answering machine on his home telephone bleeping, requiring attention. Two messages pending, Andy changed out of his uniform and hung it up, while his shirt and socks found their way into the washing machine, Andy packed his kit bag ready for the gym and swimming pool.

With a cup of black coffee in his right hand, he activated the answering machine with his left. The first call was from Catherine informing him that her shifts had been changed and that she would be working over the weekend, but not on Friday night, so, if he wanted to, they could maybe have a drink together.

The second call was from Alice. "Hi Andy, sorry for bothering you, I just needed to let you know that I've - um, I've left Ricky. I'm staying at my parent's for a while. At least until I can get stuff sorted out. Bye - and, oh, hope I see you soon - you do cheer me up." Andy smiled as he sipped his coffee. *Better get a move on,* he thought.

After parking at the sports centre, he leaned into his car and removed his sports bag from the back seat. Locking the doors and slinging the bag over his shoulder, he made his way towards the revolving glass door. His plan was to go straight to the swimming pool to clear his head, but that idea was instantly dispelled when he saw Catherine standing in the reception, apparently enjoying the company of a young staff member going by their relaxed and friendly body language.

"Oh, Miss Smith, you chatting up the young guys again?" observing her wet hair and her rolled-up towel under her arm.

She swung around, laughing.

"Hello Andy, let me introduce you to Eric Shearer, swimming instructor here at the centre. Eric this is my... em... this is Andy Blackmore, a friend of mine."

"Pleased to meet you, Eric," as they shook hands before Eric excused himself and walked away, leaving them together.

Andy just stood looking at Catherine before raising an eyebrow, "New admirer, Miss Smith?"

"Well, Andy, I'm free, single and not getting any younger. I did leave a message on a guy's answering machine, but I got no response from him."

"Maybe because he was on an early shift, and got the message when he got home, then left a reply saying he was free tomorrow night but now no longer sure that she may be."

"Oh, I'm sure that she'll let you know, Andy," walking away, looking over her shoulder and flashing him a smile.

Two hours later there was a message waiting on Andy on his answering machine at home.

"Do you honestly think I would not be free for you on Friday night?" Catherine's tone was teasing in her short message.

Andy smiled before pressing the delete button.

Chapter Three

A ndy dialled the phone.
"Can I speak with Mr. David Diamond, please,"
"Who's calling?" David's assistant inquired.
"Tell him it's Jethro."
"Yes, sir, putting you straight through."
"David, it's Jethro," when the call was transferred.
"Hi Jethro the inquiry is finished. Thanks for your help."
"No, it's not. It's just starting."
"What do you mean?"
"New evidence has come to light."
"How new?"
"Very new."
"How good?"
"Beyond belief."
"In what format?"
"Script and VHF videotapes."
"Are you aware of the contents?"
"Yes, sir."
"Okay, usual place tonight, nine o'clock."

As Andy hung up his phone, he heard a click, which was unusual, and the line sounded hollow as he listened in, Andy strongly suspected that his or David's line had been tapped, Andy decided to keep his appointment, later that day, he entered a busy, workingman's, city-centre bar, Andy sat facing the door with his back to a wall and laid down a plain brown envelope at his side so that it was visible. David Diamond walked into the bar and sat across from Andy, watching him closely.

Two plainclothes police officers, both male, flashed their warrant cards as they approached Andy, telling him not to move. One then grabbed and opened the envelope by his side, finding a copy of the official programme and video from the 1970 World Cup Final inside.

"For sale guys, if you're interested," he quipped with a wry smile.

If looks could kill, the looks from the plainclothes officers would have finished Andy off there and then.

One turned to David "Can I ask why you're here with him, sir?"

"Certainly. For a pint and to buy this video and programme I'm a collector of football memorabilia."

Andy stared at the officers, saying nothing initially, then; "Hey guys, if you want to top his offer, the items are all yours."

Both officers turned and left without further comment. Within minutes, they sat in their car and called into FHQ via their radio; "Tell the boss it was a negative result."

Andy watched as David Diamond went into the gents' toilet, Andy followed and found David in a cubicle.

"Copies," handing a package to David, who put it down the front of his trousers. David went back into the bar and finished his drink before leaving and getting the train home.

"Good morning, Catherine," Andy was in a jovial mood, calling Catherine, pleased with the way his meeting went with Diamond.

"Good morning, Andrew, time for bed for me," Catherine had just finished a busy night-shift in the hospital Accident and Emergency Department.

"Oh damn, I forgot."

"That's okay, I'm just pleased to hear your voice."

"Right, go to bed, please, and I'll speak to you later. Sweet dreams, Catherine."

Andy hung up the receiver and called June. When she did not pick up, he left a message; "Hi June, it's Andy. I have been in touch with the school; we can do the presentation on Monday or Tuesday at eleven o'clock. Let me know what's best ASAP for you, please. Thanks, honey."

Afterwards, Andy drove up the driveway and parked outside Ricky's house. There was no sign of his brother's car at its usual parking spot - Ricky was a creature of habit.

"Hey, come in, why are you back so soon, Andy?"

"I'm here to speak to Ricky about making an offer for the house."

"He's already told me that even if you offered a million, he wouldn't accept it."

"Okay, thanks. I'll go through and see Mum for a little while, then I must go back down the road."

"Yeah, no problem," Alice smiled at Andy she held a special place for him. They had known each other for years before she met her husband.

About an hour later, Andy went into the kitchen where Alice was standing and told her he was leaving. She seemed sad and withdrawn.

"Are you okay, Alice?"

"Yeah, thanks."

"Well, I'm away," Andy said, kissing her on the cheek.

As he reversed his car away from the house, Andy glanced over and saw Alice gazing out the window, an unreadable expression on her face. He turned his car and slowly drove down the driveway and out of the large gates.

When Andy got home, he followed his usual ritual of checking his answering machine.

"Hi Andy, it's June. How about Monday before we go late shift? If it's okay with you, I'll bring my uniform and get changed at yours rather than drive home again. Let me know what you think. See you Monday."

Andy returned June's call and agreed with her suggestion. Then he called the school and confirmed that the presentation of the trophy would take place on Monday. At six o'clock, Andy called Catherine.

"Hiya,"

"Hi Andy,"

"Geez, you don't sound rested at all," Andy remarked.

"No," Catherine sighed. "Gas workers outside the flat, hammer drills digging up the road to find the leak… I feel shattered."

"Do you want to give tonight a miss and we can go out tomorrow?"

"Would you mind, Andy?"

"No, absolutely not. I'll just stay here or go for a pint."

"Thanks. I wouldn't be great company tonight, to be honest."

"I'll see you tomorrow,"

"Yeah, that would be nice."

"City Centre drink and maybe even a quiet dinner or whatever, your choice."

"Sounds great. Bye for now," Catherine hung up the phone.

A short time later Andy's phone rang again.

"Andy, it's Ricky."

"Yeah, I know who you are," he joked.

"This is no laughing matter. I heard you were here again today."

"That's right, I wanted to speak to you about buying the house."

"You're not getting it no matter what you offer, but I believe Alice has already told you that."

"Yes, she has."

"Tell me something, Andy. Why is it that every time you come and go from here, Alice is on a downer? What is going on between you two?"

"Nothing - so get that out of your head."

"She's looking at me now, but then again, she's not going to be around for long." His voice faded as he turned away from the phone. "Are you, dear?".

Andy heard Alice say, "tell you what, I'm going to my parents now, if you're that desperate to get rid of me."

"Ricky, what's going on there?"

Andy heard the phone being slammed down, cutting him off. He was concerned about what might be happening at the house, but he dared not go there for fear of making matters worse, if that was possible, or rousing further suspicion from Ricky.

About an hour later Alice called Andy

"Andy, I'm at my parents' house with the kids. This is the number to call if you want to see me about anything. Please don't worry about me; he never touched me. Really, I'm fine."

"That's good. I'm pleased you called - I was worried about you."

"I thought you would be. I think I'll stay here for a while now."

"Yeah, that's a good idea; it's hard enough on you and the kids already, staying in the house with Ricky is just tempting fate," replied Andy. "I'll have to see to Mum, though, he is getting out of hand."

"He's too far gone now, Andy, and don't worry, I'll be popping in and out to check your Mum is okay too."

"Great. I'll be in touch. See you soon." Andy ended the call.

About four o'clock on Saturday afternoon, Andy arrived at Catherine's flat before leaving a short time later together. They drove back to his place, then walked to the local railway station to head into Glasgow. The train pulled into Queen Street station in no time, which was mobbed with football fans heading home and people heading into the city for a night out like they were, Andy loved this, as he could "people watch" as passengers ran towards various platforms taking them out of the city, where they were going to meet girlfriends, wives, boyfriends, husbands, or secret lovers. Would it be the movies, a club, fancy restaurant, or just out for a drink?

Drivers, guards, platform staff, and ticket collectors all seemed so oblivious to what was going on around them, then again, this was everyday life to them as whistles blew, electric doors closed, and trains pulled away from the platforms, Andy observed everything as he and Catherine walked across the concourse to the steps leading out to George Square and its surrounding pubs. Streets led from the square to adjoining streets and yet more pubs and restaurants before going into the Merchant City, so-called as this was the merchants' area, part of a bustling industrial city; a shipping history now long gone.

Catherine slipped her hand into Andy's as they made their way through the streets, visiting some pubs but watching how much they drank, since they had a dinner date later in the evening. This was one of Andy's "let's see what happens nights."

"This is what I've missed about you, Andy"

"What's that?"

"Just go with the flow, not a care in the world when you're up here in the city."

"Well, this is my town, my city, and I feel at home here and safe."

"How can you feel safe in Glasgow of all cities?"

"I just do, and I know that if required I can take care of myself. Er, I mean, us. Now then, how do you feel about getting something to eat?"

"What time is it?"

"Just heading for seven-thirty."

"Time flies when I'm with you Andy honestly, and yes, please, feeding time,"

"Anywhere you fancy Catherine? My treat,"

"Steakhouse then, please," she responded with a beaming smile.

"Great, let's go."

As they arrived at the steakhouse without a reservation, Andy knew they would struggle for a table, judging by the queue outside and the bustle from within. "Andy, let's try somewhere else, we're not going to get anything here."

"Andy?" a voice said. "Andy Blackmore?" Andy turned and looked in the direction of the inquisitor.

"Geez, Frank Bond, how are you?" recognising his old friend from the building trade years ago. "It's been a few, mate, what are you doing here?"

"I gave up the building trade and got into hospitality; the trade wasn't for me," Frank explained, gesturing to his uniform.

"Catherine, I'm sorry, let me introduce you to Frank Bond. Frank and I worked together for a while."

"Oh, pleased to meet you, Frank," shaking his hand.

"Likewise, Catherine."

"To put it short and sweet, Frank," Andy said. "We were hoping for a table here, but it's mobbed."

"Now let me see, you have a booking for seven-thirty, sir… Come this way, please," while the queue for tables started to lengthen.

Andy looked at Catherine, confused, as they followed Frank through the maze of tables to a far corner, secluded from the other diners and offering a perfect view out onto the street.

"Frank, what are you doing?"

"My guests table,"

"Eh?" responded Andy, even more confused.

"I'm an assistant manager here, and the manager and I have a table each for special guests."

"Wow, thank you so much, Frank,"

"I'll get a waiter to bring you the menu and the drinks list. I'd better get on with things."

"Cheers," responded Andy as they shook hands.

"I'll see you both later, Oh, and you're one lucky guy with a wife like Catherine."

"Frank…"

"Thank you, Frank," Catherine interjected, looking at Andy mischievously, "you're so right."

"You devil," Andy whispered to her.

"Well, let's just pretend at that last bit," Catherine giggled.

"What are you thinking, Catherine?"

"Mrs. Catherine Blackmore's got a nice ring to it, don't you agree?"

"Oh Catherine," shaking his head.

"Sorry, I'm just teasing you," putting her hand on his.

A waiter arrived at their table. He was wearing a smart black waistcoat and black trousers, a white shirt, and a black bow tie. His shoes were perfectly polished, and a small white towel was folded over his arm. He looked every inch a waiter, with his perfectly manicured nails and short cut hair. "Good evening, sir, good evening, madam," was his opening before introducing himself. "I'm Simon, your waiter for this evening. Mr. Bond has instructed me to look after you both. Here is the wine list that we have and here are your dinner menus. I'll return shortly."

"Thanks, Simon,"

"How about the house Cabernet Sauvignon to go with the steaks?" suggested Catherine.

"Sure," said Andy, in his "couldn't care less" attitude.

"Have you had enough time to choose from the wine menu?" enquired Simon when he returned a short time later.

"We certainly have, a bottle of the house Cabernet Sauvignon, please."

Simon brought the bottle of wine to the table showing it to Catherine, "Would madam like to taste the wine?"

"Yes, please," raising the glass to her lips and sipping the contents. "Perfect for me!"

"Sir?"

"No thanks, if it's good enough for Catherine, it's good enough for me."

"Very good, sir. Just call when you're ready to order dinner."

"Thank you, Simon," She turned to Andy, menu in hand. "Starters for me have to be crayfish and prawn cocktail, I can't resist it."

"Me neither,"

"Fillet steak medium with everything to go with it," Catherine requested.

"We are too alike, you know that?" smiling at her. "Make that two."

"Means you can't taste anything off my plate, as you have your own," Catherine laughed.

"See that laugh of yours, I love it,"

"Is it just my laugh, Andy?" averting her eyes from his after a glance at him.

Andy just looked at Catherine without replying, merely giving her a look that said much to her.

"This really is some place," commented Andy, taking in his surroundings. Despite the steakhouse's expansive open-plan layout, with its rustic cobblestones from years gone by, there was not one spare seat to be filled, Andy's eyes were drawn to the large similarly open-plan kitchen manned by what appeared to be an army of chefs cooking steaks over the open fires while pans were rattled on the stoves frying the accompaniments. Frank was busy ensuring the guests were satisfied with the service and watching the staff like a hawk, Andy watched as prospective clients were turned away at the entrance as there was a curfew time to ensure all patrons were given top quality service at least two hours before closing time.

Simon escorted a waitress to Andy and Catherine's table with each of the courses they had ordered, ensuring they were to their satisfaction. Following dessert, two shots of apricot brandy accompanied two cups of coffee. Simon assured them all guests got them to finish their evening.

Catherine looked at Andy; she could read him like a book and knew that his mind was ticking over. "Andy, spill the beans"

"Eh?"

"Spill the beans, what are you thinking about?" she queried.

"Listen, Catherine, on Monday, June and I are going to the high school to present a trophy to the school in memory of Susan. It'll be presented to the most outstanding pupil on an annual basis."

"That is so nice."

"I think after that, it shall be a closed book for me, if you understand what I mean?"

"Yes, I do, and I shall wait for you for as long as it takes."

"Thank you, Catherine," Andy gently placed his hand on top of hers across the table.

"All finished folks?" Simon enquired in a polite, jovial manner standing at their table.

"Not even started," glancing at Catherine. "Yes, Simon, thank you, I was only joking."

"Very good, sir."

Catherine gazed out of the window and then something caught her eye. "Andy," she tapped his hand, still looking across the road where Maggie and June were just leaving a pub arm in arm, holding each other close and kissing briefly as they walked away. "What do you think of that?"

Andy raised his eyebrows for a moment then turned back to Catherine. He was silent - not really knowing what to say.

Catherine broke the silence. "Mr. Blackmore, that was fantastic, thank you so much."

"You are very, very welcome." Turning back to the waiter he requested. "Simon, can we have the bill please?"

"Certainly, sir. Please, follow me."

Andy went with him over to the till and paid for their dinners in full.

"Simon, your service has been exceptional." handing him a healthy tip.

"Thank you, sir."

Andy went back over to their table where he found Frank chatting with Catherine. Both Andy and Catherine agreed that the service and the food were exceptional and that they would be back soon. They also thanked Frank for his table for the evening.

"Andy, next time, book in advance, mate; this is a busy place. But, saying that, you can reserve my table whenever you guys want it."

"Thanks, Frank." They shook hands. "See you soon."

Frank then turned his attention to Catherine. "Catherine, you are stunning. How an ex-brickie ended up with a model for a wife is beyond me," he jested.

Catherine saw Andy was about to speak, so she raised the palm of her hand towards him, silencing him once more. "Right, Blackmore, let's go."

"That's you told," said Frank as the couple left the Steakhouse arm in arm.

"One for the road," was Catherine's suggestion. "Then we'll head for the station, if you're good with that arrangement, Andy."

"Certainly."

As they sipped one last drink in a small bar near the station, Andy asked Catherine if she'd rather go home to her flat or if she wished to stay overnight and he would respect her wishes. "If you decide to sleep in the other bedroom, I am going home; if we are together, I am staying over,"

"Who makes breakfast?"

"Both of us, Andy".

As they made their way into the station, they found themselves face to face with Maggie and June.

"Hey, what is this girly night out?" not letting on they had seen them earlier.

"Never mind us, Tenerife, now this, Mr. B! Great to see you, Catherine."

"You also June, I hear you two are going out together."

"No, Maggie is new on the shift. Maggie, this is Catherine, Andy's em, a friend of Andy's."

"No, not you two, you and Andy on Monday,", trying to save the situation.

"Us, yes, we are. Geez, wondered what you meant there," June being a bit flustered by the question.

"Right, time for a train, Catherine. See you girls Monday."

"Bye June, nice to meet you, Maggie."

"Aye, you too, Catherine," as they parted company.

"Well, Catherine, that was a Freudian slip if there ever was one," commented Andy.

"Nearly," she replied, then burst out laughing. "Did you see Maggie's face?"

"Yep."

"She has no more a boyfriend than I have had recently. She's a girl's girl, Andy."

"Oh well, that's the night shift ruined then!" he exclaimed before receiving a sharp dig in the ribs from Catherine.

As agreed, they both made breakfast in the morning before sitting at the table, gazing out of the window at the magnificent views through the village, out towards the green rolling hills and beyond.

"Catherine, I am moving out of here," his arms folded, leaning on the table, staring out of the window, and avoiding all eye contact with her. "I want a place of my own, but I want it to be big enough to share with someone someday. I want to buy a house."

Catherine looked at him and nodded in agreement. "You are doing the right thing; one step at a time is the best way forward." She looked at him, awaiting a reply that never came. As they washed the cups and plates, there seemed to be an awkward silence between them.

"You okay Andy?" glancing towards him.

"Yeah," still not meeting her eyes.

Soon after, Andy dropped Catherine off at her flat, as they both had personal things to take care of during the day before the working week started again on Monday.

At two o'clock on Monday afternoon, Andy stood in the school assembly hall with June by his side. On a table to the right of the stage stood a gleaming trophy dedicated to the memory of Susan Berger. Teachers, staff members, janitors, cleaners, and pupils were in attendance. Deservedly so, the place was packed.

Mr. Sweeney, Headteacher, rose to his feet and lifted his right hand which brought silence to the whole hall. "Ladies and gentlemen, pupils, may I introduce to you Mr, Andrew Blackmore," before sitting down.

June patted a uniformed Andy's hand in support as he stepped up to the microphone to address the assembly. As he looked around, all eyes were on him, and for the first time in his life, he was struggling for words.

"Good afternoon, ladies and gentlemen, teachers, office staff, cleaners, janitorial staff, and everyone that makes this place the school that it is. Good afternoon, pupils, the most important people in this hall!" bringing loud cheers from the pupils and smiles and laughs from the teachers. "My name is Andy Blackmore. I am a police officer, as is my colleague June Brown who's sitting over there." He pointed to June to his right-hand side. "We are not here in fancy dress, in case you guys are wondering, but I'm sure some of you already know that, since me and June have been in your house." He raised his arm, pointing outwards as if scanning his young audience before turning towards the teachers behind him and doing the same. The assembly hall roared with laughter from everyone, relaxing him into his speech. "Today, we are here to present to your school this beautiful trophy in memory of your Deputy Headteacher.... turning to June he looked at her, "she was a friend; to me, my fiancée, Susan Berger, who died in tragic circumstances recently." Andy took a sharp, deep breath, letting it out slowly. Even from the pupils, you could have heard a pin drop.

"Susan, or 'Miss Berger' as you all knew her, loved this school, the pupils she taught, and the staff she worked with. Susan and I had met a former pupil of hers, and she referred to Susan as an inspiration in her life. So much so that she is now at university, against all the odds, and hoping to become a teacher, and you know something? She will be a teacher soon; I am sure of that.

"It was from this meeting that I spoke with a friend about making this trophy a reality, the one you see here before you today. The reason June is here is that she was with me the day I met Susan in this very building, so she is part of this officer's tale, too."

Andy glanced at the trophy sitting on its plinth. "This is... The Susan Berger Trophy... and shall be presented to the Most Outstanding Pupil annually. That does not mean that the pupil with the highest marks shall win it, but someone that Susan would have chosen." Andy paused, looking around the assembly hall, "It shall be someone who has positively contributed to school life, someone who has been an inspiration to others, either in or out of school, making a positive contribution to his or her community." Andy paused, deviating from his original speech. "So, this is a spur of the moment decision; I am going to ask the local newspaper editor, in conjunction with this school, to be judges, from this year onwards," he paused, "to judge who is a worthy winner of this trophy. So, it doesn't matter if you are top of the class or bottom of the class, you all have a chance to get your hands on this trophy," he said, laughing, cheered on by the pupils. "So, you know what?" June sensed he was warming to the kids and them to him. "You know what?" he said, pointing at his young audience, having them in the palm of his hand. "Teacher's pet might never get this trophy, ever!" he said to loud cheers from the kids. As order was restored in the hall, Andy took another deep breath, then the time came.

"Mr. Sweeney, and June, you too, please join me." Thunderous applause broke out around the hall as Andy and June handed over the trophy to Mr. Sweeney. tears flowed from many of the staff and senior pupils who held Susan Berger in high esteem.

A reporter, Jeannie Allison, was present to report on the event for the local newspaper along with a freelance photographer. Many photographs of the trophy with the staff and pupils were taken before it took pride of place in the school trophy cabinet for all who visited the school to see in years to come.

Since Andy and June had a night shift coming up later that night, they excused themselves from the champagne reception that the staff had organised in the staff room away from the gaze of the pupils.

Tonight's muster was going to be interesting after what Andy and Catherine had seen in the city but more so with the news of the promotions and transfers that Sergeant Black had locked in a drawer away from prying eyes. Although the other shifts in the office knew whether they were staying or going from the Bankvale office, Sergeant Black's shift would be the last to find out their fate.

Chapter Four

That same Monday evening, as the officers filtered in for the night shift, Sergeant Black stood at the front and nodded to each of them as they took their seats. It was unusual for him to be in the muster room first and listening to the chit chat of what each had got up to on their weekend off.

At a quarter to eleven precisely, Sergeant Black opened the proceedings by reporting on events that had occurred in the area since they went off duty last Thursday. Some serious crimes had taken place force-wide, also, and there were several appeals for assistance and information from other divisions.

Drawing the promotion and transfer papers out from under a pile of other official documents, Sergeant Black went quiet. He stood, arms folded, leaning on the table, staring only at the papers before him. He steadied his breath, then, finally, looked up. "Now, I have a further announcement, or rather announcements, to make," he was solemn, everyone's attention on him alone. "This is the list of the force promotions and transfers along with the divisional transfers that the new boss has decided to make at the same time. To me, they're changes for change's sake with no reason behind them at all. There have been three promotions from the office, two from constable to sergeant and one from sergeant to inspector which you can peruse over at your leisure. All the other shifts have been affected by the divisional transfers, including us. As expected, Inspector Smith has been promoted to Chief Inspector at Force HQ.

"Due to the arrival of Maggie McGill, June, you are being transferred to ZA Sub Division Group 1 at Divisional Headquarters." This was met in silence and disbelief by all the officers. "Billy and Daniel, you guys are heading out to ZC Sub Division to be among the rich and famous, along with the Armed Forces housing that occupies the area. They're keeping you both together on your new shift to make your travelling easier." Again, this news was met with silence.

The muster room door lay open; Andy and June, seated together, were facing down the link corridor leading into other small offices. Into view came the newly promoted divisional commander, Chief

Superintendent Ralph McGrory, alone. He was short, skinny, and balding, with narrow brown eyes and thin lips.

Without being obvious, Andy and June tried to attract the sergeant's attention, but to no avail, as he started going into a rant about the way the matter of the divisional transfers had been handled without any thought to the decimation of expertise left on the shift.

Andy and June watched as the "Chief Super," as his rank was known, stood in the corridor, listening to what was being said by Sergeant Black. Both officers resigned themselves to the fact that all hell was about to break loose very shortly. Chief Superintendent McGrory walked into the room, and everyone stood up in the presence of a senior officer "Sit down, you lot," he was a stern little man. "Well, Sergeant Black, you've made your views on the moves to your shift very clear indeed. I think it would have been better if we had discussed this in private, don't you think?"

"Sir, I don't know how much you heard."

"Enough to know that you don't think much of the moves that I have had organised and approved."

"Well, sir, you've removed over thirty years' service from this shift alone, which is detrimental to the training of the probationer constable and young officers I have here."

"As you see, Sergeant, time for fresh blood on this shift. They're too tight, being together so long."

"Is that a bad thing, sir?"

"I don't believe in groups of officers being together for too long; it develops bias and conflicts of interests while establishing a lax working environment, which I cannot stand. You will find out if I'm here any great length of time."

There was a silence around the room as the clock ticked past their actual start time for when they should have been going out on the street.

"So, Sergeant Black has had his say," McGrory boomed out. "What about you lot? Do you have anything to say about the transfers?" He looked around the room. "Nobody, nobody at all? Blackmore, for one so young in service, you always have something to say," he said, staring at him.

"Since you've invited a comment, sir, you'll get one," Andy remained seated.

As the whole shift watched on with bated breath, McGrory, had heard about Andy's nature, "I knew it."

"Well, sir, see everyone sitting here?" Andy was calm and in control. "Since I first got here, they've been great with me. They will always be colleagues and, more than just that, friends. No matter where we are or what office we are in, moving us about will make no difference."

"Anybody else got anything to say?"

"Yes, sir," The eyes were now on Daniel

"Go ahead, then, spit it out," McGrory snapped.

"Andy is right, sir."

"Is that it? Nothing else?" McGrory was quietly seething.

"No, sir."

"Sergeant Black, do your officers not have streets to patrol?"

"Yes, sir."

"Well, get them out, and you and I can go to your office."

"Daniel, can you see to the detail on the sheet?" Sergeant Black requested. "I'll go with the chief superintendent."

"Yes, Sergeant."

As they watched their sergeant lead the irate chief superintendent into his office, the shift had a dark cloud hanging over them and would do until they parted company next Sunday night for the last time as a group of colleagues and friends. What made things even worse was that Joe was off on his "long weekend" and would not hear of the damage done until Tuesday night.

June stayed behind to get some writing done and tie up the loose ends of her time on this shift, Andy got paired up with Maggie, as predicted the previous week. Billy paired up with Stevie, while Daniel was out and about with Brian. John was in his office, as usual, getting everything that had been left by the early and back shifts in order.

As the shift went and updated John with the news, vehicle keys were handed out as per the areas they were about to cover. As they left the office, a heated argument was raging in the sergeant's office between him and the chief superintendent. There would only be one winner there.

All three vehicles, as they left the office, had an air of quietness about them, knowing that this, the shift they had come to call family, was coming to an end after so long. There was not the usual buzz and chat about the weekend's sports programme or being out and about. There was no doubt all were wondering what was going on in the office and dreading the answer they would get on their return.

Andy's thoughts turned to his past two years and the fun that he had had with the shift. Through good times and bad, they had all stuck together. From the first serious crime he had worked on at the graveyard and the resulting parting of ways from Catherine to the attempted suicide of his brother and the death of his beloved Susan, they had all been there for him every step of the way. There were the good times with the arrests they had achieved together and the fun of his first Christmas night out; they were all memories he would treasure for years to come.

"You're very quiet, Andy" as they sat parked up, watching late-night cars go by.

"Sorry, Maggie, I was a million miles away,"

"I could see that, you're going to miss June, aren't you?"

"Yeah, I am. I'll miss the others, too, but June and I have been together for over two years now… We've spent more time together than most husbands and wives."

"You know, I never even gave that a thought!"

"C'mon, let's go for a drive, see what we can get you,"

Together, they stopped a few late-night cars and examined documents; where they could not be produced by the drivers, Maggie got the chance to issue forms for the drivers to produce their documents at an office chosen by them within seven days.

"You never know what will come out of this," remarked Andy. "No licence, no insurance, no MOT… You'll get something out of it." Andy noticed something. "Now this looks interesting. Four up in a vintage car at this time of the morning… Activate the blue light please, Maggie."

As the blue light reflected off the houses on either side of the road, the vehicle in front was pulled over to the kerbside, Andy drew up behind it with his vehicle and parked protecting both him and Maggie, Andy left his car and approached the Austin Mini while Maggie carried out a check on the vehicle via the Police National Computer, noting the details, Andy noticed that the driver's window was down, prepared for his arrival.

"Driver, switch off the engine, take the keys out of the ignition and step out of the vehicle, please," Andy instructed.

"Why?" demanded the driver, who had a Glasgow accent, and given his casual appearance seemed familiar to being stopped by the police.

"I prefer not to get knocked down while standing on the road talking to you, for a start."

"Cop with a sense of humour… No problem, big man," the driver did as instructed then stepping out of the vehicle.

"Do you have your documents on you, sir?"

"Yes." He handed Andy his licence.

"Who do you have in the vehicle with you?"

"Three of my mates. We were up the Lochside for a day out."

Maggie came over and handed Andy her notebook with the name and address of the registered owner of the vehicle, Andy compared that to the driving licence, and they matched.

"Can you check out the passengers, please Maggie?"

Maggie did as asked and the (PNC) Police National Computer checks proved positive, as all four had previous convictions for housebreakings in remote areas, Andy and Maggie, with the driver's permission, searched the vehicle with a negative result. Nothing incriminating at all was found. They were allowed to go on their way, but Andy kept a watch on the vehicle until it reached the dual carriageway, heading back to Glasgow.

"Maggie, something stinks with them and that vehicle," Andy remarked.

"But they had nothing on them and nothing in the vehicle."

"Exactly, come on, let's go."

Andy drove to the roundabout where the dual carriageway started after leaving the two-lane Lochside Road. He parked the marked police car where they could not be seen until approaching vehicles were at the roundabout. This was something Joe had shown him not long after he started two years ago, and it worked a treat for spotting stolen vehicles coming down the Lochside.

"Settle in, Maggie, this could be a long wait."

"For whit?"

"The next vehicle to come through here. As each one goes through, PNC it immediately."

"Nae problem. What are you going to do?"

"Go for a kip while you keep watching," Andy said with a chuckle. "Should have brought the mattress."

"Andy!" exclaimed Maggie.

"Only joking, Maggie." he said with a smile, raising his hand.

About an hour later, Andy got out of the vehicle, as nothing had passed them by in all that time. The radios were silent around the division, which was typical for a Monday night. They still had their property to check for break-ins, particularly the shops, which would take an hour or so.

As Andy walked up to the corner of the grass embankment, looking north along the road which followed the side of the loch, he saw the headlights of a vehicle speeding towards him. He got back behind the wheel of his vehicle and had Maggie on standby with the radio. Engine running, Andy was ready to follow on if necessary.

As the black Datsun motor car went through the roundabout at speed, Maggie was on the radio for the PNC check while Andy activated the blue lights on his vehicle. The vehicle, registered to an address in Glasgow, was brought to a halt on the nearside lane of the dual carriageway. Both officers left their own vehicle and approached the driver.

"All yours, Maggie,"

"Good morning, sir, switch the engine aff and step oot the vehicle, please."

"Why've I been stopped?" the driver questioned as he exited his vehicle.

"It's just a routine road patrol check at this time of the morning. Can I have your details, please?"

The driver calmly provided his details to Maggie, as James McCann, age 29, and residing in Glasgow, Andy circled the vehicle, shining his powerful torch through the windows, illuminating the inside of the car. Lying on the floor of the vehicle at the back seat was a baseball bat and a crowbar, Andy remained silent. He stood with the driver, making small talk, while Maggie carried out the relevant checks. She found several warrants including a failure to appear in court.

"Turn around, sir, and put your hands behind your back," Maggie handcuffed him. "There are warrants out for your arrest."

"What are the warrants for.?"

"Serious assault, housebreaking and breach of peace, failing to appear at court."

"We need to get another car up here with a driver to get his car back to the office."

Within minutes of putting out the call, Billy and Stevie were at the scene.

"Maggie, before we put him in the car, let's get his vehicle searched," Andy suggested. "We don't want any accusations after we get to the office that anything's been planted."

"Okay."

Billy drew the keys out of the ignition and opened the boot, which, upon opening, shined like Aladdin's Cave of Wonders. The boot glimmered with jewellery and other expensive property possibly accrued from a housebreaking, or more likely, more than one.

"Looks like you have a cracker here, guys."

"Stevie, there's a baseball bat and a crowbar in the rear,"

"No problem, pal," before he drove towards the office.

Maggie and Andy conveyed their prisoner to the office for processing on the warrants alone and then would set about the task of searching the Datsun and logging what was suspected to be stolen property in the boot.

With the handcuffed prisoner standing at the charge bar flanked by Andy and Maggie on either side, Sergeant Black stood and watched as John processed him through the custody book pending his incarceration.

"Name, please,"

"Mickey Mouse," the prisoner replied with a smirk.

"Age?"

"About eighty, I think. Aye, eighty."

"Date of birth?"

"First of January nineteen-o-two."

"And finally, your home address."

"Disneyland Florida, USA."

"Thank you for all that, an additional charge of attempting to pervert the course of justice by providing false details can be added to the rest of the charges. Take him away, photograph and fingerprint him, please, then I'll lock him up. While you do that, I'll get the details of the warrants and you can charge him when you get back."

"Hey big man, I was just having a laugh with him," the prisoner protested.

"You should have given him your proper details,"

"Shit, okay. I'm not here for bother, it was just a laugh."

Andy photographed and fingerprinted the prisoner who supplied his details as James McCann, age 29, as per the details he had given Maggie before returning him to the charge bar.

"James here has something to say to you, haven't you, James?" nudging him.

"Listen, Constable, I'm sorry about earlier, the lassie here has all the right details."

John nodded. "Right, I have the details of the warrants that are out for you. Who's doing this one?"

"Maggie is,"

"Who, me?" spluttered Maggie.

"Yes, you."

Sergeant Black was right behind them as Maggie cautioned McCann at common law word perfect before launching into the contents of the warrants issued at Glasgow Sheriff Court. McCann made no reply to each charge. Like many before him, he picked up a mattress and blanket before being led down the cell passageway. His shoes were deposited at the cell door and as he cleared the doorway, Maggie slammed the door shut behind him, its large bolt dropping automatically, locking him in.

"Right, you two, we have to work fast; these are city centre warrants, and we don't want them getting to him first, as this rogue has been up to something in this area," Sergeant Black said in that highland twang that Andy missed so much in the past six months.

Andy explained to Sergeant Black about the vehicle they had stopped before McCann's, how the four people in the Austin Mini all had previous convictions for housebreaking in remote areas, but were happy enough to have their vehicle searched, and that since nothing was found, they had to be let go.

"The reason that vehicle was empty is that the one you've brought in has everything from God-knows-where. Look at the jewellery that's in here. Do you have their details? We need to find out where this lot came from."

"Yes, Maggie has everything," replied Andy.

"Great, now let's see what we have in the Datsun."

About to open the door Andy suddenly shouted, "Maggie, stop! Gloves! No bare hands while we do this."

"Sorry, Andy, never even thought." Maggie stopped pulling back from the vehicle.

"No problem, every day's a school day."

"Nice one, Andy," as he looked on, holding a pile of paper and plastic bags. "Your secondment wasn't a total waste of time, then," he joked.

Andy just shook his head as he went into the car under the lights of the garage in the rear yard. The first item to be removed was the crowbar, followed by the baseball bat.

"Sergeant, Maggie, look at this," Andy paused examining the baseball bat closely "Is that blood and hair?"

"Looks like it," taking the bat straight into the office for a clearer view under the fluorescent lights in the muster room. He placed a paper bag on the floor and the bat on top of it in the empty room. The note read **DO NOT TOUCH.** What may have been blood appeared quite fresh and damp.

Nothing other than the crowbar was found inside the car, so they turned their attention to the boot of the vehicle. It was full of household goods as well as jewellery boxes containing rings and watches of high quality by named makers, ones that only those with real money could afford. Every item was taken into the office and laid out on the muster room floor.

"June, get yourself in here, please, and bring Maggie with you," ordered the sergeant. "June, bring the production book with you and a pile of labels."

Over the next hour or so, Andy and Sergeant Black emptied the boot of the Datsun and the property found was logged in pencil as "contents of vehicle" in the production book. Each item was labelled to save time later, as there was little doubt that it was the proceeds of crime.

Sergeant Black was a man who liked to get things done there and then, and it was hours until the CID would return to duty at eight o'clock. The sergeant was also aware of the warrant from A Division, and they would be picking up McCann for court even though he was brought in after midnight.

"Right, Andy, come with me," His Sergeant heading for the cells in a no-nonsense mood.

"McCann, wake up!" giving him help with the toe of his boot - accidentally, of course.

"What is it?" McCann grunted.

"That baseball bat has blood and hair on it."

"Let me sleep, guys." He turned towards the wall of the cell.

"Right, interview room for him."

"James, let's go," Andy was calm shaking McCann awake.

A few moments later, McCann sat dazed and sleepy in the interview room.

"Anyone got a fag?"

"Aye," Sergeant Black, lit one for him and handed it over. "Right, laddie, listen to me. I have had that bat rushed to Glasgow for forensic examination and on it is human hair and blood. Do you hear me, laddie? Where have you been tonight and who is injured, or worse still, dead?" His tone was low, menacing, and usually wore down even the hardest of men.

Would McCann fall for that one? Andy wondered.

"Are you sure it's human hair and blood?"

"Do you think I'm lying to you?" Sergeant Black growled, thumping the table with his fist.

"Listen, I was never in the house."

"What house? Up the loch side?"

"I have done nothing …. right," as they sensed some panic starting to creep in.

"Right, now where's the house?" Sergeant Black demanded to know

McCann remained silent. He began squirming in his seat, then rubbed his face with his hands. His elbows remained on the table when he started clasping and unclasping his hands. Suddenly he threw himself back in his seat and was still.

"I'm waiting," growled Sergeant Black before banging his fist off the table again.

McCann knew that he was one short step away from a possible life sentence and decided to cooperate. "Go past the hotel to the first road on the left, go up there to the dirt track, then turn right and follow that up to the big stone house."

"Right, get back to your cell, if you're lying, God help you."

"All I did was take the stuff away; the others, they went in, then left in another car."

"What kind of car?"

"A mini, just a wee mini."

McCann did not realise that Andy and Maggie had already stopped the car and they had the occupant's details.

"John, get the details of all the scoundrels in that car from Maggie, get their divisions to detain them as soon as possible on suspicion of housebreaking to start with," Sergeant Black barked. "Maggie, you come with us in case we need you."

Sergeant Black got into the driver's seat of his car and set off with Andy and Maggie to the house described by McCann. For Andy and Maggie, it was a roller-coaster ride operated by the worst driver they had ever sat beside. How the suspension survived going up the dirt track to the house was beyond belief.

As they got to the house, the front door was slightly ajar, and the lights were on both upstairs and downstairs. The scene that met them was disturbing as they made their way around the house. The downstairs rooms had been ransacked by the thieves looking for valuables. A concealed hole in the wall safe had been opened without force, indicating that it had been opened by someone with the combination number for the lock. In the kitchen, lay the body of an elderly gentleman. A visual examination by the officers indicated that he was dead. There was nothing to indicate he had been hit by the baseball bat; there were no signs of blood on the floor or around his body. Maggie had gone upstairs alone and pushed open a bedroom door, letting out a piercing scream as she did so.

Sergeant Black and Andy ran upstairs. "Maggie, don't touch anything, do you hear!" yelled the sergeant.

Maggie was standing in the hallway shaking violently at the sight of an elderly woman's body lying on a bed with her forehead badly beaten inwards, her hands tied behind her back, and the white bedsheet crimson with blood from her injury.

A deep voice yelled, "Maggie go outside and radio for assistance from the ambulance service and get more officers to the scene."

Sergeant Black slowly pushed the first door open but found it empty. Remaining cautious, he checked the second bedroom - still nothing. Then, as the final bedroom door was opened, Sergeant Black saw the harrowing image of a young woman in shock. Sitting on the bed, partially clothed blood trickled slowly from her nose. Her left eye was swelling and closing like that of a boxer who had been smashed by a right hook. She turned and stared blankly at the sergeant, saying nothing. With trembling hands she slowly pulled the blanket on the bed upwards to her chin, shaking her head from side to side.

"It's okay, we're the police. You're safe now." Sergeant Black's voice was soft and gentle.

"Sergeant Black to control," he called into his radio. When he gave out the code for murder, everything swung into place from the control room, like a well-oiled machine, with the detective chief inspector on call receiving the first call out, followed by many more being summoned to the local office for a briefing at zero five-hundred hours.

When the rest of Sergeant Black's shift reached the house, they immediately sealed the scene to preserve it for forensic examination. Further assistance came from the other subdivisions, who sealed the dirt track road to the house before the major incident caravan arrived later in the day. As the day progressed, officers from the Serious Crime Unit took over the inquiry as forensic scientists combed the house room by room for clues. A detective chief superintendent was in overall charge of the inquiry by nine o'clock the following morning.

Sergeant Black and his shift finished about eleven o'clock, twelve hours after starting their shift, having submitted their statements about the events of the night. The four from the Austin Mini had been picked up and detained in the city centre as they waited for McCann to arrive with the stolen property at a pre-arranged venue.

McCann, who was still in custody at Bankvale office, would be seen by senior detective officers concerning the events at the house the previous evening.

Maggie stood at her car outside the office, waiting on Andy.

"Ah don't think I'm cut out for this, Andy, first of all, the faintin' at the post-mortem, then screaming tonight when ah seen that old wummin lying on her bed."

"Go home, get some sleep, then come back tonight and we can have a shift chat when you get here," placing a reassuring hand on her shoulder.

"Ah dunno if ah can sleep, man."

"June is due out, she might let you stay with her for today," Andy suggested. "See you tonight."

Maggie watched Andy walking away, knowing that she and June had been rumbled from their night out in the city. Next time I'm out with him, I'll find out exactly what he knows.

At a quarter to eleven that night, less than twelve hours after they left the office, they all reported back for night shift, this time including Joe, who was back from his "long weekend" off duty.

"Looks like I missed a busy night," Joe remarked.

"That's not all you've missed, Joe," said Sergeant Black, handing him the list of transfers.

"Tell me they're having a laugh, Sergeant!"

"No, and after the night I had with McGrory, I could be going too."

"Meaning?"

"Let's just say we had words last night. The man's an idiot, just an idiot," shaking his head. Everyone knew that it was a linguistic trait of their sergeant that when he was in a mood, or angry, or worse, he always repeated the last word or couple of words of his last sentence; it made him unique as nobody else they knew did that.

As the muster ended and the shift was about to be dismissed to their duties, Sergeant Black wanted to thank everyone for their efforts the previous evening. Everything had to be checked and double-checked after the tea breaks later, or when the night became quiet.

"Andy, you and Maggie are going nowhere, I have things for you guys-"

"Good evening," said a gruff voice, casually interrupting them.

All eyes turned to see a tall man, who was easily described as being - built like the side of a house and, filling the doorway with his massive frame he smiled at Sergeant Black. Fitted jeans, cable knit sweater and boots that tapped evenly across the floor completed his look.

"And you are…?" Sergeant Black, leaned back in his seat, his jacket unbuttoned, puffing on a cigarette.

"Detective Chief Superintendent Graham Barlow, Crime Squad."

"Oh, sorry, sir," Sergeant Black, straightened up.

"Sergeant, I wanted to address your shift, if I may? Given your relaxed look, you're finished with the briefing," Barlow said jovially, which caused a few chuckles around the room.

"Nah, it's just the way we work here, sir," explained Joe jokingly.

"You must be Blackmore, then,"

"Hell no, sir!" laughed Joe. "He's the young stud at the other end." He pointed in Andy's direction. This brought more laughter as Andy buried his head in his hands, getting a pat on the back from June.

"Okay, listen. I don't do night shifts, gave them up years ago, so shut up for a minute," Barlow requested in a relaxed manner. "I just want to say that today I was briefed on everything this shift did last night; working on your initiatives, stopping cars on a quiet night, getting details of cars and occupants, the recovery of the stolen property, and your actions at the crime scene… It was all highly commendable. As a result, we have five people in custody charged with various crimes ranging from murder, robbery, and rape to minor driving charges, and we are awaiting the result of the post-mortem into the death of the male in the house, but at this time it looks like it could be natural causes, due to the shock of what was happening to him and his family.

"To conclude, well done, everyone, you guys have a lot to be proud of. Now, when your sergeant buttons up his jacket, he can come into the chief inspector's office with Constables Blackmore and McGill," Barlow departed the muster room with a laugh and a shake of his head.

"Not a word, you lot, not a word," Sergeant Black fastened his jacket, doused his cigarette in the ashtray, and left the room. He knocked on the office door. "Come in," called Barlow. Sergeant Black, along with Andy and Maggie, trooped in one after the other. "Take a seat, you guys."

Barlow filled the chief inspector's chair as he sat behind the desk. His thick black hair was swept back from his forehead and hung over his collar. His unshaven appearance hinted to the two young officers that he had been operational for a few days or was an undercover officer, Andy immediately took a liking to this senior officer - he reminded him of his days on the building sites and the people he had worked with. He did not seem to have any airs or graces about him.

Barlow looked at the three of them. "I'll keep this short and sweet for you three; I'm recommending you all for a Chief Constable's Commendation for your actions last night. You have no idea how many man-hours and protracted inquiries you have saved us. Now, whether you get it or not is beyond me, but thank you anyway."

"Thank you, sir, on behalf of all of us," replied Sergeant Black calmly, but bubbling with pride on the inside for his two young officers, - no, for his whole shift. They had made him proud today.

"You're welcome," Barlow replied.

"Whit's a commendation, sir.?"

"A night oot on the bevvy and the chief pays for it,"picking up on her Glasgow slang.

"Oh, 'am up fer that," Maggie replied.

"Aye, and it's no this chief, Maggie,"

As Andy, Maggie, and Sergeant Black started to leave the office, Barlow said, "Mr. Blackmore, close that door and sit down, please." Andy did as he was told without hesitation while Maggie made her way down the corridor with her sergeant.

"Sir, see if this is anything to do with Brian Berger or anything connected to it, I'm walking," anticipating what Barlow might want.

"Gonnae just listen to me for a minute, Christ!" Barlow snapped. "I was told you could be a time bomb." As the two of them looked at each other, Andy was the first to break.

"Okay, who's going first?" That brought a burst of spontaneous laughter from the senior officer.

"Brilliant," Barlow replied, bursting into more laughter.

"Well, sir, rank has its privileges - well, so I've been told," replied Andy with a broad smile. This was the type of banter Andy missed with his mates on the sites and his gut said Barlow was a good guy.

"It has, Constable, so go get me June Brown."

"Eh, what?" taken aback a bit.

"You heard me, get June Brown and bring her here."

Andy found June in the locker room with Maggie chatting, "June, the boss wants to speak to us."

"What about?"

Andy just shrugged his shoulders and walked out of the locker room.

He returned to the office with June a few minutes later, both confused by the whole situation since she had only played a minor part in the murder inquiry.

"Right, first of all, Andy, are you sleeping with June?"

"No, sir, she's gay.

"Right, if you say so, good answer. June, are you shagging Andy?"

"No, sir," she smiled just Maggie McGill her answer remained a thought.

"You two are just what I need," Barlow did not know what to believe of their answers. "Brilliant, a double act. Right, listen to me, you two, I need you."

"For what exactly?"

"You know what. To bring a lot of people to justice."

"You know something, sir?" Andy interjected "This job, this justice system, it's rotten to the core."

"I'm sorry you feel that way, but we're not all that way," a little saddened by that reply.

"Sir, why should we trust you?"

"Because June I have been told that I can trust you both."

"So we should trust you - because you say you trust us? And what do you trust us to do? before Andy could say a word.

"To bring the guilty to justice and to get justice for Kerry and the likes of her."

Andy leaned forward, staring at Barlow. "Kerry? How do you know about Kerry?"

Barlow looked at the floor like a child caught with his fingers in the cookie jar. *Just how could a police officer of his senior rank get caught out like this?* thought Andy. Something was wrong here.

"You two are a team, and I know all about both of you," Barlow looked at them both "Andy, your past relationship with Catherine before the murder inquiry you were involved in at the graveyard. Your relationship with Susan Berger and your subsequent engagement to her. Meeting Catherine in Tenerife and renewing your, er, friendship with her, and June you know everything about that. June, I know about your relationship with Sheena and your current situation…" letting his voice drift away on that one. "The last update was the presentation of the trophy at the school in memory of Susan. June, your friendship with Andy, built up since he started here, is commendable." Barlow turned his attention back to Andy. "Then there is also a little incident in a garage which did cause me concern."

"In what way, sir?"

"Would you have lit the lighter?"

"Sir, as I said to the person concerned, try me." looking into Barlow's narrowing eyes and pausing. "Right, where's this going?"

"How well does David Diamond know Jethro?"

"No comment,"

"Who's Jethro? What's going on here?" June was confused, flashing looks at Barlow and Andy. "Who the hell's David Diamond?"

Barlow stood up, towering over the seated Andy and June.

"If there's anything I can do for either of you, call me."

"Anything, sir?"

"If you come on board, Andy, what can I do to get you to trust me?" looking at Andy.

Andy looked at June and took her hand before replying. "Keep us and the rest of this great shift together, sir."

There was an uneasy silence.

"Okay, Andy, time I went home. I have a murder inquiry to get on with."

Andy requested a private moment with Barlow. June left the office, shutting the door behind her.

"You lot, or someone, has been watching me, and I think my phone's been tapped," Andy complained. "You know too much."

"Sorry, Andy, but you've upset a lot of people,"

"So, I've been told before," before changing his tone of voice to one more soft, "Do you know how high this goes?"

"All I know is, it's high. How high, I don't know."

"Crown Office high, sir?" looking at the whitening face of the detective chief superintendent.

"Do you know who?"

"Benny McLaughlin is the one that pulled the plug on the last inquiry."

"How do you know that, Andy?"

"Doesn't matter, sir."

"If you say so,"resigning himself to the fact Andy would not reveal his source.

As Andy left the office and walked down the corridor, June looked at him.

"What shit are you in now Andy?"

"Not here," Andy murmured as he walked past her.

"Hey, you two, get yourselves over here," called Sergeant Black. "June, get Maggie back here, and you replace her in the car." The sergeant turned to Andy. "Andy, it's time we started getting things together, or we're going to be here for days with all the stuff that was in that car and the follow-up. What was Mr. Barlow wanting with you two, anyway?"

"Another inquiry away from all this, Sergeant, but I think you already know that" wanting to change the subject.

Sergeant Black looked at Andy, "Don't worry, Andy, you're being well looked after."

Maggie returned to the office. Each production label was checked and double-checked for signatures to identify the property recovered in the car, preparing them for court. The statements of Andy and Maggie were checked for accuracy to ensure everything was correct, as this was going to the High Court for sure. Neither Andy nor Maggie had ever been there, and they were rookies in that world of Queen's Counsels, High Court Judges, fickle juries, and tenacious defence lawyers earning thousands of pounds per day. A few others on the shift were in the same boat - what had they all gotten themselves in to?

Would Barlow keep the shift together? Andy wondered. He just had to wait and see what happened. With less than three years' service, Andy felt that he was way out of his depth. He had said to Catherine that when he presented the trophy bearing Susan's name to the school it would bring down the final curtain on his relationship with her. Barlow could change everything... again.

Chapter Five

A ndy arose from his bed and wandered about the house in his dressing-gown, contemplating having breakfast at six o'clock at night. He retrieved the package he had previously concealed, then picked up the phone.

"Detective Chief Superintendent Barlow, please."

"Who's calling?"

"Constable Andy Blackmore."

"Certainly, please hold the line."

A moment later; "Andy?"

"Yes, sir."

"What can I do for you?"

"It's what I can do for you, sir. I have something for you if you can pick it up."

"Do you want me to come to your place?"

"Yes, please, sir."

Within the hour, there was a knock at the door and a meeting between Detective Chief Superintendent Barlow and Andy.

"I want this to end, sir I've had enough. I'm trying to get my life back on track after everything that's happened in the past, so I'm entrusting this package to you to get justice for those who deserve it."

"What's in here?"

"Documentary evidence and a video."

"Does anyone else know about this?"

"Yes, sir, a friend has copies of everything."

"Why?" raising an eyebrow.

"My insurance policy in case I end up like Susan or if nothing gets done about it."

"Thank you for this."

"Can I ask you something sir why are you the only one interested in all of this?"

"Because someone has to do it," glancing away from Andy.

"I think that someone has a special, vested interest in all of this," Andy, looked at Barlow.

"Maybe so, Andy."

"What children's home were you in, sir?" in a soft, caring tone.

"It doesn't matter, Andy. Was a long, long time ago."

As Chief Superintendent Barlow was slowly making his way to the door he turned and looked at Andy "Oh, I forgot to say. Your pal June is staying where she is. There was nothing I could do about the other two."

"Thank you, sir," closing the door behind Barlow.

Every cloud has a silver lining, Andy thought to himself as he drove to the office that night, knowing that June was staying. But it was not up to him to break the news, as much as he wanted to.

"Good evening, Miss Brown," Andy said as he entered the office and opened his locker.

"Hiya," June sounded a bit down.

"What's up?"

"Just seems like the end of the road for us before I move on."

"You never know what can happen in this life." Andy's voice sounded reflective.

"Also, I've decided that I'm not going in with Barlow."

"Me neither June"

June looked at Andy, her brows furrowed, her look confused. She thought for sure he would go in with Barlow and fight the system from within to get justice for Kerry, at least.

"Why aren't you?"

"I've had it now, June. I need a rest away from it all - I need to get my life back together."

"Well, I know a lady that can help you there."

"And who would that be, may I ask?"

"Catherine."

"Right," he replied, shrugging his shoulders.

"We'll always be mates, Andy, sadly nothing more," June jested.

"Come on, let's go."

Sergeant Black went through the day's news in his usual fashion. "Now, here's a turn up for the books." "Our Divisional Commander has had a change of mind. Constable June Brown is remaining at this office for the foreseeable future."

"Good on you, June!" Joe called out.

June stared at Andy, knowing he had something to do with it, but he just sat there, not even looking at her. A little smile on his lips, betrayed his feelings. Going down the corridor, she squeezed his hand as a way of saying thanks. Normal service had been resumed and they were staying together for a while, at least.

The night shift ended quietly at seven o'clock on Monday morning, with nothing of any great interest having taken place. It was a night shift that started with a bang and ended in a whimper. That wasn't a bad thing, though. The past few days had been long and heavy, so having nothing to do for a change was a blessing; it allowed the officers a much needed break.

Andy went to the gym later that day for a training session in his various martial arts before retiring to the swimming pool, where he slowly built up the lengths. About an hour later, he got dried and changed and drove to his flat, from where he called Catherine.

"Hi, do you fancy a lunch date?"

"Yeah, that would be nice, Andy"

"We have to talk about a few things."

"That sounds ominous."

"No, it's certainly not," Andy reassured her. "Nothing to worry about. I'll get you at one."

As Andy and Catherine had lunch together at a local pub, where they dined on a platter of sandwiches, with coffees, Andy focused on the future.

"What do you want for the future Catherine? For you and for Barry?"

"I just want us to be together. What I also want to know is how you feel about the fact that Barry is such an essential part of my life - I cannot leave him."

"And I have my mother to think about. What I really do feel is that together we can get through anything - face any situation, problem, circumstance, and also have some fun along the way."

"So, Catherine does that mean I should go get us a house?"

"If you want to be with me for a long time, then we, and I mean we, shall get us a house."

"Well, I was thinking about that, how long is a long time?"

"With me, a long time, Andy B."

"Well, let's see how we get on together for, say, a week together, maybe on holiday to an island far away. What do you think?"

She gave him a funny look. "It sounds like a lovely idea, Andy…"

"Good, I've booked it for us in September."

Catherine's eyes bulged. "Are you joking?"

He shook his head.

"Andy, I can't afford another expensive holiday!"

"Did I ask you to pay? It's all sorted," Andy assured her.

"What have I done to deserve you, Andy B?"

"By being you, Catherine, we can't change the past, we could have been heading for a future alone, so let's change the future together." *Destino,* he thought, *destiny.* "Also," he continued after a pause, "shall we start looking for a house? Shall we stay local? After all, all our friends are around here, and I can always go back to see mine in the East End."

"Yes, I agree with that. But Andy, are you sure about all this?"

"I certainly am," was his reply. "After all, you'll need someone to look after you in your old age."

"That is so the wrong answer!" Catherine laughed.

"Please, there's something I have to tell you."

Over the next hour or so, Andy told Catherine everything about Colin and Sandra Berger, the abuse inquiry, all those associated with it, including Sheena and her relationship with Sandra and June.

Catherine sat stunned not realising how much pain and hurt he had been through.

Andy continued the story, about the evidence that was uncovered in the Berger house. Although he had previously told her that the presentation of the trophy to the school would be closure for him, the new evidence opened the whole sordid sorry tale again.

"Now I am being dealt with by Barlow and I really do think it is time to move on."

"Why are you telling me all this now, Andy?" She took his hand and stared into his eyes.

"Because I feel I have to lay everything bare now that it's over, and I trust you in case anything happens to me, and if it does, you must talk to June." His head was down as he gazed at Catherine's hand in his.

"What makes you think that anything could happen to you?" Catherine was concerned.

"I have caused a great amount of personal damage to many individuals and their reputations, and I've since been reliably informed that I am being well looked after.

"Now, you know the way our jobs work; the rumour mill will start, there's nothing more certain. Just remember, you know nothing about anything."

"Tell me something, Andy. What if, just what if, Barlow comes to you and asks for your help?" She paused. "You know more about this than the whole force put together."

Andy shook his head very slowly, his lips sealed together. He listened closely, but never took his eyes off their hands.

"Right, whether you like it or not, I am going to tell you something," drawing Andy's attention away from their hands to meet her eyes. This was a side of Catherine he had never seen or heard before; it was more her tone of voice as he waited on her to speak.

"I think," she paused, looking at Andy taking a deep breath, "I think that Barlow will come for you, and I want you to take the opportunity to be part of something massive. You have nothing to lose; you must close this chapter in your life. This is not about getting revenge for Susan or Kerry or anyone else, this is about getting them justice, something that you signed up to the job for, Andy, and if you are concerned about us, forget it. I will be with you every step of the way."

"I don't know, to be honest. But I don't think that'll ever happen, as he's with the Serious."

Catherine nodded as she knew he meant the Serious Crime Unit. "Okay, let's put it this way, if he does not seek your help, would you be disappointed?"

"Being honest, probably. I would like to be able to refuse the offer rather than be left out in the cold entirely."

"I think, being straight with you, if this inquiry gets underway without you, your body will be in Bankvale while your head will be in whatever office the inquiry is going to be run out of, just dying to know every detail of what's happening there."

Andy sat looking at Catherine and with a smile, "Has Barlow put you up to this, trying to persuade me to join him?"

"Never met the man, Andy, honestly."

"If the offer comes, I will decide then."

"Right, Andy let's get off this subject for a bit and go do something."

"What do you want to do now?".

"Let's go see Barry."

"I wasn't expecting that," she smiled.

When they arrived at her place, Catherine opened the front door and shouted that Andy was with her. Barry clambered down the stairs from his bedroom.

"Hey Andy, have you been out with Catherine?" Barry's voice was excited.

"Yes, I have."

"Barry, we want to speak with you,"

Catherine and Andy sat with Barry and told him of their plans. Barry told them that he understood what they were saying, and he was happy they were together.

"Can I stay here, Catherine?" Barry was nervously rubbing his hands together.

"Are you sure you'd like to stay on your own, Barry?"

"Erm, maybe not," looking towards the floor.

"Would you like to live with other people?"

"Yes, that sounds nice, if I can't stay here."

"I'll see if you can stay here or live with other people," Catherine voice was breaking.

"Will you and Andy visit me?"

"Of course, Barry, of course, we will visit you here or wherever you are," hugging him tightly as tears started to roll down her cheeks.

"Okay, then," returning her tight cuddle.

Catherine went into the kitchen, tears streaming down her face at the thought of leaving Barry permanently for the first time, Andy followed her and held her close.

"Would you like to come with me tomorrow to meet Ricky? we must get Mum sorted."

"Yes, I'd like to meet him, and especially your mum."

As Andy took that familiar turn through the gates and up the driveway, Ricky's Mercedes, with its personalised "RB" licence plate, sat in the driveway.

"Wow," Catherine remarked, looking at the large sandstone villa. "Most impressive."

"Yeah, this is what it was like to be well off at one time,"

"What does that mean?"

"I'll tell you on the way home," he muttered.

Andy tried to open the door, but it was locked. That was unusual; something was wrong. He took a silent deep breath, steeling himself for the worst, and rang the bell. Through the glass, he saw Ricky approaching; he looked dishevelled and unshaven and suffering from a hangover. It was Catherine's first visit, and this was the last thing Andy needed.

"Hello," swinging the large door open.

"Hi," as Ricky walked away.

"Come into the parlour, have a drink, join the party," His behaviour was erratic, arms outstretched and mumbling to himself.

Andy glanced at Catherine, and she read the signal that this was not what Andy had planned at all, Andy looked around the kitchen, which bore no resemblance to the kitchen he had seen the last time he was here. Empty whisky bottles and take-away cartons littered the worktops, dirty dishes filled the sink.

"So, who is this, Andy?" looking at Catherine. "Are you not going to introduce us?"

"Ricky, this is Catherine."

"Hi Catherine, I'm Ricky, the disgraced brother of Andy, but he'll have told you all that."

"Get a grip, Ricky, where's Mum?"

"Where's Mum, he asks … Oh yes, she's out with your best friend, or girlfriend, Alice, my soon to be former wife Alice. Isn't that right, bro?" slurring his words.

"Ricky, what's going on with you?" Andy was brusque. "Look at the state of this place. Catherine, please come with me," taking her hand.

Andy went through the house to his mother's adjoining flat and looked around. She was nowhere to be found, but thankfully the flat was clean and tidy.

"Well?" Ricky had followed Andy.

"How the mighty have fallen, eh, Ricky? Someone who had everything, and a family to go with it."

"Meaning what?" Ricky snapped.

"Do you know what Ricky looking at you now, I'm sorry I found you that night in the field. I should have let you die. At least Alice and the kids would have a place to live in peace away from a drunken loser like you." Leaning against a kitchen worktop facing Ricky, Andy folded his arms and just shook his head.

Catherine stared at Andy, aghast at what he had said to his brother.

"Yeah, yeah, yeah, then you could have moved in with the widow Blackmore."

"No, Ricky, you'd sold your soul to the devil by then, all this will do is pay your debts" he paused "I'm so sorry, Catherine, let's go."

As they got to the door, Alice's car reached the top of the driveway, Andy and Catherine stepped out of the house and stood in the porch. Alice got out of the car and greeted Andy with her usual tight hug, then extended a hand to Catherine as Andy did the introductions.

"This is Catherine."

"Well, a long time ago he went out with a Catherine; he must like the name."

"Pleased to meet you at long last, Alice and I am that Catherine."

"Really! You're that Catherine?" While surprised she had a huge smile on her face.

"Yes, I'm that Catherine unless there have been other Catherines," she exclaimed with a laugh.

Andy interjected, "Yes, there have been other Catherines; Aragon and Parr and four others, but that was years ago." He wondered if the ladies were on his wavelength as he went round to the passenger side of the vehicle and helped his mum out of the car. Taking her gently by the arm, he led her at her slow pace to the door of the house. Catherine was seeing sides of Andy she had never seen before.

"Hello son," Mrs. Blackmore said.

"Hi Mum," Andy replied. "Listen, there's someone I would like you to meet."

"I've been for a lovely day with this girl," looking at Alice. "She took me for something to eat."

"That's nice of her,"

"So, what were you saying, son?"

"Mum, this is Catherine."

"Nice to meet you, dear," Mrs. Blackmore said, going into the house.

"Nice to meet you too, Mrs. Blackmore,"

"We need to talk, Alice I got your phone call."

"Yes, now, if possible,"

"Is that okay with you, Catherine?"

"Sure, I'll sit and chat with your mum."

"Straight to the flat then Alice?"

"Yes,"

Alice told Andy that Ricky's condition had deteriorated at an alarming rate and that he had gone from gambling to drinking large amounts of alcohol and that, as he saw, the house was a mess.

The door to the adjoining flat opened and Ricky walked in.

"So what's this?" he demanded. "A meeting to get rid of me, is it? Now you got your boyfriend here everything's fine, then, Alice, is that how it is? Did you know that she left me?"

"Ricky, listen, this is not your finest moment, so go back into the house."

"Are you gonna make me?"

"If I have to. Please do not do this, Ricky."

"Hey, the last time we fought I beat the shit out of you, little brother."

"I know, Ricky, I've not forgotten."

"I can do it again, you know," Ricky boasted. "Cop or no cop, I'll do it again."

"I'm sure you can," Andy replied calmly. "Now go back through to the kitchen, please."

"What you gonna do bro? Set me on fire like you threatened to do to my friends?" Ricky was goading Andy as he waggled his finger. "What you gonna do, jail me?"

"Ricky, please go and sit down, I'll speak to you shortly."

Realising everyone was watching closely Ricky slowly moved back into the main area of the house, muttering obscenities as he went towards the kitchen.

"This has gotten too serious now Alice,"

"I know," Alice sighed.

"I think now's the time to see to Mum. Her welfare is paramount."

"Andy, I'm here every day to make sure she gets washed and fed. I also have carers coming in, even though I'm back working again. My parents are watching the kids."

"Even so, she's my responsibility. I need to do more."

"Andy, I have a friend that can help out and get you guys emergency respite."

"How long will that take?"

"Can I make a phone call?"

"Yeah, sure, there's a phone over there."

A few minutes passed, then Catherine returned. "Andy, if you and I go now, my friend has one available place left for an emergency respite admission. All we must do is get a doctor to sign the papers, but I can see to that tomorrow. My recommendation is emergency respite due to deterioration of home conditions and a risk to the client."

"Alice, are you okay with that?"

"Yes, definitely," relieved that something could be done so quickly.

"Okay, I'll phone her back. You guys go pack a bag for your mum."

Alice and Andy went through to his mother's bedroom, where they packed a bag for a short stay.

"You alright Alice?"

"Yes, I'm fine." Alice's slow movement reflected the sadness in her voice. "Catherine's lovely, Andy, and she's a lucky lady to get you."

Catherine returned to the small flat. "Andy, everything's sorted whenever you're ready to go," being as gentle in her tone of voice as she could be.

"Come here, you," Alice softly kissed Andy on his cheek.

"Come on, time to go," he then went to his mother. "Mum, listen to me, please," he said in a way that she would understand, holding her hands.

"Yes?"

"How do you fancy going on holiday for a few days?"

"Oh, that would be nice," she smiled.

"We have found you a place to stay."

"Is it nice?"

"Yes, it is very nice, Mum. A lovely hotel with nice people there."

"Great, when do we go?" looking into his eyes.

"Would you like to go today?"

"Yes, that would be nice, son."

"Mum, what's my name?" he asked her softly, his eyes filling with tears. He waited a few moments for her to reply, looking into her eyes.

"Your name is…" She hesitated, smiled and finished, " son." Then she turned staring blankly out of the window as the trees swayed in the breeze.

"Yeah, that's right, Mum." Andy took her hand and briefly held the back of it against her cheek wondering if she would feel the tears.

Andy guided his mother to the car, Alice and Catherine followed slowly behind them, both knowing in their hearts that Andy was hurting inside. This was the last thing he wanted to do, but he knew it was necessary for her safety and welfare. They watched as Andy loaded her case for her "holiday. "Catherine," I knew Susan, she was so lovely. Now I would love to get to know you - more than I do already, as he used to speak about you all the time when you two were together. Ignore everything that that idiot inside was saying about us. You were then and are now his life. Do you know that when you two went your ways he was gutted? and I mean gutted. Then he met Susan, and everything seemed good, but as a woman I know he never got over you."

"So, does that not demean his relationship with Susan?" Catherine asked bluntly.

"Oh God no, he loved her, don't get me wrong, he did love her, but he was in love with you before you went your separate ways."

"Alice, can I ask you something?" she stopped her before they got too close to Andy for him to overhear them.

"Sure."

"We're the same age, I think, the mid-thirties, right?"

"Yes, that's right."

"Are you in love with Andy?"

"Am I in love with my brother-in-law? Wow, what a question."

"Well?" raising an eyebrow, awaiting a reply.

"I love him to bits… as a brother-in-law."

"Thank you, Alice."

Andy helped his mother into the car and then Ricky appeared at the front door, shouting and swearing, asking where Andy was taking her and what right he had to do that, Andy said he was taking her away for a holiday and they would be back in a few days.

"No way, get her out of the car!" Ricky yelled, marching towards Andy.

Catherine stepped between the brothers; she knew Andy was about to hit Ricky, looking at the way he was standing.

"Ricky, we've just met," now, please let Andy take your mum for a holiday."

"No, she stays here," he insisted.

"Please, Ricky, don't do this."

"And what are you going to do to stop me, you stupid woman?" Ricky snarled as he headed for Andy.

"Wrong answer," Catherine took hold of Ricky's arm with one hand while swinging her other across his neck and her left leg behind Ricky's legs, taking him off balance and flooring him on the spot, leaving him helpless on the ground.

"What the hell!" Andy exclaimed, seeing his brother on the ground.

"Ah, we can talk about this later," Catherine got into the car. "Alice, we'll be in touch. Now, let's go."

As he drove out of the gates of the house, "Catherine, can you tell me where I'm taking Mum?"

"Oh yeah, Lochside Nursing Home."

"Really? Ten minutes from the office, that one?"

"Yes, that one so you can see her whenever you like."

Back in Ricky's driveway, Alice looked down at her husband lying on the ground. "Can I suggest you get up from there before I drive over you," while getting into her car.

Andy drove along the smooth road leading to the front doors of the nursing home. It was a large grey sandstone building standing two floors high, with its white painted timber windows offering extensive views over the home's meticulously manicured gardens and, of course, the loch itself. It was a short drive from where Andy and Catherine lived. This was ideal for visiting and making his mother feel that she was not being excluded, Andy got his mother out of the car, telling her this was her new holiday home. She looked around and caught sight of the loch.

"Oh, look at the water, that's lovely."

As they walked in, the nurse in charge looked up from her desk. "Catherine?" greeting her warmly.

"Mhari, I'm so glad you're here, this is brilliant!" Catherine said. "Mhari, this is Andy, my, erm, friend."

"Pleased to meet you, Andy," Mhari said with a smile and a handshake.

"Likewise."

Mhari and Catherine had nursed together in the local hospital before Mhari left to have her family and thereafter take up a post in the nursing home. She had never lost her charming smile that shone like a beacon of reassurance from her small slim figure.

"Mhari, we need to talk," Andy, you sit there with your mum."

A few minutes later, Mhari and Catherine returned, "Right, Andy, let's get your mum booked in."

With everything sorted between Mhari and Catherine, Andy was delighted with the single room his mother was given. It looked over the loch and the yachts, which would hold her interest. After unpacking her small bag and hanging her clothes in the wardrobe, Andy led his mother to the common room, where other residents were sitting.

"Right, Mum, enjoy your holiday,"

"Thank you, son, who is this girl with you?"

"This is Catherine, Mum. She managed to get us into this hotel."

"Oh right, thank you,"

"What's your name again?"

"Catherine,"

"Thank you, my dear."

"You're most welcome, Mrs. Blackmore."

"How do you know who I am?"

"Andy told me." Catherine put her arms around the frail old lady and gently hugged her. "Thank you for giving me Andy," she whispered into her ear.

"You're very welcome, my dear," pausing momentarily. "Look after him when I'm not here." That sentence shook Catherine as she looked into her eyes.

As they left his mother in the nursing home, Andy drove down the long driveway to the green gates at the entrance.

"Andy, head for my place, please, I have to get Barry fed."

"Sure." There was something about Catherine's tone of voice that sounded strained.

They rode the rest of the journey in silence.

"Hiya Andy," when they arrived. "It's good that you're here."

"Why's that, Barry?"

"'Cause Catherine and I love you."

"Aw, Barry, that's so nice, I love you too, mate," wrapping his arms around Barry's shoulders.

"Catherine says you send people to jail to keep us safe. Is that true, Andy?"

"Sometimes, mate, yeah, sometimes."

"Can you stay with us and keep us safe?"

"Well, that's up to Catherine, Barry."

"Catherine, can Andy stay and keep us safe?"

"Andy, do you want to stay and keep us safe?"

"Barry, for you, mate, no matter what, I'll stay and keep you safe tonight, if that's okay?"

"Yes, that's good," Barry sat down in the living room.

After dinner, they were chatting and watching television when Barry asked where Andy would sleep, as they only had two bedrooms.

"Well, Catherine, how are you going to answer this one?"

"We'll think about that later," Catherine replied. Barry nodded.

As the clock approached midnight, and with Barry in bed, Catherine and Andy retired to her bedroom, with its queen size bed.

"You were the first and the last ever to sleep here, Andy," Catherine told him as they lay in bed.

"I understand because you're protective of Barry, but you... you are so beautiful; I can't understand why anyone wouldn't want to be with you."

"Nobody is interested in a single woman with a brother tagging along all the time."

"I think that's about to change"

"I would love that to be true, Andy."

"Tomorrow, we'll go house hunting and visit a few estate agents, if you want?"

"That would be great. It can be the start of a new life for us. Barry has his club, so we're free to go together."

"There is one thing I need to know, though, before committing to you fully Catherine"

"What's that?" snuggling into Andy.

"Where did you learn to drop a fully grown man, as you did to Ricky today?"

"Oh, just something someone taught me a long time ago at my judo class."

"You did judo?"

"Yeah, long time ago," as she turned off the small bedroom light.

At nine o'clock the following day, Catherine dropped Barry off at his club, where he mixed with other people with special needs. It was there that he was able to be himself among his peers. Then Catherine and Andy made their way to the estate agents.

"Hi," Andy said to the estate agent, a young blonde-haired woman. "We're looking for a house, three or four bedrooms, a living room, kitchen, bathroom, and garden."

"Detached or semi-detached, sir?" the agent asked.

"Let's see what you have and what price range they're in."

"Do you have a mortgage arranged?"

"No,"

"Well, we can help you with that, if needed. We have lots of properties currently for sale, and they say that there is a big hike in prices coming soon, so this is a good time to buy, if you ask me. Here is a book of photographs you may look through. I'll leave you to it, just give me a shout if you see something. My name's Annette."

"Thank you, I'm Catherine and this is Andy."

"Yeah, I know," she looked at Andy "I went to Bankvale High; I remember him."

"Does that get me a discount then?"

"So, how long have you been working here, Annette?"

"Six months now, and I love it. Now let's see what we can do for you."

About an hour later, Andy and Catherine had chosen four houses to go and view. Annette started to phone the owners and make appointments for viewing times.

"Right, possible future Mrs. B, let's go see what we've got here."

"Possible Mrs. B?" Catherine laughed.

"Well, you never know, I might meet someone rich and famous today who will whisk me away," Andy joked, wrapping his arm around her neck in a friendly headlock.

Driving down the street to house number three on their list, they looked around at the neat gardens and the cars in the driveways. There was a feel-good atmosphere about the place. The house itself was a three-bedroom detached villa with a garage. As they looked around the property, they experienced a homely feeling, and the back garden was large, just as requested.

"Can we have a minute, please?" Andy asked the owners, who went out of the room, Andy turned to Catherine. "What do you think?"

"I just get a great feeling in here," Andy nodded in agreement.

The owners returned to the living room, "Okay, give me a price, please, that's acceptable to you and we'll take it, subject to mortgage approval. Will you take it off the market today?" The owners were stunned by the suddenness of it all and agreed to do as requested.

By five o'clock that night, Andy Blackmore was the prospective owner of a house, with just the paperwork to complete through their respective lawyers. The entry date was eight weeks away, but that suited Andy, as he needed to get ready for the move. He also had annual leave to arrange so he could get the place the way he wanted it - then again, it might just be the way Catherine wanted it.

Back at Catherine's, Andy sat facing her and burst out laughing.

"What's so funny?"

"I was just thinking about how much we spent today... Is there enough left for a fish supper?"

"Not sure," joining in the laughter. "So, what are your plans now, Andy?"

"Take each day as it comes, meet someone special, share a new home with her if she'd like that, and hopefully get married. What about you?"

"Well, I've met someone special to me, I'd like to share his new home with him, and hopefully get married because I love him so much."

"You know when Ricky sells his house, I will have money coming to me, so life should be good in the future if you would like to share it with me?" Andy, gazed into her eyes as they sat facing each other.

"Andy Blackmore, are you asking me to marry you?"

"I love you, Catherine, so yes, I'm asking me to marry me."

"Then I accept your proposal." She laughed and wrapped her arms around his neck. "We'll just have to let Barry know when he gets dropped off from his club."

"Yeah, who's going to do that?"

"We will, together,"

"Let's make it special for him," Andy suggested. "Take him to the pub for something to eat and tell him there, as it'll probably be the last time we'll be out for twenty-five years until the house is paid off."

"Oh, you," kissing his cheek.

As they sat in the pub, Catherine gave Barry the news, "Barry, Andy and I have something to tell you." He looked at her inquisitively. "Andy bought a house today."

"Can I see it, Andy?" Barry was excited.

"When I get the keys soon, you can see it, Barry," Andy assured him. "You'll be the first to see it."

"Are we going to live there?"

"Well, remember we talked about it? you're going to get your own house."

"Oh aye, I remember. Does that mean Catherine will be all alone?"

"Well, that brings me to something else, Barry,"

"More surprises?" Barry was rubbing and clapping his hands like a child.

"Andy and I are going to get married someday and be together."

"What about me? Will I be alone?" Barry frowned.

"No, Barry, you won't be alone," Andy promised. Barry nodded.

"We are going to see that you get somewhere very special to live," Catherine told him.

"Then we'll all have somewhere to live," smiling and happy.

Andy dropped Catherine and Barry off at their house before heading to his flat. It was only then, when he was alone, that the significance of the day's proceedings suddenly dawned on him; he was about to become a homeowner and a married man. He phoned Catherine.

"Hiya, missing me already?"

"You know, we were so wrapped up in us today, we forgot - we have to get Barry sorted. We need to make him feel included in everything that's happening. What are your thoughts?"

"Yeah, I agree. I'll go see about the sheltered housing tomorrow."

"Great," Andy was relieved. "Hey, love you loads."

"I love you too, Andy"

Both Andy and Catherine were scheduled for late shifts, so time was of the essence for both. Life in a hospital setting was never easy, being at the sharp end; life as a cop was not easy, either, but it was something they had learned to handle. Now they had to handle it together.

"Good morning, Swinton and Docherty lawyers, how can I help you?" when Andy called the solicitors.

"Is Mr. Sweeney available? It's Andy Blackmore calling."

"Please hold the line, sir," A moment later; "Putting you through now."

"Andy, how are you doing'?"

"Good thanks, Gerry, can the house I'm buying be put into joint names?"

"I thought you were unmarried, Andy?"

"At the moment, but I want a secure future for someone. My future wife."

"Oh, I see. Yes, I can sort that out for you, no problem. It just means I need both of you to sign the papers."

"Thanks, Gerry."

As he drove to work, Andy realised that his whole way of thinking had altered. He now had responsibilities.

Chapter Six

T he radio blared. "Zulu 1, attend at the Barnaby's Public House. There is a report of a large-scale disturbance about to take place." "Roger, attending," replied Georgie who was partnering with Andy.

"Large scale disturbance about to take place, what the hell does that mean?"

As they pulled up outside the premises, all was quiet. That was until they went inside and saw that both sides of the village's poaching gangs were facing off each other, in a stand-off that would have made a movie producer proud to film. The fish was poached not just for the eating, but sometimes for other illegal shenanigans.

Andy and Georgie had walked into a scenario they did not want to be in.

"Georgie, I get the feeling we're outnumbered here - if this all goes wrong,"

"I get that feeling, too Andy." Georgie tried to keep his tone even, to make light of a serious situation.

Andy looked around and immediately recognised that these were two of the families involved in the poaching trade. *Clearly something had gone wrong with whoever ran what part of the river,* he thought. He also saw the family hierarchy among the groups. He had confronted them on several occasions and established an easy if not friendly relationship.

"Andy, hang on, I've requested urgent assistance," raising his hand.

"Somehow I don't think this can wait, my friend."

"Don't do anything stupid, Andy." Georgie was getting nervous now.

"Would I do anything stupid?" as he walked onto the dance floor between the groups. "Okay guys, one from each side please, on the floor with me!" One from either side slowly stepped forward. "Now guys, as you know, we've always had an arrangement about what goes on down at the river. That arrangement is about to come to an end right here, right now, and I'm going to make your lives an absolute misery, which will cost both of you and your families a lot of money. So, what's this all about?"

Andy listened as the two men explained, both trying to talk over the other. One of the men, Frankie, accused the other, Jackie, of poaching in their area. Jackie alleged that Frankie had been poaching in his area. So, it was a stalemate.

"Okay, as of tonight, you take the east of the river from the bridge, you take the west of the river from the bridge, agreed?"

"Agreed Mr. Blackmore, and I'll ensure it's enforced." Andy swung on his heels when he heard the voice from behind him.

"Hello Pat, how is the head of this mangy group?"

"Hello, Mr. Blackmore. I think it's time this lot went home, don't you?"

"Yes Pat, because if we start searches, I'm sure a few would be in bother."

"Nah Andy, everything is planked," one of the poachers said.

"Can I leave you to deal with this Pat?"

"Will do it now, everybody home now, this is finished, Mr. Blackmore has spoken." Although not everyone was happy with the outcome, slowly but surely, they trooped out of the venue, the outcome of the meeting unsure.

"Nice to see you again, Pat."

"Well Andy, don't get used to it. This is the new training for freedom scheme, so I must behave."

"You're off to a flyer then, Pat."

"Thanks, Andy."

"For what?"

"For looking after my family while I've been inside," he whispered.

"Pat, nobody knows about that."

"I know, and I know everything has been good for you here because of that."

"Yes, it has. See you around, Pat."

"Yeah, sure thing."

As Andy and Pat went outside, there must have been at least half a dozen police vans and cars from around the subdivisions, blue lights flashing, each of the vehicles double-manned, except for one that had picked up the foot patrols, boosting the numbers.

"Geezuz Pat, it's like Blackpool out here,"

"Wouldn't know mate, never been."

"Ever been to Lapland, Pat, to Santa's grotto?"

"Everyone needs helpers in this life, Andy, and my Santa was you looking after my kids," as he walked away.

"You know something, Andy," Georgie muttered as they got back into the car. "You've been out a lot with Joe and June; you and I haven't been out a lot together in the vans or the cars. They've told me stories about you and the things that you've done, and some seemed a bit ridiculous when they told me, but man, I believe everything they told me after tonight."

"Sorry, have I missed something here?"

"You're a nutter mate, no wonder they've nicknamed you the Iceberg! Do you even know what fear is?"

"Do I know what fear is, he asks," Andy echoed. "Yes, but not for a long time now."

There was a strained silence in the vehicle for a while.

"Andy, can I tell you something? I'll deny this forever, but you stepped up to the plate and sorted it tonight. When these two gangs get together it's usually a bloodbath."

"It's about knowing your limits, Georgie. Trouble is, I don't know mine."

"Well Andy, nearly time for home."

"Yeah, I'm going to see Catherine before I head home."

"Catherine who?"

"Smith," he responded.

"Do you mean Catherine Smith from the hospital?"

"Yeah, why? Georgie, do you mean to tell me that you didn't know we were seeing each other?"

"Nope, I thought you were seeing June."

"Geez man, you're so out of touch," he replied, laughing as they walked into the office.

"Wait a minute, you were seeing her years ago, right?"

"Right. Now we are back together"

"Great, good luck big man."

"Thanks."

"Hey mate, another star performance tonight in Barnaby's."

"Oh behave, June," laughing. "Only thing missing was you, June."

"Hey, how were your days off?"

"Interesting, to say the least."

"Oh? What does that mean?"

"Well, I bought a house and proposed to Catherine, other than that it was the same old, same old."

"Same old, same old he says, come here you," kissing his cheek. "Congratulations Andy. I mean it."

"Andy, I need a word with you," "Yes Sergeant" who had walked into the locker room.

"Sure." Andy followed his Sergeant down to his room.

"Come in, close the door and sit down, Andy."

Thirty minutes later, Andy walked out of the office, his head spinning, and went straight to his car. Any thoughts of going to Catherine's had passed him by, but one way or another, he had to speak to her, Andy went back to his flat and sat thinking about everything that had come to light in the last hour. He hardly slept that night.

"Hello, Andy here," answering his telephone.

"Hey Andy, how are you, I thought you were coming to see me?"

"Yeah, that was the plan Catherine, but it all went a bit haywire, and that's what we need to talk about."

"Sounds serious, Andy."

"No, it's not serious, you were so right, we just need to talk, please. When I finish tonight, can I come see you then?"

"Yes, Andy, my door's open."

"I'll see you after I finish, and there's something else."

"And that is…?"

"I'm looking after your future."

"You're a mysterious man, Andy."

"See you tonight then," ending the call.

"So, Andy, have you given any thought to our discussion?" Sergeant Black asked, when Andy arrived at the office before the start of his shift.

"Yeah, but I need until tomorrow. I need to speak to someone."

"Okay, I'll make the call, but tomorrow's your deadline."

"I know, thank you."

"June, you're out with Andy, or should I say, Andy, you're out with June. Now then, try and stay out of trouble, Andy. Everyone knows about your escapade last night. June's the only one that will go out with you now, her and Joe," The Sergeant was laughing.

"Aye Sergeant, even you have stayed well away from me," Andy remarked, wearing a cheeky grin.

"Aye, I want to see retirement!" in that accent which Andy had grown to love.

The late shift faded into insignificance, to be forgotten when they all finished, Andy made his way to Catherine's house as they had arranged.

"Tea, coffee, brandy.?"

"Tea and coffee, which means I can drive home, brandy means I stay overnight."

"Brandy it is, then," pouring him a large one. "What's up, Andy?" She could see that something was bothering him.

"You were so right. I didn't come here last night because Sergeant Black spoke to me before leaving the office, and my head was up my rear end to be honest."

"In what way?"

"Because you're the only one who knows everything."

"Has Barlow asked for you?"

"Yes."

"Do you want to be part of it - the investigation?"

"I'm tired of it all, to be honest, Catherine."

"It's your call and I'll be there for you all the way, I told you that."

"Cheers, I appreciate that, I do. Now, there's something else."

"What next?"

"I need you with me when the papers are signed for the house."

"Why, can you not sign your name?" smiling again.

"Well, it's going under joint names," looking at Catherine.

"Whose names?" she was puzzled.

"Yours and mine. Or more correctly ours."

"You're joking!" Catherine exclaimed, stunned.

"Nope. It means if anything happens to me, you have a house for the rest of your days."

"Geez Andy, what can I say?"

"Don't need to say anything just come here into my arms."

In the morning, Andy returned home from Catherine's and sat staring at his telephone, his fingers tapping on the receiver. Even now, he was not one hundred per cent sure that he was doing the right thing. He picked up the receiver and made the call.

"Detective Chief Superintendent Barlow, please."

"Who's calling?" asked the female officer in the control room.

"Andy Blackmore."

" Barlow here, hello Andy, hope that you're calling me to tell me you're coming here?"

"There are a few things I have to get clear, sir, and that is my lack of experience."

"Well, the squad I'm putting together is going to get specialist training in this matter, if that helps. It means that everyone will be in the same boat, right from the start."

"I understand, sir. Then, in that case, I'm in."

"Good man, I'm pleased to hear it."

"I'll notify Sergeant Black when I start the late shift today."

"Yes, and get the weekend off, as you start here next Monday. Five-day week, shift times are nine to five, day shift only."

"Thank you, sir. See you on Monday."

Andy sat back in his seat. He had made his decision. Whether it was the right decision, only time would tell, and as Catherine had said to him, he was doing this for Kerry and all the others that were involved in the cycle of abuse. What struck some fear into him was the thought of leaving the office again and losing all his shift, and June, Andy picked up the phone once more and listened to the ring tone on the opposite end of the line.

"Hi, Catherine here."

"I'm going, Catherine. Start on Monday, five-day week."

"How are you feeling now that you have made the decision?"

I feel I want to put an end to this inquiry, now all I must do is tell the shift I'm leaving again."

"How are you going to break it?"

"At the moment, I just don't know," was his slow staccato reply.

"Well, I am going to be with you every step of the way."

Later that day, Andy arrived for work early. He went into Sergeant Black's office and broke the news of his decision to him. Sergeant Black sat back in his seat rocking back and forth, with his hands in his open tunic pockets which was a habit of his looking at Andy with a smile on his face, Andy looked at him, narrowing his eyes.

"You knew this was coming, you have known for a while this was coming. That is why you said what you did, that day down at the loch."

"Close that door Andy," flicking his hand.

He leaned on the desk. "First, I want to let you know that the last three pages on your secondment assessment are forgeries, and you received brilliant assessments from all the senior officers. Because these papers go to Force Headquarters and onto your record, we did not know who would access them, hence the reason that was done." He hesitated and looked directly at Andy. "I'm not going to apologise for this action, as it has achieved the anticipated result."

"Sergeant," Andy's voice was unnaturally quiet. "You have just used the word we, who is the we you are referring to?"

"For confidential reasons, I only know some of the people and the plans. We are a group of people that believe in you, and what you tried to do for Kerry. On Monday, you're going to Force Headquarters. After that, you will be under the command of Detective Chief Superintendent Barlow. From there, I'm not party to any information."

"Who all knows about this in here?"

"Me. Now listen to me laddie." That phrase brought a smile to Andy's face as he recalled his first day on the shift and being called laddie. "This investigation you're going on could make or break you, but knowing you as I do, the experience will be great for your future, that is if you can keep your mouth shut long enough," Black had an affectionate chuckle after saying that.

A short time later, Andy's colleagues, fellow officers, and more importantly his friends, gathered for their shift, Andy was sitting with his thoughts, knowing that his days with them were numbered. He did not say anything. Following the muster, and with all the business having been taken care of, Sergeant Black turned and looked at Andy.
"Constable Blackmore has an announcement to make," announced Sergeant Black.

As his shift looked in his direction, Andy stood up, thinking about how to break the news he had to deliver to them.

"Today is my last day here for the foreseeable future," Andy said with a heavy heart. "All I'm allowed to say is that I'm going to work at Force HQ for a while."

"You're coming back Andy, aren't you?" June's jaw dropped at the news.

"Being truthful, I don't know what's going to happen. This all happened very sudden."

"How sudden? How long have you known about this?"

"Less than forty-eight hours, Joe."

"You've known for forty-eight hours, and you said nothing?" June's voice was shaking.

"He wasn't permitted to say anything," Sergeant Black interjected.

"Hell, we just get you back from the CID and you're away again."

"I'm sorry, but this was nothing to do with me, I just had a decision to make."

"Does Catherine know?"

"Yeah, she does. I had to tell her I was moving."

"Right Andy stay in, clear up and empty your locker before you finish."

Andy could feel the mood in the shift change to a more sombre tone. He looked at June and Joe as they passed him by and he knew they were upset, but not as much as he was. As Andy walked past his office, Sergeant Black beckoned him to enter.

"If it's any consolation, I think you've made the right decision."

"Thanks. We'll see in time."

"You'll do well in this job, Andy, if you just watch what you're doing. Also, get those promotion exams under your belt. You're a good cop and it's been a pleasure working with you."

"Thank you," before pausing. "Can I say that I'll never forget you, you have been a real inspiration and I'll never be able to thank you enough for everything you have done for me." He nodded towards his Sergeant before making his way down the corridor.

As Andy cleaned out his locker, he felt a hand on his shoulder.

"Hey big man, what am I going to do without you?"

"Be good and behave yourself," wrapping his arms around June. She rested her head on his chest.

"Can you tell me where you're going?"

"June, even I don't know. All I was asked to do was go to Force HQ. I think you know why I'm going, though."

"I understand, I think. Honour the memory of Susan and get justice for Kerry."

Andy looked at June and nodded.

"We'll stay in contact, eh?" asked Andy.

"Christ yeah, of course we will. That's a stupid thing to say," June replied.

"When Catherine and I get married, your name will be first on the wedding list."

"Is that a promise?" June had tears in her eyes.

"Yes, it is, and you can bring whomever you wish as your partner."

Tea breaks came and went, and everybody was very supportive of Andy and his move, but it was like the end of the line for him and them, Andy had packed his bags and moved his belongings into his car. As he sat in the front office with John McMurdo, seeing out his final hours, he listened to the radio calls being put out from the Divisional HQ, voices he recognised and was unlikely to hear again for a long time.

"How do you feel about the suddenness of your move, Andy?"

"Shocked, to be honest," replied Andy.

"Do you know, you've not been here as long as us, but you've made a great impression on everyone that's worked with you, and you would be welcome back anytime." Andy smiled and nodded "Thanks John.

"Andy," shouted Sergeant Black as he walked in on them. "Do you want to go home?"

"Honestly, Sergeant, no. I want to see it out until eleven, for possibly the last time. I'd like to go for one last walk around my beat, if that's okay with you, Sergeant."

"Sure son, absolutely."

As Andy went around the streets, he looked in through shop windows and pulled on the padlocks to make sure they were locked fast.

On his way back to the office, a slight drizzle of rain began. It was as if the skies were mourning as Andy made that last slow walk to the back door. When Andy came in and handed in his radio to John, the night shift and the late shift all gathered together. The only person he would have wanted to make that last leaving speech was on hand to deliver it.

June had tears running down her face, "Andy Blackmore, in a short time you've become a legend here. Only a few of us have had the pleasure to work with you, but on behalf of everyone, we wish you all the best until you get back here."

Andy looked around, from one face to the next, and felt himself choking up. "Thanks, everyone, and thank you, Sergeant. Thanks for everything."

"You're welcome, Andy," as he his Sergeant shook hands, knowing he was losing a good officer.

Andy received a warm send-off from both shifts. He left the office by the back door for the last time accompanied by his two mentors; June and Joe.

"Well, I wonder who is going to replace you big man."

June interjected. "He is irreplaceable, do you mean you wonder who we're going to get?"

"She is right you know, you are a one-off and it has been a hell of a ride knocking you into shape. Caused me a few sleepless nights I can tell you, and if June had her way you would have caused her a few sleepless nights but for different reasons," jested Joe, bursting into laughter and receiving a slap on his shoulder from June.

"I want you both to know, that through everything that we have been through together in such a short time, I have loved every moment of us being together and all that you have taught me, so I am going to make you both a promise; I will not let either of you down." He paused. "This is not goodbye, this is just hasta luego."

He shook Joe's hand firmly and warmly, giving him a short hug. He looked at June, and they just smiled at one another. Then he hugged her tightly and kissed her forehead, as Joe watched on.

Without saying anything more, Andy got into his car and drove off into an unknown future without his best mate in the job, June, Andy's future months would be the most trying in his career, without a doubt. He had a ghost to lay to rest.

Chapter Seven

The following morning, Andy took stock of his days in Bankvale; so much had happened in such a short time. He walked across the floor barefooted, picked up the phone and dialled out.

"Good morning, Alice,"

"Hi Andy, how are you?"

"I'm good. What about you and the kids?"

"We're fine, Andy, but Ricky's a mess, and I have to decide when he's fit to see the kids."

"Is he hitting the drink?"

"Yeah, he is."

"Are you working?"

"Yes, I'm just getting back into the swing of things after being away for so long. Thankfully I have today off."

"You're brilliant and you've got a brilliant brain, you'll get there."

"I need to speak to you about your Mum, can we meet up?"

"Sure, any night next week would be good."

"What about tomorrow, are you working?"

"No, that's another thing I have to tell you about."

"How about…" Alice paused. "I know, do you remember the pub we all used to go to as teenagers?"

"Yeah, The Rooftop."

"Let's meet there, say, at two," Alice suggested.

"That's good for me," Andy confirmed.

"See you tomorrow then."

Later that day, Andy picked up Catherine and they drove up the Lochside, pulling into a small, picturesque village with grey stone houses that were built to last by the stonemasons of yesteryear. The slate roofs, the small windows and doorways… In the summertime, the window boxes were always a blaze of colour, which brought the whole village to life. All the residents were in a friendly competition to see who could produce the most colourful garden, and most were already in full bloom.

Andy parked the car and they sat for a few moments looking across the loch, with its islands dotted around and green hills that seemed to rise out of the water, Andy and Catherine meandered hand in hand along the shale beach, watching the water gently lapping at the edge, miles away from that night in Tenerife when they were together with the waves rolling in.

Sitting together in a little tearoom, it was like a blast from the past, with its wooden tables and chairs, china cups and saucers, real stainless-steel knives to cut the cakes if required, and red and white checked tablecloths, with the condiments in the middle of the table, Andy looked around. It had a maximum capacity of twenty-four, he judged. He watched as the hostess and her employee served the customers with a smile and a chat. Nothing seemed a chore; there were none of those false smiles that you got in the city. As they finished up and freed their table for the next customer, Andy and Catherine discussed how much they had enjoyed their time away from it all.

"That was beautiful,"

"Yeah, and now I'm going to take you somewhere else," Andy replied.

"Where?"

"Further up the loch, to a village local for a drink. The strangest pub I've ever been to."

"In what way?"

"Well, let's just say it's strange if you're not a local."

"Right."

As they stood outside the local pub, Catherine looked it up and down.

"Okay…" looking at the dark grey sandstone. It had two turrets, one either side of the building. The windows were like something from a castle, very narrow. Two heavy oak doors, with their wrought iron hinges, were open, inviting them inside.

"This is like something out of the Hammer House of Horrors Andy,"

"Wait 'til you meet the locals, now, if they have two eyes, they're not local."

"For god's sake Andy, that's a terrible thing to say!"

"One eye in the middle of the forehead means they're local," he joked. "This is like a movie scene from the backwoods."

"Andy…" slapping his back in a raised voice with a laugh.

"Okay, here we go," pushing the door open.

The place was as good as full of locals and, as if on the signal of a conductor, a sea of heads turned to see who had entered their pit, Andy noticed that the whole room had fallen silent upon their entry. Catherine took hold of Andy's hand.

"Can ah help you pal?" grumbled the barman.

"A large red wine and a can of coke, please," requested Andy.

The barman served them up. "Here you go, mate."

"Cheers." Andy handed him a five-pound note.

"There you go mate, your change." Andy checked it.

"Excuse me, sir, I'm a pound short in my change."

"No, you're not," replied the barman, staring at Andy.

"Andy, leave it," Catherine pleaded.

"Barman, can I have a word please?"

"Sure, which one?"

"Closure," he replied, staring at the barman.

This was a word that the locals didn't appreciate at all, Andy could feel their stares digging into the two of them.

"I'm sorry, sir," holding his hand out in friendship. "My mistake, I miscounted."

The barman made the fateful error of also holding out his hand. They gripped each other, and Andy smiled as he pressed his forefinger into the barman's wrist before he released him. The painful expression on the barman's face made Andy smile.

Andy and Catherine sat down, Andy making sure he faced the bar. As Catherine was speaking to him about their new house, which was due to be finalised in the coming weeks, he watched as the barman raised a glass to a font to pour the whisky.

As the glass filled, it fell to the floor with a crash. The barman lifted another glass and repeated the process with the same result.

"Hey, you got butter on your fingers today?".

"Naw, my hand just feels funny,"

"Andy, what are you watching?"

"The barman seems to have a problem pouring whisky."

"Why?"

"How should I know," shrugging his shoulders.

Andy strolled over to the bar and ordered another large red wine for Catherine.

"Get you in a minute, pal."

"You okay, sir?"

"Why?"

"I've noticed you've dropped a couple of glasses."

"Who are you?"

Andy, knowing that Catherine was within earshot, replied, "I'm a doctor."

"And?"

"Sir, I've seen these symptoms before, and they should be investigated immediately at the hospital."

Catherine sat there stunned and lost for words at the interaction, not knowing whether to put an end to this farce. As she looked around, all the heads were facing Andy and listening intently.

"Listen, doctor, what's wrong with me?"

"Well, could be several things. Trapped nerve or brain tumour affecting the right side of your body. Or, it could be nothing."

"Andy," Catherine called out

"Sorry, large red coming up."

Andy walked around the bar, lifted the measure, and poured a large red for Catherine.

"Hey Malky, get me a pint mate," shouted a local.

"No problem,"

"Really? try it."

As the barman started to pour the pint of beer, his hand gave way almost immediately, spilling the beer everywhere.

"Sir, can I suggest you seek medical advice as soon as possible?"

Andy went and sat beside Catherine.

"Listen, folks, I'm going to the hospital," the barman announced. "See if you take a drink, leave the money at the till please."

Andy watched as the barman left the bar open, and as the locals filled up their glasses, they left the money as requested. As Andy returned to Catherine with her drink, he heard a chair being pulled backwards at his table and, out of the corner of his eye, saw a man take the seat opposite.

"Andy, Andy, what have you done to our barman?" asked a familiar voice, casually.

"Just a little fun, Pat."

Pat turned to gaze at Catherine.

"And you are?"

"Catherine Smith, meet Pat Callaghan," Andy introduced them.

"Oh, do you two work together?"

"We used to," Andy replied with a smile.

"Yeah, we used to," repeated Pat, laughing.

"Time we were leaving, Pat, sorry to leave you, but we have to go."

"No problem, Andy, nice to meet you, Catherine, good luck with your new job, Andy." Pat raised his glass towards Andy and nodded, Andy returned the nod of acknowledgement as he left the premises.

Sitting in the car, Catherine asked Andy, "Who is Pat?"

"Pat used to play Santa Claus in my pantomimes."

"Oh, that's nice. Now then, the barman, own up," Catherine demanded in that tone only she could deploy.

"Well…" he paused "He owed me a pound and refused to reimburse me, so for a laugh, I paralysed his right hand for a couple of hours. Tweaked a little pressure point."

"Why the hell do I want to marry you?"

"Maybe because you love me, and life would be boring without me? where to now?"

As they drove down the Lochside road, the discussion turned to his mum and her long-term future. On their way home, they stopped at the Lochside Nursing Home for a short visit with his mother and thereafter Andy drove to his flat and parked his car before he and Catherine went to their local pub for a meal.

"Tomorrow I have to meet Alice to discuss mum's future. Would you like to come along?"

"What about Ricky?"

"He's back on the sauce."

"Maybe it is best you sort that out with Alice. I will give her space to speak with you. Anyway, I have to see to Barry, so you go see her, it's not a problem for me."

At two o'clock on Saturday afternoon, Andy sat in the lounge of the Rooftop. He was there for the first time in years. In the horseshoe-shaped bar, with its dank, red and white embossed wallpaper still attached to the walls, it felt like time had stood still as he sat in the corner where they had all lounged together as a gang of teenage friends, going into their early twenties when some decided that married life was for them. It was a great time.

One of the bar staff, in her mid-fifties with fiery red hair now fading to grey, was looking over at Andy. She walked over to the table where Andy was seated.

"Something tells me I know you,"

"Hello, Marie,"

"I know you," she repeated.

"So, you should New Year, many years ago, your husband was at sea."

"Oh Christ, Andy... Geez, you married yet?"

"Yes, it's me, Marie, and no."

As Andy looked at Marie, he remembered how her husband had been in the navy when he was in his late teens. Marie was always a flirt with the crowd that he was a part of for years. Her eyes and her smile were a magnet to him in years gone by. Now they were showing signs of age, just as he probably was to her, Andy remembered that he was warned off her by all his mates, who feared for his safety if her husband knew that he was sniffing around her, or rather, that she was sniffing about him.

"You haven't changed a bit, Marie."

"What does that mean, Andy?"

"Your red hair, now with its wisps of grey, your smile, that sultry sexy look in your blue eyes, your black dress and stockings like always... you were a temptress in years gone by," teasing her.

"Oh Andy, stop..." Marie playfully objected.

"You still married, Marie?"

"No, he's long gone, been on my own for years, Andy..."

"Oh, don't take that the wrong way please, those were fun days Marie," he pleaded, putting his hands up defensively.

"Yes, they were," as she went back to work. When Alice arrived, Andy called over to Marie, "do you have a table for two, please, or are we okay to sit here?"

"For you, darling, just stay there."

"Who's that?"

"That, Alice, is an old, old friend of ours. Do you not remember Marie?"

"You're joking!" slightly shocked that she was still there.

Marie approached the table and handed Andy and Alice their menus, along with placemats and cutlery.

"So, Andy, is this the lady in your life then?"

"This is my sister-in-law, Alice."

"Oh, sorry," Then she muttered; "Alice, Alice... Oh, Christ, Alice! You were part of that crowd."

"It's been a while Marie, no problem." She looked at Andy then Marie. "Are you still lusting after him?"

Marie laughed. "Not at my age, Alice."

"Well, our whole crowd knew you were, back then."

"What woman didn't, married or not?" Marie replied in a light-hearted manner.

"Erm, can we order something to eat please, Marie? I'm here, you know,"

"I'm not on the menu," laughing so loud that it attracted the attention of other customers. "What about you, Alice?"

"Girls behave, I'm starving!" This was the reason why he loved coming home; the banter was always magic.

"I'm married to his brother, Marie,"

"Doesn't mean you're off the menu, not if you know what's on the dessert list."

"Meaning what exactly?"

"Girls, can we get back to the case in hand... like lunch?" suggested Andy.

"To be continued..." Marie smiled at Alice. "Now, can I take your orders?"

As Andy and Alice had their fish and chip lunch, they discussed Ricky at length and the future of their mother, who was enjoying her time in the nursing home, or as she would say, "being on holiday."

Andy told Alice that he and Catherine had bought a house and that his lawyer was dragging his heels in getting the paperwork completed to finalise the purchase. He asked Alice if she was available to see the transaction through to its completion.

"What will happen with Mum and meeting the costs of the nursing home?" Andy asked.

"I have to look into that, considering what Ricky did with her house."

"What can I do to help you out with Ricky Alice?"

"Nothing, Andy, he's a lost cause with the drink, and see, to be honest, I couldn't care less about him anymore."

Andy remained silent and shook his head despairingly.

"There's something I have to tell you, Alice,"

"Go on,"

Andy told Alice that, with immediate effect, he was no longer working at Bankvale and that he had been transferred to new duties at the Force Headquarters. His voice trailed off as Marie returned to their table.

"Brother and sister-in-law, yeah right," Marie commented "Not with looks at each other like that."

"Marie, can we have the bill please?" Andy asked, before making his way to the gents' toilet.

Marie remained at the table watching Andy then inquired if Andy was single. Alice told her firmly and politely that he was engaged. Marie smiled before going to get their bill.

She returned with a leather folder containing the bill for the food and drinks.

"Can I get that?" Alice reached out towards the folder.

"Certainly not," drawing it away from her. "Maybe next time."

"Thank you,"

Andy walked to the till area where Marie was standing and handed her the payment for the lunch. She handed a receipt to Andy which he put in his pocket.

"Thank you, Andy. Enjoy the rest of your day together, and welcome home."

Andy looked at her with fond memories and thanked her.

Marie watched as Andy and Alice left the lounge together, Andy said that he was going to see his brother and mother, while Alice told him that she was going back to her parents.

"I shall be in touch with you about the house, and to make sure that you're okay."

"That would be nice, Andy"

As they were about to go their separate ways, they hugged each other, and he kissed her cheek gently with his parting word "I shall see you soon Alice."

Once again, Andy turned his car off the roadway facing the large gates to his brother's house, but this time the gates did not open on command, Andy pressed the intercom button and waited for a reply.

"What?" came the demanding response. There was a pause. "Who is it?" Ricky shouted down the intercom.

"Ricky, it's Andy, open the gates please."

"No chance."

"C'mon man, please let me in."

"Alice isn't here, so piss off."

"I know, I've just left her. I told her I was coming here."

"Secret liaison again?"

"Ricky, this is not funny."

"Never was Andy, so get lost." Those were Ricky's final words before ending the call.

Andy went back to his car and thought about his next move. He had to get into the house somehow and speak to Ricky. He sat for about five minutes thinking, then got out of his car again and pressed the intercom.

"What?" came the drunken reply.

"Post sir," Andy said in an Irish accent.

"Okay," Ricky opened the side gate.

Andy walked up the long driveway, leaving his car at the main gates. He knocked on the locked door and waited. Ricky opened the large door and stared at Andy. As he tried to shut the door, Andy stepped forward, pushing Ricky backwards with one hand.

"I'm the postman, here to deliver you a message," making his way into the kitchen. "Today you can tell me everything, this is your amnesty. Tomorrow all bets are off."

"What do you mean?"

"Oh, you've not heard then. I'm moving to Force HQ."

"Why?" looking at his brother through narrowed, bleak eyes, puffed from lack of sleep.

"That is for me to know," Andy replied before pausing. "Now start talking!"

"I need a drink."

"No chance. Start talking, brother." Andy stared at Ricky.

"Okay, here's the deal, one for one."

"I don't do deals.".

"Do I get immunity?"

"From what?"

"Jail if I give you everything." Ricky looked up at his little brother.

"Christ sake Ricky, where is this going?"

"This is going where you don't want it to go, brother."

Over the next hour or so, Ricky went into full flow, spilling the beans on everyone who had taken part in the Games Nights and who was still active in arranging and participating; senior figures well known to the public. He left no public service untouched.

"Before I go, answer me one more question." Andy demanded, getting to his feet.

"What's that?"

"Do you, or did you, know Kerry Ferguson? I know that your pal Berger did, intimately." He paused, waiting for a reply. "Don't answer that. Your face has says it all." Andy shook his head in disgust while Ricky stared at the floor in abject misery. His body crumpled.

Andy left closing the large door quietly at his back. As he stood at the gates to the large villa he turned around and looked at the magnificent building. Something inside his head told him that, the next time he would be there, it would be under different circumstances. Armed with a mountain of information, Andy got into his car and, switching on the engine, glanced one last time at the house. His next stop was to be at the Lochside Nursing Home to visit his mother.

When he arrived at the home about thirty minutes later, he walked into the large lounge. He looked around and saw his mother sitting on her own in a corner. She was dressed smartly, and her short hair was neatly brushed back from her face. Other residents sat around the room, some sleeping, some others having slowly drifted into a world of their own. A few staff members greeted Andy and were trying their best to communicate with the vulnerable residents. He watched as a small group played dominoes while others played card games.

"Hi Mum," searching her eyes for a spark of life.

"Hello," came from the woman on the other side of those sad eyes.

"Hello Mum," Andy repeated.

"Oh, it's you. Everyone is so nice here."

"Are you happy here, Mum?"

"Oh yes. You know, my mum and dad were here yesterday."

"Were they, how long were they here for?"

"Erm, I'm not sure, but we chatted for a while."

"What were you talking about?"

"Oh, just this and that."

"That's nice."

Andy gazed at his mother as she watched Only Fools and Horses on the television. She seemed oblivious to his presence.

After a short time, he went to the small office and saw the nurse in charge. He stated that he thought his mother's condition was deteriorating. The nurse agreed and informed Andy that her doctor had made a routine visit and he had noted her condition on her records, Andy then returned to the sitting room.

"Mum, I have to go now, I'll be back to see you in a few days. Maybe I'll bring Catherine with me."

"Right you are, that would be nice. What's your name again?"

"It's Andy, Mum."

"Nice to meet you, Andy," his mother replied.

Andy sat holding her hand. It was so thin he could feel the bones in her fingers. As she began to slip into a light sleep, Andy rose from his seat and gave her a gentle kiss on her forehead before leaving the home.

When he got back to the flat a short time later, he sat down, his head still full with the day's encounters with his family. The phone rang. It was Catherine, inquiring how his time with Alice went. He told her they'd had lunch and she had agreed to act as their lawyer in the purchase of the house. He also told her about his meetings with Ricky and his mother.

He did not tell her that Ricky had given him information about the Games Nights or those involved. Catherine suggested that they should make the effort to visit his mother more often and to gather some items from her past to help her remember people and places. Photographs would be ideal, and cassette tapes with her favourite music on them, Andy agreed that would be a great help.

"Hey, good luck Monday." She was facing two more nights of night shift.

"Thank you, I'm going to need all the luck I can get, to be honest."

"I'll come in and see you Monday night."

"I'd like that, see you then," ending the call.

Shortly afterwards, the phone rang again.

"Hi Andy, it's Alice, listen just want to wish you all the best in your new job, and also thank you for today."

"Thanks, I saw Ricky today, he's in a mess."

"Yeah, I know. He's not seen the kids for days now, I can't let them see him like that."

"I agree, he has to settle down again. I also saw my mum."

"Oh, how is she?"

"Deteriorating rapidly. She didn't remember my name today."

"I'm sorry about that, Andy," she paused briefly. "What about that Marie, she's some woman, is she not? Hasn't changed a bit."

"Yep." Andy paused. "Does Ricky know anything about our night together?"

"No Andy, and he never will. Why?"

"Because he keeps alluding to it now and then."

"It's just the way he thinks, Andy."

"Okay,"

"Can I see you soon Andy, so we can discuss the house purchase?"

"Sure, I'll call you."

"Great, thanks, bye for now."

Andy sat down and began to make notes concerning everything that Ricky had told him earlier in the day; names and places and approximately what year it all began. Then the phone began to ring once more.

"Hello?" Andy here. "Who's calling please?"

"Andy, it's Marie."

"Oh, hi Marie."

"Sorry to call you, but I wanted to apologise for my behaviour today."

"Don't worry about it, Marie," surprised at the call from her. "Marie, how did you get this number?"

"Oh, let's say we have a mutual friend. Will we get to see you again at the Rooftop?"

"Yeah, probably."

"Great." She paused for a second. "Andy, check the receipt you put into your pocket please."

"Andy reached into his pocket and, written on the receipt, was a phone number."

"You got it?"

"Yes,"

"That number is mine, don't lose it. It's for you to use any time you want." There was silence between them.

"Goodbye, Andy."

"Bye, Marie."

Little did Andy know just how important that phone number would become ... very soon.

Part Two

Operation Hope

Chapter Eight

A t eight-thirty on Monday morning Andy stood outside the red-bricked Force Headquarters in the middle of the city centre, with its large windows draped with venetian blinds, keeping out prying eyes from the high-rise office blocks surrounding it, Andy pushed the glass revolving door open, entering the large foyer with its marble floor, the force crest and motto embedded into the tiles.

To his right stood the concierge, who was usually a retired police officer, looking smart in his black uniform, white gloves, and cap with its red-band and white top.

"May I help you, sir?"

"Yes, I'm here to meet with Detective Chief Superintendent Barlow."

"Your name, please?"

"Andrew Blackmore."

Andy watched as the concierge checked the list of visitors scheduled to be in the building that day. The concierge lifted the phone and dialled an internal number.

"I have a Mr, Andrew Blackmore here to see DCS Barlow, but he is not on my list, sir," he paused "Yes sir, certainly," Andy heard him say before he hung up the phone. "Why did you not tell me you're a cop?"

"You just asked my name, sorry,"Andy was apologetic.

"Put your warrant card around your neck. Here, you'll need this," throwing Andy a lanyard.

"Thanks."

"Go over to the lift, press five and someone will be waiting for you."

"Thank you very much."

"Hey, don't look so nervous," the concierge remarked.

Andy just nodded and smiled before walking over to the lift.

As the lift ascended, it stopped at each floor, where high-ranking officers came and went about their business. Each in turn just nodded at Andy while looking at his warrant card, seeing the word 'Constable'. Eventually, the lift reached floor five and the door opened.

"Andrew Blackmore?"

"Yes sir,"

"I'm Detective Chief Inspector Donald Jenkins. Nice to meet you, Andrew."

"Pleased to meet you, sir." Andy offered an outstretched hand, which the DCI accepted.

"Follow me, please,"

Andy followed the DCI along the corridor, stopping at a door with a keypad entry system, Andy noted that not a word was spoken between the lift and the door following their introduction.

"Here you are Andrew; this is your desk."

"Thank you, sir," observing the nameplate on the desk; DC Andrew Blackmore.

"Sir, there's been a mistake, I'm not a Detective Constable."

"Well, you are as long as you're on this inquiry, and we have to get that warrant card of yours changed." DCI Jenkins replied. "The others will be in shortly, or at least before nine. You're first in."

One by one, the team got together and sat at their respective desks. All were seated just before nine o'clock when the door opened. Detective Chief Superintendent Graham Barlow walked in and stood at a desk, facing his newly formed team.

What struck Andy about those gathered around him was that none of the officers showed any sign of recognition of each other, which was rather unusual. Usually, someone would have worked with someone else somewhere during their service. That did not seem to be the case in this office.

DCS Graham Barlow and DCI Donald Jenkins joined the police service at the same time. Between them, they had served more than fifty years. Outside work they were firm friends, often socialising along with their wives. They had reached their ranks via different routes; Barlow was ex-Special Branch, while Jenkins was with the Serious Crime Unit and had been seconded to this inquiry. Away from the office, they were just Graham and Donald, but in the office, rank was respected above friendship.

"Good morning, ladies and gentlemen. I'm Detective Chief Superintendent Graham Barlow and I'm in charge of this inquiry, the details of which have remained secret from all of you, except for one person in this room." Barlow glanced at Andy. "Now, going around the room, I want you all to state your name and brief career details, so we all get to know each other. As I said, I'm Detective Chief Superintendent Graham Barlow, I've spent over twenty years in the CID, and I'm currently head of this new Serious Sexual Crimes Investigation Squad."

"I'm Detective Chief Inspector Donald Jenkins. I'm currently serving at S Division, and I have been invited into this inquiry by DCS Barlow. Like him, I have over twenty years CID experience." Jenkins was in his mid-forties, tall and well built, athletic-looking, immaculate in a grey suit, white shirt, and grey tie.

"I'm Detective Inspector Alan Watt, currently serving in J Division CID. Experienced in serious criminal investigations. Coming up to eighteen years CID experience." Watt was in his late forties and had joined the force just before his thirtieth birthday. He was small and slim in stature compared to Jenkins. His blue piercing eyes and smile made him an instantly likeable individual.

"Good morning, all, I'm Detective Sergeant Frank Wallace, Force HQ. I work in this building, twenty plus years CID experience." Wallace, sleeves rolled up man, slightly overweight, about fifty years of age, balding with a Mexican bandit style moustache, would not have looked out of place in a spaghetti western.

"Detective Constable Lindsay O'Donnell, currently on secondment to the Crime Squad with ten years' police service." O'Donnell was over six feet tall, early thirties, built like a middle-weight boxer, short brown hair, with dark brown eyes and flashing smile. Like Andy, he was unmarried but in a relationship, and he liked to check his appearance in the mirror at every opportunity.

"Detective Constable Grant McLean, I'm serving in M division and I have seven years' service." McLean was about five feet ten inches tall, mid to late twenties, cropped hairstyle and square-jawed, muscles bulging under his shirt sleevesWhere O'Donnell looked like a boxer, McLean really was a boxer of some repute.

"Detective Constable Sharon McLeod, I have almost ten years' service, currently working within a unit dedicated to Child Protection here at Force HQ." McLeod was approaching thirty. She had been a university student before dropping out to follow a career in the police. Tall and slim with long fair hair, she was as sharp as a razor with a great memory for facts.

"I'm Detective Constable Andy Blackmore, as of today I believe, and by far the least experienced here, with almost three years' police service."

"Hiya, I'm Amanda Carson, I'm your log-gist and I've been working here at Force HQ for five years. Happy to meet you all." She was the youngest in the team at 23. A small, bubbly, slightly built individual;

badminton was her first love, and she was a Scottish Internationalist. There was some concern about her age and the nature of this inquiry, but she was recognised as being a thorough and accurate log-gist who missed nothing and would question anyone about the authenticity of their information, no matter their rank.

"Okay," in a no-nonsense tone, "lying on your desks in front of you are sealed envelopes, the contents of which are marked 'strictly confidential,' therefore nobody in this room can discuss this matter with anyone outside this room. This inquiry is going to be harrowing, as it involves child abuse inquiries, taking statements from victims and witnesses and the interviewing of suspects. What I can tell you is that you have all been hand-picked for one reason or another. Before we open the envelopes, is there anyone in here who does not wish to be part of this inquiry? If you do not, then it will not be held against you in any way. This isn't for everyone." The DCS paused and looked around the room. "Right, I take it by the silence and everyone still being here that you're all in for the duration, so you may open the envelopes. They've been compiled over several months by our surveillance teams, force intelligence officers, and others."

Andy opened the envelope and took out the contents, as did all the others. They were faced with photographs and information on high-ranking, serving police officers, some of whom were known to those gazing at the faces in the photographs. Senior politicians, local businessmen and, to their surprise, some women also featured in the inquiry. As they took in the information provided, there were looks of both shock and anger on the faces of some of the detectives.

"This is unbelievable." DC McLean was the only one to have spoken as the contents were put back into the envelopes. Nothing in the envelope came as a shock to Andy.

"I have only one other thing to say," announced Barlow. "This inquiry is so sensitive that we cannot allow anyone into this room, and that includes the cleaners, so, we are going to have to do everything ourselves in here. There is a shredder in the corner. Every piece of paper with notes on it must be destroyed. There are no keys to this place, so everyone in here must remember the code to the door. Under no circumstances must this office be left open. If you're asked by senior officers or others what is happening in here, refer them to me, please.

"DCI Jenkins and DI Watt shall be the links between you guys and myself, as I can't just disappear altogether from my current role or that would just raise more suspicions about this inquiry. They are the ones who will decide who is doing what and when, and what the daily actions will be. Each of you will be given a small case with a security lock on it; that's the only place where you can keep papers, and under no circumstances should they be left in cars or taken home. I know that this sounds like you can't do this or that, but it's for your protection. Also, when word gets out that we are sniffing around - and let's be honest about this, it will eventually happen - the suspects will circle the wagons and try to protect one another. We shall all become personae non-grata."

The officers, looking at DCS Barlow, remained silent as he looked around the room at each of them.

Blackmore broke the silence and stood up, surprising DCI Jenkins, but not Barlow. "Listen, everyone, you're probably wondering why someone with little experience and service is here on this inquiry. I have been working with DCS Barlow for several weeks now; most of what is in your envelopes came from me. Yesterday I spoke with someone who knows all the players' names, dates, and places where things have gone on, which I'm going to put into an intelligence report, then I'll pass it onto Amanda for processing. There is one other thing you should know. If you remember, four people died in a car that went into the loch at the Lochside Hotel. The deceased were retired senior police officer Brian Berger, his wife university lecturer Sandra Berger, her lover Sheena Gough, and my fiancée Susan Berger, who was a high school teacher.

"Brian, Sandra, and Sheena were all part of a 'games team' involving young adults who were or are in care and were taken to various venues to be used and abused, for which they were paid handsomely by those who could afford it. The deaths in the car were put down to brake failure and a tragic accident."

"Do you believe it, Andy?" interjected DCI Jenkins.

"No sir, not in the slightest," Andy replied, aware that all the eyes were on him.

"So, what are your thoughts on the matter?" Jenkins continued.

"One suicide and three murders, sir." There remained an expectant silence around the room. "You see, Brian Berger didn't want me to marry his daughter because I knew far too much about him and the goings-on involving him, his wife, and her lover. Brian Berger left a message on my answering machine telling me I would never marry Susan; hours later they were all dead."

"Was there an inquiry into the deaths, Andy?"

"Traffic inquiry, brake failure was the reason given I'm not here for revenge, I'm here so that I can assist your inquiry in whatever way I can. My name will likely come into this inquiry at some point, so I wanted to tell you all upfront what the past year has been like for me and my involvement in this inquiry. Now even DCS Barlow does not know this, but I have met the organiser of these games nights, I know who she is, and I am here to bring this abuse to a conclusion." With that, Andy sat down, noticing a nod of approval from Barlow

"As you will see, each of you has a telephone on your desk," came from DCI Jenkins "Each has its unique number, and beside that, there is a pile of contact cards. All that is on them is your number, and on the other side, which is blank, is for your first name only. No rank or position should be on them. So, on mine would be 'Donald', nothing else."

"At the back of the room is the statutory kettle," DS Frank Wallace chipped in. "And we've got everything you guys need for the moment to make tea and coffee. There is also a microwave over there. I suggest we get a 'kitty' together and we can remain stocked up with weekly shopping."

"Who gets the weekly shopping sir?"

"You do Andy, thanks for volunteering," bringing some much-needed laughter to the room.

"Can I suggest, as it is approaching midday, we get something to eat, as we have a guest coming in to speak to you all concerning this inquiry at one o'clock," .

"Where do we eat, boss?" came from DI Watt. "Can we go to the canteen, or has everything to be done in here?"

"I don't see any reason we can't use the canteen today, just make sure that nothing gets discussed away from this office," Barlow enforced. With that, they departed for lunch to the canteen. As they waited in the queue to be served, their joint presence did not go unnoticed by senior officers, and former colleagues who knew some of the officers. The cover story was that they were in the building for meetings. This was the last time they would be in the canteen and thereafter become self-sufficient for the duration of the inquiry.

At one o'clock on the dot, DCS Barlow walked in with a short balding man in his early sixties, followed by a middle-aged woman, both carrying briefcases.

"Ladies and gentlemen, let me introduce you to David McConnell and Chloe Agnew they are going to be our contacts at the Crown Office, and they want to speak to you about what is required to bring all this to a successful conclusion."

Over the next two hours, McConnell and Agnew gave the officers advice concerning the standard of reports that would be required by them and gave their assurances that they would do everything they could to bring the perpetrators to justice."

"Does anyone have any questions they would like to ask?" McConnell asked.

"Yes sir," said Andy. "Why did someone by the name of Benny McLaughlin, who works in your office, put the pen through a previous case submitted to your office?"

"I'm sorry, I didn't catch your name,"

"Blackmore, Andy Blackmore."

McConnell and Agnew looked at each other as if they recognised his name.

"Mr. Blackmore, that is something we would have to look at when we go back to the offices in Edinburgh."

"Do you know who I'm talking about?"

"Yes, we do,"

"You know that he has masonic links and that anything that crosses his desk will get lost?"

"That is a serious allegation." Came from Chloe Agnew, her voice slightly raised.

"Yes ma'am, and no disrespect to the Crown Office but he is as bent as a hairpin." Andy was ruffling feathers now on his first day there and he could see the management were uncomfortable with his line of questioning, Andy continued; "can you guarantee that he'll not get access to anything connected to this inquiry?"

"Why would you ask that?"

"I refer to my previous comment, and if he's part of all this then we're wasting our time."

"I shall make your concerns known to the appropriate people and I'll call you personally."

"Well, if there are no more questions, we'll head back to Edinburgh," McConnell announced.

Andy knew he was going to get flak from the bosses but, as it was day one, he was still prepared to walk away.

"Well Andy, that got us off to a great start with the Crown Office," DI Watt commented.

"It's as well coming out now, sir, rather than spend months on inquiries to get it snuffed out,"Andy replied. "Also, it lets them know that I know about what is going on there."

The room was very quiet, with all eyes directed towards Andy.

"Andy, some of the guys are wondering how you know so much about all of this?"

"Because I was part of the inquiry which led to the report going to the Crown Office,"

"And what happened to that?"

"Myself and my DI got taken into the Divisional Commander's office and told there was to be no further action."

"Did they say why?" Grant inquired.

"They said it wasn't in the public interest, then I heard someone say that Benny had 'sorted everything out at the Crown Office' then I found out Benny had the case papers and that he had links to others through the Masonic Lodge. So, this is what we're up against, right from the off."

"This isn't going to be easy, and it also accounts for some of the questions we were asked before coming onto this inquiry," Lindsay stated.

"I'm sorry, I don't understand."

"A prerequisite of coming onto this inquiry was that we had no links to any lodge," Lindsay replied.

"I see, and whose decision was that?"

"Mine," DCS Barlow answered. "What we have to do is start gathering evidence together, and we have to find out who was the organiser of the games nights. Starting tomorrow, we will start bringing in the owners, of the properties used, in for questioning."

"Sir, I thought you knew who was organiser of the games nights?"

"No. Why, do you?" Barlow demanded looking directly at Andy

"Yes sir, her name is Anika Marina Salamon. As I said earlier, I've met her."

"Andy, I know you said you had new information, so get all that onto paper before today is over, and we can review it in the morning and see how it integrates into the other information we have."

Andy nodded as he scribbled a note.

"Is your source reliable, Andy?"

"Yes, sir."

"How reliable?"

"Very."

"He is?"

"Who said it was a 'he', sir?"

"Smart arse," the DI replied with a smile.

"As of today, this inquiry will be known as 'Operation Hope,'" Barlow announced. "We'll start looking at everything we have tomorrow, Andy, you get your intelligence in, please. Then when you finish doing that, come into my office and you can explain to us how you know about Salamon."

"The rest of you can go home, get back here for nine tomorrow morning."

DCS Barlow went through to a small office set aside for him off the main office and sat down with DCI Jenkins.

Andy answered the phone as Jenkins looked up at him.

"McConnell here, Andy."

"Nice to hear from you, sir."

"I'm calling about Benny McLaughlin. I made a call when we left your office, and when I got back here, I had a result from the boss saying there was more than enough to proceed, so that has been re-opened as part of the larger inquiry."

"So, what happens to Benny now?"

"Well…" McConnell hesitated. "He's been moved to parking tickets with immediate effect; he'll be lucky to prosecute a pisser in the future."

"That was quick,"

"This isn't being recorded, so I can say we both knew who you were when you introduced yourself and we both know of your connection with David Diamond and the danger you pose to the Scottish legal system by going public, Andy, you're going to have to trust Chloe and me in this."

"We shall see, sir. Thank you for calling."

"Who was that?" the DCI shouted through as Andy hung up.

"The Crown Office. The game's on now, sir,"

"Christ, Barlow was right," Jenkins remarked.

"In what way, sir?"

"You're an iceberg."

As Jenkins was leaving the main office, he stopped and looked at Andy.

"Can I ask you something?" Jenkins whispered,

"Sure."

"Does Catherine know what you did to the barman the other night?" Andy looked away as Jenkins smiled at him. "Was it a brain tumour or a trapped nerve, doctor?"

"You know sir, I am still awaiting the x-rays"

Jenkins looked at Andy then shook his head as he walked away.

Andy submitted his intelligence report, then gave the three most senior officers on the inquiry an account of his dealings with Salamon in the past, detailing his meetings with her at the bookstore, Andy stood to leave the office. "Gents, I'm going home now." Andy turned to DCI Jenkins. "Oh, and just to let you know, I'm going to Catherine's for dinner. I'll be driving my car to my flat and I'll enter there alone and be back here for nine in the morning, for the information of your surveillance teams. See you tomorrow."

When Andy had left the office, Barlow, Jenkins, Watt, and DS Wallace, who had joined them, sat discussing their approach to the inquiry.

"You know, he doesn't give a shit about rank or anything."

"But he's a liability, sir,"

"In what way?" queried Barlow.

"I take it you know he temporarily paralysed a barman's hand at the weekend, then told him he was a doctor, and he should go to the hospital?"

"Well, these things happen," Barlow smiled shrugging his shoulders. "He has a reputation for that sort of thing." commenting with a broad smile on his face and a shake of the head.

Jenkins, Watt, and Wallace were at a loss for words. They knew nothing of Blackmore's reputation.

"Listen there's something you should know about Blackmore, he came to this job from the building trade, he's a martial arts specialist and he can hurt people if he wants to. We know of two retired detectives who were put onto him by sources unknown to us, but we suspect it was Berger or someone in his circle, Andy got hold of them in a garage and, well… there was a small petrol spillage which he threatened to set alight; the thing was, it was all over one of them."

The other two detectives sat there in silence. Then DCI Jenkins questioned, "are you saying that we have a madman, or even a psychopath, on this inquiry, boss?"

"No, we have a rough diamond that just needs polishing and a little guidance"

"Donny, have you worked with this guy? No, you haven't. I have, and I promise you, he won't let you down."

"Are you sure?"

"Yes. So, as of today, I'm taking the surveillance team off him."

"Why were they on him in the first place?"

"Because I wanted to know who he was linked to, and for other reasons. Now, let's get to business.

The men sat around a large teak table, their jackets off, their ties loosened and pulled down from the collar of their shirts, and their sleeves partially rolled up. There were mugs on the table and a plate of biscuits within easy reach. Biscuits were mandatory on the table and the shopping list. A list of actions was compiled for the inquiry officers, ready for first thing in the morning.

"Now gentlemen, finally, given the information Andy provided, we've got our target; Anika Marina Salamon. Let's get a photo of her, then she is Andy's responsibility, as he's met her. What we need to establish is; does she know he's a cop? If not, then he goes for her. Get intelligence on her. Who is she? Where's she from? Who is she linked to? All the usual stuff. You know what? We need a dedicated intelligence officer in here. Can anyone get me one for tomorrow morning?" asked Barlow, looking up at his team.

"I can get you the best," DCI Jenkins said.

"Great, get him or her here for the morning," "Anything else gents? If not, home time."

"Hiya Andy," as Barry opened the door.

"Hey, pal. Is your sister in?"

"Yes, she's making dinner."

"Nice one," as he walked in. "What is it tonight?"

"I think it's pasta again, but I've got exciting news for you."

"Great, let's go into the living room and you can tell me all about it."

"Catherine, Andy is here!"

"Right, I'll be there in a minute!" she shouted from the kitchen.

"Can I tell Andy my news?" Barry asked her, as if seeking permission.

"Yeah, of course you can, you've been waiting to tell him all day!" shouted Catherine.

"Andy, I'm getting my flat in a few weeks, I got told today."

"Aw mate, that's brilliant! Can I come and visit?"

As Barry nodded, Catherine came in and kissed Andy on the cheek.

"Hi honey,"

"Hiya,"

"How was your day?"

"Difficult, to be honest. This is going to be a long haul, and it was made clear that under no circumstances can we discuss this with anyone. It's a closed and locked office away from everyone else; it feels unreal." Catherine placed a sympathetic hand on his shoulder.

Over dinner, they discussed Barry's news. Catherine made it known it was going to by difficult for her, knowing he would be moving out in two weeks into his flat for the first time.

"Listen Catherine, this may be the best thing ever for his independence. Right Barry, your sister made the dinner, I think we should wash and tidy everything up," Andy suggested, as he started to clear the table of plates and take them into the kitchen.

"Hey mate, how do you feel about moving into your new flat?"

"I'm looking forward to it!" Barry was excited.

"Good lad. Anything you need, just ask, okay?" Andy placed an arm around Barry's neck.

"Yeah, sure Andy." as he wrapped his arm around Andy's waist.

As Andy turned around from the kitchen sink, he saw Catherine leaning against the door, where she had been listening to the conversation. She walked over to Andy and Barry and wrapped her arms around them both, telling them they were "her boys." She was delighted about the way Andy and Barry were bonding.

"Do you have plans for the weekend, Catherine?"

"Yes, I'm working," "You?"

"I'll see Alice and see what's happening with the house, then visit mum."

"I'm off on Sunday, so after some sleep, we could go for something to eat."

"Sure, that would be nice."

"Do you think you're going to be able to deal with your new posting, Andy?"

"Oh yeah, and if it gets crazy, I can just leave."

"Good," sounding pleased.

The rest of the night was spent chatting before Andy made his way back to his flat, conscious of the fact that he had told the bosses of his timetable. He did not see anyone following him home.

At 8.45 am the following day, DCS Barlow greeted his new team with a cheerful "Good morning, everyone." He introduced Chris Harvey, an intelligence officer of some repute within the force. Chris had been around the intelligence system for several years, both gathering and disseminating information force-wide. This guy was more of an analyst than an intelligence officer, as every little detail was checked and cross-checked with what he already had in his intelligence system. Twenty-five years' service, he was the man to go to for information for the past ten years, if you had the appropriate clearance. Never interested in promotion, Chris held the rank of Constable; he was happy with his lot, among the high-flyers. Everyone in the building knew him from the Commissionaire right up to the Chief Constable as he stood six feet eight inches tall. He had blond hair and was a former basketball player in his younger days. DCS Barlow knew he had a good team together and he felt that Chris Harvey was the last piece of the jigsaw. By mutual consent with DCS Barlow, Harvey would remain in uniform to allow him to move around the headquarters freely, where senior officers would not be suspicious of him being in plain clothes.

Actions for the inquiry had been set up by the senior officers and statements were the order of the day, to be obtained from victims of the games nights. Each of the officers was given a list of people to interview and sent on their way.

That first week, several youngsters were interviewed by the officers and their statements were logged by Amanda. A couple of them stated they wanted their social workers present when being interviewed, even though they were over sixteen and out of the care system. Those who were under sixteen had to have a responsible adult with them, either a parent or social worker. It was generally the latter, as they were still in the care system. The officers recorded every harrowing detail of what the young persons had been subjected to at the games nights.

The care workers in the homes, who had long ignored the kids' comings and goings at all hours of the night, were interviewed at length by the team. They were advised that having the custody charge or care of the children during their shift may leave them open to criminal prosecution in the future. This rocked the care system to its foundations, with numerous staff suspended from their positions by the local council.

It did not take long for the detectives to work out who the caring staff members were and who were just there to collect their money at the end of the month. They had a duty of care toward those kids, and they had failed them badly. Not only was the Crown Office looking at the perpetrators of the horrific abuse that had taken place, but this was going all the way down the line, right to the foundations of the system. The collateral damage and fall-out were potentially immense.

On Friday afternoon, Barlow gathered his team together in the office. He explained that, because they had been out gathering statements, the secrecy of the inquiry would diminish as the days went by, as there was no doubt that the interviewees would start talking.

Chris was asked to get all the intelligence he could from the statements that had been taken. Come Monday, the first phase of detentions and arrests would be made if there was enough evidence. If not, then it was back to getting more statements.

Amanda was tasked with compiling a card index system naming the suspect, allegation, and victim with any corroborating evidence.Everything was to remain "in house." The team felt the whole inquiry was starting to gather pace, even this early into it, with many more actions to be carried out. Was this to be the start of the downfall of the high and mighty, with justice for the victims?

DCS Barlow lifted the phone and dialled an internal number at the Crown Office.

"Mr. Barlow, I presume," It's McConnell imitating Stanley finding Dr Livingstone.

"Yes sir, even at this early stage of the inquiry, we have identified several people involved in the Games Nights and there is corroboration for a few who I intend to have detained on Monday morning."

"Excellent news, Mr. Barlow. But I get a feeling that is not all?"

"No, sir. I'm concerned about the effect this inquiry will have on my officers."

"We have access to professional assistance if required," McConnell offered.

"I would be grateful if that was made available to my staff, sir."

"I'll arrange that immediately when I get back in on Monday morning."

"Much appreciated." Barlow put down the phone and sat back in his chair, his hands behind his head. The office was empty, and he stared at the ceiling, wondering where this inquiry was going to end and who would fall from grace along the way. He leaned forward and pulled open the deepest drawer in his desk. He lifted out a bottle of Cardhu single malt whisky. From the top drawer, he took a cut-glass whisky tumbler, which he placed on the desk. With a twist of the cork, the smell of the single malt reached his nose. He poured a 'dram' into the glass before returning the bottle to the drawer.

As Barlow lifted the glass to his lips, the phone rang. It was Assistant Chief Constable Mackenzie.

"How is the inquiry going?"

"Fine, sir," Barlow replied, raising the glass to eye level and examining the golden nectar within, knowing Mackenzie was fishing for information.

"So, are you going to give me a progress report?"

"As I said, sir, it's progressing nicely," as he swirled the contents of the glass.

"Keep me up to date, please."

"Yes, sir." He replaced the receiver on its cradle, Barlow thought to himself, *aye right, no chance.* He brought the glass to his lips and sipped the contents, all the while contemplating his next move.

Chapter Nine

A s big Chris Harvey gave up on his Saturday off to go through all the information in the statements obtained, he slowly began to put together a picture of the participants in the games nights. If there was one thing about Chris, he was thorough and accurate in his work, which is exactly why he was brought into the inquiry.

He sat in the office alone in silence, referencing and cross-referencing names, dates, and places. The previously unknown Salamon featured heavily in all the statements, and she was known to all the youngsters as the recruiter and paymaster.

Chris searched every system available to him, but there was no intelligence held by any force concerning Salamon. Was that even her real name? Was she someone who got caught up in the Games Nights and was being used by someone higher? Had she been brought in from abroad to organise the Games Nights and had then left the country? These were all questions that had to be answered.

Chris sat and had a long think before making a telephone call. He had the authority of the boss to do what he thought necessary without asking for permission from a senior officer.

"Hi mate, Chris Harvey here, how are you?"

"Alright, Chris. What can I do for you?" came the reply.

"I need a woman checked out."

"Okay, go for it."

"Anika Marina Salamon. No further details, sorry."

"With a name like that, it should not be a problem. A couple of hours, okay?"

"Sure thing. Hit the jackpot and I'll owe you a pint."

Chris got back to work, searching, and researching. Just before he was due to leave the office, the phone rang.

"Hi,"

"Chris I can't discuss this over the phone, but I can hand it to you in a sealed envelope on Monday."

"That would be great, thank you. Call me when you're on your way."

"Yes, certainly. See you Monday, at ten o'clock."

Chris knew this was the breakthrough he was looking for…possibly.

With Catherine working, Andy headed east, back to his old stomping ground, where he met up with his childhood friends. All it took was a phone call to one and the drums were beating for everyone to gather at The Rooftop Bar for a session of drinks and good banter. This was away from the hustle and bustle of work, as none of Andy's friends were cops.

This was the first time in years everyone had been together again, and Andy was glad that he had made a phone call inviting Alice to be there. The evening was turning into an old-fashioned, early seventies night when they all met and drank together, friends forever.

"Hey Andy," Frank shouted over. "Look who's joining in the fun!"

"Andy baby, you're back,", sidling over to him and sitting on his lap. "Hey Alice, this is what I used to do with Andy when he was younger." The corner where they sat was in hysterics as Marie wrapped her arms around Andy's neck and gyrated. Wives and girlfriends were in fits of laughter and the guys were banging on the tables with their hands.

"Oh Andy, you tart!" yelled Elizabeth, Frank's wife.

"If she keeps this going, she'll just make things hard for herself," Andy shouted, watched by Alice.

"That's what I'm hoping for."

When things calmed down, Alice whispered to Andy that she was a little jealous that Marie could do that, Andy just laughed.

The chat during the evening was that of another glorious failure by Scotland at the World Cup in June and what the forthcoming football season would bring for their respective teams.

As the night came to an end, everyone began to file outside before they drifted back to their homes, but they knew this was not the last time they would be together. Although they had gone their separate ways in life, this was a team of friends that would be together for life. As Andy and Alice were leaving the bar, Marie looked at them and remarked, "hey, you two look great together."

"Marie, it is not going to happen,"

Yeah right, Marie thought to herself as she nodded her head.

When Marie was tidying up the tables in the lounge, with their empty and partially filled glasses, she looked out of the window overlooking the street. She watched as Andy put Alice into a taxi, taking her back to her parents' house, where she was staying with her children. She put the empties on the bar and went downstairs, where she found Andy outside.

"Hey you, fancy a late-night drink?" as she began bolting the outer doors.

"You mean a lock-in?"

"Yeah. Long time since I had one of those…"

Without saying a word, Andy made a gesture which suggested; "Sure, if you want," looking at Marie with some trepidation.

"Do you still have staff in there?"

"Yes, a few."

"Well, maybe not the best idea, huh?"

"They'll be gone soon, then we can talk."

"What about?"

"Things you need to know."

Andy wondered if Marie knew he had changed his job. It was a long time since he had seen the bar empty and had been asked back for a late-night drink.

Andy sat on a stool and leaned on the bar. He watched as the slim Marie poured a brandy for him and a Bacardi for herself. She saw Andy's reflection in the large mirror behind the bar, watching her pour the drinks. Marie turned around, placed the glasses on the bar top before making her way around the bar and sitting on the stool next to him.

"Cheers Andy," lifting her glass.

"Sláinte Marie"

"Still a brickie?"

Andy nodded.

"Brickie my arse," staring at him.

"Meaning?"

"You're a cop, Andy. You became a cop and never even told me!"

"You never asked."

"Well, I've been doing a little investigating myself."

"About what?"

"Oh, this and that. Your brother Ricky was in here a few months ago. He had no idea that I knew who he was. He was with a lot of friends, male and female. It was a private hire here in the lounge and all curtains were tightly drawn."

"Where's this going, Marie?" as if he did not already know.

"Last week when you came in here with Alice, everything started to come together, then, someone had said you were now a police officer, and it was your girlfriend that had been killed in the car at the loch. I'm sorry about what happened to her."

"Thank you, Marie," he paused. "Now you were saying about the private hire?"

"I was paid a thousand pounds for one shift to work the bar and to keep my mouth shut about what went on in here that night. That is a load of money for me, Andy, and it was in cash."

Andy sat there in silence, recognising the catch twenty-two situation he was now in.

"Do you have any idea what I'm talking about?"

"No," Andy lied.

"C'mon Andy, it's me that you are talking to."

Marie looked deep into Andy's eyes and instinct told her that he was lying to her. She considered long and hard about what she was about to say to him.

"Listen," her eyes looking downwards, away from the gaze of Andy, as she took his hand in hers. Then, taking a deep breath, "they brought girls and boys in, they were around thirteen years old or so, maybe a little older, not by much, and it was just a night of... sex."

"Have they been here before or since?"

"Yeah, twice before. I'm the only one working at the bar, nobody else is allowed."

Andy nodded.

"They're due back here on Wednesday night."

"Who's booked it?"

"The same person as usual, Anna Szymańska."

"Marie, did you see Ricky take part in anything?"

Marie went very quiet and bowed her head towards the floor.

"You don't have to answer that," Andy knew she already had.

"Can I ask you something, Marie, why are you telling me all of this?"

"Something needs to be done to protect those kids, Andy. When I leave here after those nights, I'm one thousand pounds tax-free better off, but I feel like shit, for being a witness to everything that happens. Some nights, when I get in and throw the money on the settee, I'm physically sick."

She paused and wiped the tears away from her eyes.

"What happens now, Andy? If there is one person, one cop, I would trust with my life it is you. Can you get anything done about this, Andy?"

"I don't know, Marie. I just don't know."

"I can't believe I wanted to get you into bed last week," changing the subject and laughing.

Something occurred to Andy. "I need your phone number, Marie, and the one for here, not your personal one, I already have that."

"Oh, I like that."

"Well, here's the deal; if this works, I'll take you for dinner."

"Where are you going tonight at this hour, Andy?"

Andy looked at his watch and realised the time.

"You'll be safe at my place, and I'll tell you everything I know;"

"Westhouse Road, mate," Andy directed as they got into the taxi.

"Hey Marie, new boyfriend?"

"Jesus Bobby, he's young enough to be my son!" "No, just a neighbour of mine, and what do you mean, new boyfriend? When did you last see me with a guy?"

"Never, Marie, never."

"Right then. You'll give Andy a bad impression of me."

"How are you doin' Andy? I'm Bobby."

"How do you do," shaking his hand.

"Do you work in the pub?" Bobby asked.

"Nah mate, I'm a brickie."

"Aw great, I'm lookin' for a brickie, take my card mate, gimme a call."

"Thanks, sure thing. Monday, okay?" as they set off.

A short time later they arrived in Westhouse Road "Here you go, Marie's passion palace."

"Do you want to be barred from the pub, Bobby?"

"You'd never bar me, Marie."

"True," she admitted, paying Bobby.

Andy told Marie to wait until the taxi went out of view as they stood chatting on the street. When the taxi had gone, they went into the close and up the stairs to Marie's flat.

"This is lovely, Marie."

"Thank you, Andy."

"I remember this place well," Andy recalled with a laugh.

"Do you?"

"Oh yes. How could I forget?"

"Do you want a drink?" Marie asked.

"What have you got?"

"Whatever you want." She opened a cabinet full of booze.

"Brandy?"

"Good choice," sitting down opposite him in a chair. "So, Andy, tell me about yourself."

"What would you like to know, Marie?"

"Everything."

"Well... I'm a bricklayer who was seduced by a mature woman one New Year's Eve, who became a cop and moved west, who is still single, but attached to a lovely lady, and who still loves the East End, and what about you, Marie?"

"Born and bred here, divorced, and I'll never forget my New Year with a special guy. Long for a repeat of that night and the ones that followed for a few months, but that is not likely to happen again."

"I think we have to sort out another problem, don't you?"

Marie sat and poured out her heart to Andy about the Games Nights she had worked at, about those that she knew by name and everything that she could think of about Anika and her associates, and who were the main players. Then, she changed the subject.

"What about Alice, do you fancy her, Andy?"

"She's my sister-in-law, Marie, so she's out of bounds."

"That's not what I asked you."

"She is attractive, intelligent and a great mother."

"Okay, if that's what you say, but I see things differently."

"In what way?"

"She's special to you."

"Yes, she always will be."

Marie took a sip from her glass. "I'll finish this and go to bed. You have the spare room, Andy."

"Thanks, Marie."

She knocked back her drink. "And hey, if you wanna sneak in beside me, I won't object."

"I know, bad girl," Andy replied with a wink. "Goodnight, Marie."

"Goodnight, Andy," smiling as she closed the door behind her.

At eleven o'clock on Sunday morning, Andy knocked on Marie's bedroom door; "Hey, tea or coffee?"

"Tea please," Marie replied, sleepily.

A few minutes later, Andy opened the door and carried in the tea, finding Marie still under the bed covers.

"Here you go," handing her the cup.

"I'm not used to this," sitting up.

"I'll have a coffee through there, then I'll head for the west,"

"Pity," Marie commented, looking at him.

"If I was single, I'd be in beside you, Marie."

"Really?"

"Yes. Now, coffee time for me, then we can talk tomorrow." Andy leaned over and kissed Marie on the cheek. "See ya very soon."

Andy grabbed a passing taxi out on the street and returned to the Rooftop where he collected his car from the car park before driving up to the Blackmore villa.

"Ricky, it's me," Andy called through the intercom.

"What do you want now?" Ricky demanded.

"Just a chat, that's all."

"Fine, come up."

Andy got to the door and was met by his unshaven brother.

"When did you last eat?" Andy was concerned.

"Dunno."

"D'you want me to make you something?"

"Nothing here for eating mate, look and see for yourself."

Andy opened the fridge and saw that everything in there had gone off; the milk was turning to cheese, it was that bad, and food lay rotting on the shelves, Andy closed the door, his heart melancholy at the depths his brother's life had reached. Even the bread was covered in blue mould, Andy looked at Ricky, wondering when he had last had a wash or even got changed out of the clothes he was wearing.

"Have you seen Alice?" Ricky slurred under the influence of drink.

"Yeah, a whole crowd of us were at the Rooftop last night."

"And did you take her home and spend the night with her?"

"She went home alone, Ricky, because she loves you."

"No, she doesn't, she loves you mate." Sad at his brothers' demise, this was not a time for anger.

"Oh? And how do you know that?"

"Because she told me, in a roundabout way."

"What do you mean, in a roundabout way?"

"It doesn't matter. Why are you here?"

"To give you a heads up that your days of freedom are numbered, quite possibly."

"Yeah, I thought it might come to that. What happens if I talk officially?"

"I don't know, to be honest."

Ricky nodded. "Will you look after Alice and the kids if the worst happens?"

"I'll try."

"How's mum, Andy?"

"She's bad, Ricky."

"Thanks for being honest. Good luck to you and Catherine, mate."

"Thank you don't you want me to get you bread or milk or anything from the shops?"

"Nah, I won't need it."

As he walked down the driveway, Andy had a gut-wrenching feeling that would be the last time he would see Ricky alive, but he tried to believe that wasn't true. After all, Ricky was still his brother.

Fearing for Ricky's health, Andy rushed to the home of Alice's parents.

Alice's mother answered the door "Oh hello Andy, please, do come in,"

"Thank you."

"Hi," Alice greeted him with her usual smile.

"I've just come from your house, Ricky is so down."

"Andy, there's nothing I can do. Does that sound bad?"

Alice's mother looked over at her daughter, she remained silent not wanting to get involved.

"I'm worried about him Alice."

"So am I, but only he can help himself."

"I agree, I went to make him something to eat; virtually all the food in the house is rotten. I know that you're living here with the kids, it was just to let you know, Alice."

"What are you doing now, then?"

"Heading home. You have my number?"

"Yes, I do," touching the side of his face before he left.

"Andy, did you go home last night? Your car was left at the pub."

"No, to be honest, I stayed with a friend."

"Oh, that's good, I was wondering where you would go after I was in the taxi."

"No problem, Alice, see you soon"

Andy reached his flat and waited a few hours before contacting Catherine, who would be getting ready for her night shift. They had a quick chat about his weekend and her shifts and arranged to see each other during the week.

"First of all, thank you all for your efforts last week," DCS Barlow announced. The whole team was gathered for Monday's 9;00 briefing. "I was hoping we were going out to make our first arrests and detentions this morning, but Chris was in on Saturday, and he's put together a comprehensive document for us to go over before we make our next moves. I would suggest that you look at the list of persons requiring interview and proceed with those now; we will reconvene at one today."

"Guys, before we go, I was out at the weekend," announced Andy.

"Lucky you," quipped Sharon McLeod.

"Well, actually, it was lucky me, I can tell you that the next Games Night has been arranged for eight o'clock on Wednesday night at The Rooftop Bar in the east end. I also know that Anika Salamon has organised the evening under the name of Anika Szymańska."

"Can we ask where this information came from Andy?"

"Yes, a friend in the east end"

"Now how did he or she know all this? Do they know that you're involved in this inquiry?"

"To your first question, Salamon has used the premises before and the person that told me has been a witness to the events Secondly, the person who told me has no idea about this inquiry, or my involvement."

Going on for ten o'clock, Chris informed the boss that he was leaving the office to collect an envelope containing information on one of the suspects from a confidential source. His reputation was such that the boss never even questioned him.

As he reached the reception area, a person entered the foyer wearing full biker's leathers and a helmet with the visor down. An unmarked brown envelope was handed to Chris, and they parted company without a word being spoken. The concierge just looked on, shrugged his shoulders, and got on with his job.

Chris got back into the lift, with some senior officers, all of whom knew him. There was the usual banter between them.

"What have you got there, Chris?" a young, uniformed Chief Inspector enquired, pointing to the envelope.

"Well sir, it's this week's top racing tips for Doncaster and Newmarket."

"Didn't know you were a racing man" the Chief Inspector remarked as he left the lift on the fourth floor.

Chris smiled to himself and shook his head in disbelief at the Chief Inspector's comment. He wondered what the job was coming to if those sort of people were its future leaders.

Opening the envelope, drawing out the document at his desk, he was confronted with the words 'Strictly Confidential' and 'Restricted Information' on the front sheet of paper. Turning the page over, he looked at a single photograph of a blonde woman. Below the image was the name 'Anika Marina Salamon'. Chris opened the document and began reading.

> Name; SALAMON. Anika Marina
> Age; 41
> Born; 1940
> Place; Warsaw, Poland
> Occupation; Business Owner
> Home Address; Restricted Information
> Alias Surnames; Kamińska, Szymańska, and
> Zielińska
> Marital Status; Divorced
> Children; None
> Associates; Restricted Information

> CONFIDENTIAL INFORMATION

> Paylova was taken out of Nazi-occupied Poland and brought to Scotland in 1942. She spent time in foster care; the whereabouts of her parents are unknown.

> She was schooled in and around Dumfries until she was sixteen, then she moved to Glasgow around 1958/9. She worked in local factories, then in whisky bonds.

> 1970: Arrested for soliciting in the city centre.

> 1973: Suspected of entertaining high-ranking police officers and local politicians at home.

1978: Suspected of organising parties known as Games Nights for high-ranking police officers, local politicians and businesspeople both male and female.

1980: Questioned about her involvement with young vulnerable adults. No further action.

1982: Seen in a city centre bookshop by a retired police officer, seated with Constable Andrew Blackmore who is known to the officer. Blackmore was seen to leave the premises in the company of Sandra Berger. There is a known link between Berger and Salamon, as they were/are involved in a sexual relationship. Sandra Berger is the wife of retired senior police officer Brian Berger. Any link between Blackmore and Berger is unknown to the retired police officer.

1982: Salamon currently owns an escort agency for high-end clients and organises parties.

Chris had not been involved in the initial meeting of all those involved in the inquiry, he was unaware of the connection between Andy and the Berger family. Therefore, he did not mention the contents of the intelligence he had been given to anyone. Instead, he photocopied the image of Salamon, removing her name from the document.

Chris went into the boss' office and closed the door behind him. He handed over the envelope to DCS Barlow, who examined the contents and gave Chris a nod to disseminate the information to the inquiry team. Chris was rather puzzled, given the contents of the Blackmore paragraph, and he said so.

"Chris, Susan Berger was the fiancée of Andy Blackmore, he's aware of everything, so no harm was done. Oh, and well done getting that from wherever it came from." Barlow paused. "I take it your source is secure?"

"Yes, sir and thank you."

Chris waited until Andy, who had been out getting statements, returned to the office.

"Andy, have you got a minute?"

"Sure Chris"

"Do you know who this is?" Chris showed him the photograph, minus the name.

"Yes," Andy replied. "Anika Salamon."

"Cheers mate, just wanted to be sure."

All the officers came back for the one o'clock briefing as requested.

"Okay, guys listen up. We have an identification of the ringleader of this inquiry, Anika Marina Salamon, and this is her history." DCS Barlow outlined what was known of her and appealed for his officers to get more information from the people they were interviewing. "Tomorrow we go out and start the clear up. Now, as you're aware, a police officer of a lesser rank cannot interview an officer senior in rank to him or her, so I have made arrangements for that to be covered as of nine in the morning tomorrow."

"What about Salamon?" DCI Jenkins enquired.

"I've been thinking about that one," Barlow replied.

"And what are your thoughts?"

"To play the long game and hope that she doesn't know that our Mr. Blackmore is a police officer."

"Boss, what the hell does that mean?"

"What it means, Donald, is that I'm sending Andy back to where he first met Salamon and praying that this is her meeting place for prospective clients."

"Are we going to wire him up?"

"Erm, excuse me, I'm sitting here, you know," Andy interjected. "Don't I get a say in this?"

"Actually, no, Andy," Barlow replied, which brought laughter all around.

"Thanks for your support, guys," Andy jested.

"As for wiring him up, yes, that is for sure, and the trial run is this afternoon," Barlow continued. "Right, let's get going."

Andy was taken to an office away from the rest of the officers, where he was wired up for reception and transmission. He was given a five-minute training session on the equipment before getting ready to head for the bookshop where he had met Salamon before. This was the biggest risk Barlow had ever taken and could blow the lid off the whole inquiry.

Andy walked into the bookshop on New City Road. He went to the photography section and chose a book before sitting down at a table with a cup of coffee. Hour after hour passed by and there was no sign of Salamon. As Andy watched the door, Sharon McLeod walked in and nodded that it was time to go, Andy returned his book to its shelf and made his way to the door.

"Sorry, after you," as he held the door open for the woman entering.

"Thank you," "Oh, hello again!"

"I'm sorry," pausing, "Do I know you?"

"We met here a few weeks ago." It was Anika. "I remember you, let's have a coffee, and I'll tell you why I remember, that's if you would like to have a coffee with me."

"Sure, why not, I am not in a hurry to go anywhere." He turned and went back to the café.

Andy knew exactly why she remembered him. As they sat facing each other over a table, Andy slowly stirred his coffee.

"Do you remember the last time we met?" asked.

"Not really," Andy lied. "So, what is it about me you remember?"

"You met someone here that we both know."

"Listen, I'm sorry but I have to go soon."

"Let me introduce myself. I'm Anika Szymańska."

"Oh, are you Russian?"

"No, Polish."

"Ah okay, Polish with a Glaswegian accent," he laughed

"I've been here a while," Anika admitted.

"So, who did I meet that we both know?"

"A woman called Sandra Berger."

"Oh yes, now it's all coming back to me. Geez, that was a while ago." Andy paused. "Well, this is a pleasant surprise but I have to finish my coffee.It's time for me to go."

"No, please wait," Anika pleaded, placing her hand on his. "Tell me, how did you know Sandra?"

Andy looked at Anika, wondering what she knew about him.

"What do you do for a living, Anika?" Andy changed the subject.

"I have my own business."

"Doing what?"

"I'm an organiser."

"Meaning what exactly?"

"I organise weddings, parties, things like that, and you have still not answered my question."

"Which was?"

"Sandra."

"Oh yeah, Sandra." Andy paused again. "Me and Sandra were friends."

"What age were you when you met her?"

"Fifteen or Sixteen, I think."

"Yeah, she always liked them young," Anika remarked.

"I'm sorry, I have to go," getting to his feet.

"Listen, I have a few parties arranged. Would you like to join?"

"Are you asking me out?"

"No… Well, maybe. Can we meet here again tomorrow?"

"What time? I'll be working."

"Oh, what do you do?"

"I'm a brickie and I also do some security work."

"Mmmm, rough hands then," Anika commented. "How about half three or four o'clock?"

"Yeah, good for me, see you tomorrow then" as he walked away, watched by Anika.

"Great," Sharon unhooked all the wiring from Andy. "You're light years ahead of where you should be."

"Did you get everything?"

"Yeah, we have it, just have to get tomorrow now; the boss says from now on to stay away from the office."

"Okay, so where should we meet?"

"Your place. I'll wire you up, then you go."

Sharon arrived at Andy's flat the following day at half-past one with all the equipment recharged and ready to go. Once he was taped up, Andy got the train into the city. He didn't want his car identified if he was being watched by anyone on Salamon's side. As he was going towards the cafe of the bookshop, a woman behind him spoke. "Your turn for coffee." It was Anika.

Andy now knew she was surveillance conscious.

"Yesterday, when we were talking, you told me you were a brickie." "Yes…" fearing the worst.

"You know what?" "You didn't even tell me your name."

"Sorry, I didn't think. I'm Andy."

"Pleased to meet you, Andy," shaking his hand. "Now then, tell me about you and Sandra."

"I was a paperboy in the East End and Sandra and her man were on my round. When I was delivering their papers, she used to come to the door wearing a dressing gown; she was such a tease. Then one Sunday, she asked me in, as her man was working. She made no secret about the invite."

Anika nodded eagerly. "Listen, I have a party on Wednesday night, would you like to come?"

"Yeah, sure, I'd love that."

"Great! Meet me at The Rooftop Bar, at seven o'clock or thereabouts."

"Okay, see you there," as she began walking away from the table. "Oh Anika, how do I contact you?"

"You don't, I contact you here. Let's say… How about Wednesday afternoon? Just looking at you, I feel I may have a job for you. There is something about you that makes me think I want you to work for me. See you Wednesday, Brickie boy."

Later, when Andy thought about what he had done, he knew he had to act quickly, as Marie would be behind the bar. Sharon arrived at his place and Andy stood in front of her, getting the recording equipment removed. Sharon asked him if he had a girlfriend, which he confirmed.

"Lucky girl," Sharon replied. "What's her name?"

"Catherine."

"Lucky Catherine."

"Nah, lucky Andy."

"So, is she younger than you?"

"You're a nosy little devil, Sharon," Andy remarked, laughing.

"Well, I'm a detective, after all."

"For your information, no, she's older than me."

"Okay, that's all I wanted to know." Sharon paused. "For now."

Andy called the office and briefed DCI Jenkins. They discussed the meeting with Anika and his invitation to the party on Wednesday night, which was fraught with danger, given the guests who might be in attendance and the compromising situation Andy could find himself in. They also discussed the job that Anika mentioned she may have for him. The big question was; Did she know he was a cop?

Chapter Ten

Andy walked into the bookshop and began to browse the photography section. He drew a book from the shelf and headed to the coffee bar.

"Coffee, black, please."

The waitress nodded.

Andy sat down with his book, entitled *War Photography*.

"Hi Andy," sitting across from him.

"Hello Anika."

"I like your taste in books, Andy."

"Thanks."

"Well I've been thinking, I have a job offer for you."

"Oh?"

"How good would you be on a door, making sure everything's in order?"

"I can handle myself. But if you want me on a door, I don't come cheap you know."

"Okay. Let's talk about money and conditions."

"How do you mean; conditions?"

"You hear no evil, see no evil, speak no evil, and you are well paid."

"How much are we talking about?"

"Five-hour shift on the door, let's say, one thousand five hundred pounds for the five hours."

"That is one pile of money, Anika! What the hell are you into?" Andy raised his eyebrows.

"Let's say… games. Adult Games nights."

"That is just silly money. So let's say I'll do your door this week and see how things progress."

"Great! Do you know where you're going tonight?"

Andy nodded. "Was it The Rooftop Bar you said?"

She confirmed, Andy watched as Anika left the bookshop. Then he went back to his book.

Sharon McLeod watched Andy leaving the bookshop and followed him to the railway station, where he got the train home. Sharon drove to his flat to remove and collect his wires.

As she was taking his wires off, "Sharon, we have a problem." She looked up at him. "The party tonight is in The Rooftop Bar, which was my local for years, and I know the barmaid. She knows I'm no longer a brickie."

"Shit. I need to speak to the boss about this one," Sharon paused. "Just stay away from the office for now. I'll get back to you."

Sharon drove straight back to the office, where she spoke with Barlow. The decision was taken to go through with the plan as previously agreed, as Andy cancelling would raise suspicions with Salamon. Any raid that was being considered by the bosses was also cancelled.

Barlow called Andy "Game on, please be careful."

"Yes sir," before hanging up the phone.

The next call was to the barmaid Marie.

"Hello stranger, are you finally calling me for a date?"

"Reading my mind again, how do you do that Marie?"

She rolled her eyes. "What can I do for you?"

"Well I have a favour to ask."

"Yes," she prompted.

"I'm doing some extra work to make money on the side to help out my mum, but my day job cannot find out. Can you pretend you don't know me?"

"Well, that might be a tough job, big man. But since it is to help your mum, I have to say yes. She is such a sweetheart."

"Awful nice of you to say that, I know you only met her once."

"No worries. I won't know you."

"Great - look forward to not seeing you." They both laughed and as Andy hung up the phone he crossed his fingers, she would be the only one in the building who knew Andy was a serving police officer. *Glad I remembered she really liked my mum* he thought.

Andy parked his car away from The Rooftop Bar on his arrival in the east end and walked to the venue. As he went in, he saw Marie, who, true to her word, ignored him. Anika came over and introduced Marie to Andy and told him what was expected of him. To get entry to the party, the code word was "Thirteen." Andy confirmed he understood and went to the door, placing himself by the entrance. He was wearing a large black padded jacket, dark jeans and boots with a black woollen hat pulled down over his ears, Andy looked every inch a bouncer.

The first to arrive were the young teenage girls, who were dropped off from various cars. Then a couple of boys, accompanied by what looked like their minders.

"Good evening," two well-dressed gentlemen greeted Andy.

"Good evening," Andy replied. "Can I help you?"

"I hope so, thirteen."

"Enjoy your evening," Andy nodded as he opened the door for them to enter.

There was a procession of clients entering the venue over the next hour or so, each of whom had the password. A middle-aged couple arrived at the venue accompanied by another lady.

"Good evening,"

"Good evening," replied the woman. "And you are?"

"I'm sorry, the lounge bar is closed tonight," Andy informed them as they tried to enter.

"Thirteen," the woman stated, looking at him.

"Have a nice evening," Andy intoned.

"Oh, I shall," pausing then looking at Andy from head to toe, "and I'm coming back for you later." She ran her forefinger down his chest over his jacket, looking into his eyes and smiling.

About two in the morning, the party began to break up as the girls left the venue, followed by the boys and the guys they had arrived with. The partygoers were quick to follow and left in cars and taxis.

"Hey big guy. What's your name?"

"Andy."

"Well Andy, I'm Gail and this is my friend Lorna. We'd like to take you home with us."

"Sorry ladies, but I don't mix business with pleasure, but, thanks for the offer."

"Shame, maybe some other time…"

"Perhaps." Anika was the last to leave the Rooftop on her own. She stopped on the street next to Andy and praised him for his work that evening.

"Are you available for a meeting on Saturday at the bookshop?"

"Sorry, I'm not free then, but I can do Friday."

"Okay, let us meet at half-past three. Oh, and Marie has a drink and an envelope for you."

"Thank you," watching Anika walk away, before closing the double doors and bolting them before making his way up to the lounge. Marie was sitting at a table, on which lay one Bacardi and coke and one brandy with ice, Andy leaned on the table, looking at Marie. He could see that she was uncomfortable. Something that had happened that night had got to her.

"Are you okay?.

"Truthfully, no, not tonight. Things just went a little over the top."

"How do you mean?"

"One of the girls… She was taking everyone on. It was disturbing."

"I see,"

"So, how did you get this gig with her tonight?"

"It's a long story."

"Here, she left you this," tossing Andy an envelope thick with cash.

"Listen, do you want a lift home?"

"Yeah, sure,"

With the Rooftop locked up for the night, Andy took Marie to her place before heading to his flat. Before she left his car, Andy asked what the locals were saying about the nights in the lounge bar. "I just tell them it is a birthday party or private hire; the owner doesn't bother as long as he gets his money."

"Good, thanks Marie."

As he sat, reflecting on how close he had come to being rumbled, Andy decided that he would phone into the office tomorrow to get further instructions from the boss. A large brandy in his hand, Andy thought of Catherine and just wanted the weekend to come so he could have a day off. Bed beckoned.

"Good morning, sir," Andy called the office at nine o'clock.

"Morning Andy,"

"I'm just calling in to see where we go from here, sir."

"Well, you lie low, stay with Anika and do what you must do. You will be followed twenty-four hours a day, seven days a week, by my surveillance unit and you will not know where or who they are."

"I'm meeting Anika on Friday afternoon, at three-thirty, same place as before."

"Just update me as to the next party, where and when, and stay away from here."

"Okay," hanging up the phone and slumping back into his chair. He had lost track of time and Catherine's shift pattern, so that was something he had to rectify quickly. He called Catherine's number and waited as the phone rang. No one answered, Andy's heart sank. He got up and went to the gym to get rid of his excess energy.

As he drove into the car park, he saw a car he recognised and understood why he hadn't got a reply to his phone call. Knowing that Catherine was there, Andy sat in the café, waiting for her to appear from whatever class she was in.

"Excuse me, would you like a coffee?"

"Oh, Andy!" with a surprised smile. "What are you doing here?"

"I'm here because I love you,"

"Andy, we both know that's not the reason you're here," Catherine whispered cheekily.

"Well, it was a good effort," Andy laughed.

They sat and chatted for a while, Catherine quizzing him on what he had been doing, Andy explained that he couldn't tell her anything at this time, but hopefully would be able to soon.

"I'm heading into the gym for a while, do you want to come with me?"

"No thanks but get yourself to my place when you finish for lunch."

"I'd love to," he replied, kissing her gently on the lips.

Andy lifted his kit bag from the floor and made his way to the male changing rooms. Catherine watched him from her seat, something gnawing at her mind, which she had to confront when Andy arrived at her place for lunch.

With her elbows on the table and her chin resting on her clenched fists, Catherine wondered if this relationship was about to end for the second time, even though they were almost due to sign the missives on a house, Andy was never so evasive – what was he hiding?

Chapter Eleven

As Catherine drove home, her mind was in turmoil as she mulled over how to approach a very delicate subject. What if the information she had been given by a close friend was wrong? What would that signal to Andy? That she didn't trust him.

Catherine had also been harbouring something else that she had never revealed to Andy. The time and place had just never seemed right for some reason. Was what she had to say to him that important in the grand scale of things? *After all, it is my past,* she thought.

Now seemed the right time, over lunch or just after lunch, Catherine pondered. This had to be done before they moved in together - if they moved in together. She was standing in the kitchen, preparing lunch at the worktop, when she heard the door open.

"Hi Andy, in here," Catherine called to him.

"What's for lunch?", standing behind her, and putting his hands on her hips. He felt her body tense very slightly, enough to tell him this was a 'no go.' Added to this fact, she did not turn to kiss him, which was right out of character for her, Andy sensed that something was amiss.

"Is everything alright, Catherine?"

"Yes, of course it is, I'm just busy preparing this salad for us," Catherine replied unconvincingly.

"Okay…" taking a seat at the table. Catherine walked into the living room with two plates, laying one in front of him and kissing him on his cheek. She sat on the opposite side of the table, facing Andy.

"Thank you, Catherine, this looks lovely."

"You're welcome," but Andy still had a gut feeling that something was not right. As if in unison, both began to ask each other if they had been up to much.

"Sorry, after you."

Catherine knew she was hopeless at small talk, but she asked what he had been doing since they were last together, Andy carefully considered his reply, which was not as spontaneous as usual, prompting Catherine to ask "Well?"

Andy began to tell her that, in respect of the case and the inquiry, he couldn't say anything, as the whole issue was far too sensitive. He went on to say that the less she knew, the better it would be because if any information got out into the public domain, even inadvertently by a slip of the tongue, all hell would break loose.

Catherine stared at him, incredulous. "Do you honestly think I would discuss it with anyone?"

"No, that's not what I meant,"

"See if you can answer this then." "Are you in the office mostly, or out and about?"

"Out and about," puzzled by the question.

The remainder of the lunch was consumed in silence. When he was finished, Andy placed his knife and fork on his plate.

"That was lovely, thank you," watching Catherine finish hers.

Andy placed his elbows on the table, his hands tightly clasped together in front of him. Catherine silently stared at her empty plate.

"Catherine…" Andy began, his voice gentle. "Would you like to tell me what's going on, please? This isn't like you at all."

Catherine looked at Andy remaining silent, but he could see her thinking something over.

"Andy, I accept that you can't discuss your inquiries on this case in full, but you have just shut down completely, so there's something I want to say to you initially, and then there are some questions I need answering here and now, or we can have no future together. "Secondly, when I'm speaking to you, I don't want to be interrupted, because what I have to say is something I have never said to anyone before."

Andy sat there, confused, to say the least.

"Right, where do I start?" Catherine took a long, deep breath to calm her nerves. She had her arms on the table, her hands clasped together, as she looked into Andy's eyes. "Many years ago, I was in a very short-term relationship with a guy. I think I was about twenty, I can't even remember if I was nursing or not at the time, but it makes no difference. I found out he cheated on me with a close friend of mine. So, I got rid of him, saying that I had to take care of Barry, and I never saw him again. When I told him I was getting rid of him then he told me that he didn't want to see me again either, because of Barry. You have no idea how hard that was to take."

Catherine went silent for a moment and Andy watched her closely, listening intently.

"That was a long time ago, and if I ever got asked out, I politely declined for fear of being rejected again. Then you came into my life and turned it upside down. You never gave a hint of rejecting Barry and I knew that you were in love with me, but the real reason I ended our relationship was that I didn't want us to go through life together with you thinking that we can't do anything or go anywhere without Barry being around us.

"You were my first relationship since I was in my, what, late teens, early twenties. I kept myself to myself, I did what I wanted to do, and my friends always thought there was something wrong with me for refusing to go out with anyone until you arrived. When I heard that you were seeing Susan, my heart was broken, because I had lost the only person that I had loved in so many years.

"So, that's the past, now to the present." Catherine looked at Andy. "I just want to be sure that you are committed to this relationship. I know you've been meeting a woman over the last few weeks; and I wouldn't have a problem with it - except you seem to be keep a secret from me. You see, I have a friend that you don't know who lives near the bookshop," Catherine continued. "She came to me recently out of concern, knowing that you and I were in a relationship and about to move in together. She saw you in the shop a while ago with an older woman."

Andy knew he was in a catch-22 situation. Either reveal what was going on, as much as he could, or lose Catherine, and the latter was not going to happen as far as he was concerned. He made up his mind.

"Put a jacket on, we're going for a drive."

"Why should I?" Catherine asked, narrowing her eyes.

"Because I need to speak to you, away from here... please."

Reluctantly, Catherine put on her jacket, locked the door to her flat, got into Andy's car and, a short time later, they arrived at a car park near to the Lochside shopping centre.

"Okay, let's go," having had a good look around in case they were being followed. Catherine knew Andy was a little edgy as they made their way into the coffee shop.

"Two coffees, please," Andy requested from the young lady behind the counter.

"Are you sitting in, sir?"

"No."

"Why not?"

"I have my reasons. Please trust me."

"Trust," Catherine repeated. "That's ironic, coming from you."

"Let's go for a walk," reaching out his hand.

Chapter Twelve

Catherine asked, "where are we going?"

"Around to the beach, where it's quiet and secluded, away from prying eyes and ears," Andy replied.

On their way to the beach, they passed by other shops. Catherine stopped at one of them to look at a skirt and blouse worn by a mannequin in a shop window. As she looked at it, Catherine realised that her gaze had gone from the clothes to her reflection, which stared straight back at her, Andy had walked on a few paces and stopped to wait for her, taking sips of coffee from the cup, Andy had no intention of calling to her to move on; this would have just added further tension to the situation. Perhaps she just needed a few moments alone to gather her thoughts.

What have you done, Catherine? her reflection seemed to say, as she stared at it. You're about to lose the love of your life for a second time. There must be a reasonable explanation.

"Catherine, are you okay?" waking Catherine out of her dream-like state.

"Oh, sorry, I was just looking at that skirt and blouse," softening her tone toward him.

"Yeah, for the last five minutes," Andy joked.

As they continued slowly walking in silence, Andy noticed that there were only a few folks about, tourists as usual, Andy breathed in deeply; he was almost resigned to losing Catherine.

"What's that?" Catherine suddenly asked.

"Post office raid alarm," Andy replied, as two masked men ran from the post office, one carrying what appeared to be a sawn-off shotgun and the other carrying a machete. The men were heading straight for them.

As the masked robbers separated to go around Andy and Catherine, Andy lashed out with his left hand, striking the man carrying the shotgun across the chest, directly onto his heart. As the man hit the ground, the shotgun spiralled away from his grasp and lay on the grey paving slabs, Andy immediately seized the weapon as the other masked raider with the machete turned to assist his fallen comrade, running towards Andy and Catherine, Andy placed the weapon on the ground at Catherine's feet.

"Stand on that and don't move," Andy shouted in a commanding voice.

Catherine watched in horror as Andy went into his martial arts stance, yelling; "Game on, let's do this big chap!" He beckoned the man towards him, but the robber knew when he was beaten, and he ran off and leapt onto a waiting speedboat, concealed on the other side of a retaining wall. The speedboat made off up the loch at high speed.

As Andy whipped off the unconscious robber's mask, he could hear the wail of sirens getting closer, meaning help was at hand, Andy prayed it wouldn't be anyone from his shift. He had lost track of the shift pattern.

"Andy!" Catherine cried, as she saw a blue colour appearing on the unconscious robber's face. He appeared to have stopped breathing. She kneeled beside the man and desperately tried to find a pulse before starting mouth-to-mouth resuscitation and chest compression.

"Someone call for an ambulance!" Catherine shouted. Just then, several police officers ran around the corner towards the post office.

"Over here!" a bystander called.

"Somebody gie that lassie a hand!" shouted another.

Andy watched Catherine keep the man alive until an ambulance crew arrived at the scene a short time later. They loaded the man inside and conveyed him to the nearby hospital under police escort.

"Andy, Catherine!" a familiar voice behind them

"Hi Joe," they both said in unison.

"Please tell me June's not here,"

"Why's that?"

"Because I'll get an earful if she finds out what happened here,"

"Blackmore, get yourself over here!" Andy instantly recognised June's voice.

"June, it wasn't my fault, the raider boy ran right into my hand."

"Yeah right," giving him a look only she could muster.

"June, I need an hour with Catherine, then we'll come to the office and give you all the statements you need."

"Got a problem, big man?" her expression softening.

"Yeah, a serious one,"

"Well, we can't have that then, can we?" with that look in her eye.

Andy knew June risked incurring the wrath of senior officers by allowing him and Catherine to leave the scene of a serious crime, but he was also aware that she knew he would be as good as his word.

Police officers all around busied themselves with potential witnesses and the scene went into lockdown for Scenes of Crime Officers who were en-route. As blue and white police tape was strung across the area, barring pedestrians from entering the crime scene, Andy and Catherine popped back into the coffee shop.

"Another two coffees, please,"

"There you go, on the house, we heard what you guys did."

"Aw, thanks," lifting them from the counter. "C'mon, let's go, Catherine."

Strolling along a tree-lined footpath towards the beach, soon the loch came into full view. It was home to small and larger private boats and yachts moored at the harbour, surrounded by the green rolling hills which were dotted here and there with white cottages. Small hotels and guest houses sat by the water's edge. To Andy, a city boy born and bred, no place on earth could command views like these.

"Today has been surreal," Catherine remarked, as they sat down at a picnic table. The last hour was going through her head like a video on replay.

"Can I ask something?" why did we come here of all places?"

"Because this is the only place where I can guarantee that we're not being watched or listened to."

"Are things that bad, Andy?" her eyes narrowing in a stunned look.

"Yes, and when I explain everything to you, you will understand, I hope."

"I'm listening."

"Good." Andy paused. "You asked me not to interrupt you earlier, so the same goes here."

"Alright," Catherine agreed.

"Okay, let's take this in chronological order... The mature lady I was seen with in the bookshop by your friend was Sandra Berger, mother of Susan. She was one of the subjects of a police inquiry. That's why we appeared so relaxed with each other; she was Susan's mother." Andy paused again, collecting his thoughts. "The woman who joined us, was... in some sort of a relationship with Susan's mother, and it was Sandra who introduced us to each other in the bookshop."

Andy glanced around the area. "Catherine, are you following this?" She nodded. "Good." He paused. "People, beyond me, observed and identified the bookshop as somewhere the woman regularly attended, so I was asked to go there to contact her, as we had a connection through Sandra Berger. There is a lot I can't tell you, but I was at the bookshop, knowing she would be there, and this is where your friend got things wrong by sitting near us. Yes, I told her I was a brickie. Yes, she offered me a job. Yes, I accepted, and that job has been done. Now, I have already told you I'm going to meet her again on Friday at half three. If I was in a relationship with her, would I tell you that? This woman is one of the most evil women walking this planet."

"Does she have anything to do with the Games Nights you told me about?"

"Yes," Andy admitted. "And if anyone knew we were discussing this, I would be sacked."

Catherine looked at Andy, knowing that he was telling the truth and that she had made a grave, but understandable, error of judgement.

"Do you know what, Catherine?" Andy paused and looked directly at her. "I don't think I have a friend like you have, willing to tell all if you were seeing someone." Andy took hold of Catherine's hand. "What's sad is that you were ready to walk away today." Catherine looked down. "I'm going to tell you something else. When you ended our time together before, I was gutted. I was really in love with you, you were everything to me, I would have given my life for you, but you made your decision, and I honoured that decision." Andy stared at his hand in hers. "Shortly after we parted, I met Susan, and you know the way that ended." Andy looked out onto the loch, a period of silence following.

"When we both ended up in the same hotel in Tenerife, that was crazy, and I thought to myself, why here, why us, is this fate?" Andy continued. "Anyway, I digress. A marriage, or even just us living together, is all based on trust. Your trust in me has been shattered by your friend; I accept that." Andy paused. "What I do know is that you mean more to me than anything or anyone. I want to be with you for many years to come, I trust you implicitly, I love you."

Catherine gripped Andy's arm, tears in her eyes.

"I'm so sorry, but I had to know," Catherine her eyes watering.

"Catherine, if I'd been you, I would have also wanted to know." Andy stood up and wrapped his arms around her. "I love you and I want you by my side until I die." He gently wiped away a tear from her cheek. "Hey, dry your eyes, we have to go to the office and give statements."

They embraced and shared a tender kiss. As they walked away, arms wrapped around each other's waists, they deposited their empty coffee cartons in a bin.

Catherine suddenly stopped walking and, stood back from him, "Andy, look at me, please." He did. "I love you so much and I want you to know that you can trust me, and that anything we discuss stays between us."

Andy looked at Catherine and nodded.

"I can see why women fall for you - you're so open," Catherine laughed.

"As well as my stunning personality and blue eyes," Andy laughed as well.

Catherine playfully slapped his shoulder. "Anyway, you know I prefer older women and one in particular."

Chapter Thirteen

June inquired, "problem solved?"

"Yes, thank you,"

"Well, you might have another problem."

"Why? What's wrong?"

"The guy that you hit is in hospital and not doing too good," June informed him.

"Oh, is that all?"

"What are you doing now?" watching Andy lifting the receiver on the phone

"Making a phone call to sort the situation," he replied casually.

Andy spoke to an old friend and martial arts tutor of his, asking for his assistance to resolve the situation with the robbery suspect, before hanging up.

"What now?"

"We wait for a result as I make a statement."

"Andy, mate, this is difficult, but I've been told not to take a statement from you."

"Right, okay. That speaks volumes about what they are thinking. Am I allowed to take Catherine home when she finishes her statement?"

"As far as I know." June shrugged her shoulders.

"Blackmore." Andy recognised the voice as DCS Barlow's.

"Hi boss," Andy replied. "What are you doing here, sir?"

"I'm here for you, Andy," Barlow replied in an ominous tone.

June looked at Andy, knowing more than anyone what he could do to someone, but she also knew that he would not do anything maliciously or with venom in his heart; that was not her Andy. June's thoughts were interrupted by the ringtone of a phone lying on the office desk.

"DCS Barlow speaking.Certainly. It's for you, Andy." He handed the phone over, Andy listened to the voice on the other end of the line.

"Thank you, doctor. Could you relay that information to my boss?" Andy returned the phone to Barlow. "Dr Jin Lee for you, sir."

Barlow listened intently to Doctor Lee, "thank you."

June watched as the boss hung up the phone, took a deep breath, and turned his attention to Andy. June's heart was pounding in her chest, awaiting any news he may have received from the doctor, Andy was in Iceberg mode.

Barlow put his hands behind his head and looked at them both. The seat moved back onto its rear legs as Barlow swung back and forth. His jacket had fallen open, revealing a smart white shirt and tie. He looked at June.

"I heard you two are as good as joined at the hip."

"I wouldn't let my girlfriend hear you say that sir," Andy quipped.

"Shut up Andy!" June snapped, realising the seriousness of the situation.

"That's good advice," Barlow stated. "Take it." The pause that ensued seemed like an eternity as Barlow stared them down. "Why are you here, Constable Brown?"

"Erm, I was, er…"

"Oh, for Christ's sake, spit it out!" Barlow barked.

"Sir, I was asked to stay close to Andy."

"Who told you that? Was it a high-ranking officer?"

"Yes sir, a Detective Inspector."

"Right. Well, as his boss, I'm relieving you from that duty forthwith," Barlow announced.

"Sir, this has nothing to do with June, she was only doing as she was ordered," Andy interjected.

"And who asked for your opinion?"

"Nobody, sir, but you got it."

DCS Barlow put his face in his hands, before staring at them both, his face turning red with anger. "I cannot believe that you have gone from being a potential suspect in a murder inquiry, to possibly getting a Chief Constable's commendation for your actions today, thanks to your friend Dr Lee. Whatever he did up at the hospital has meant that the guy has now gone from being destined for the mortuary to being fit to be detained in custody for court." Barlow shook his head. "I give up on you, Andy," throwing his arms upwards and shaking his head.

"Sir, you can't," Andy pleaded. "I'm your link to Anika and I respectfully request that I need someone by my side that I would trust with my life." Andy looked at June.

"No, no, no," June was gesticulating with her hands. "No way."

"Why not?" looking at her.

"Because he's a nightmare to work with, sir."

"That's why I need you to keep the lid on him," Barlow reasoned. "Are you up for it?"

"I don't even know what he's involved in, sir."

"I'll arrange for that to change immediately. You're moving to the big city, Constable Brown."

"As for you Andy laddie," Barlow snapped. "Get that stupid smile off your face and get your statement done."

"Yes sir," as Barlow left the office. He turned to June. "Where's Catherine?"

"Sitting in the front office, waiting for you."

"I need to see her. Take her into the confab room, please. I'll write my statement there if that's alright with Sergeant Black."

"Okay, I'll clear it."

Over the next hour, Andy wrote out his statement, which he handed to the investigating officers. As he and Catherine left the office, he stopped outside the back door, seeing June in the yard.

"June!" Catherine was happy to see her.

"Has he told you what he's done?" Catherine gave her a quizzical look. "He's gone and asked his boss for me to be his minder."

"Great, that's fantastic! Someone to watch over him," Catherine replied, hugging June like a long-lost sister.

"See you soon, Junie babe," waving at June as they left the yard.

Crossing the road and getting into Andy's car, Catherine leaned back in her seat, trying to comprehend the whole day.

"Good job I love you, Andy Blackmore."

"Why's that?"

"Because, I want to get back to hospital life, not the kind of life I saw today; you can keep that." There was a pause before Catherine continued. "Today I saw the real Andy Blackmore that I've heard about. Now I know all about you, more than ever because I saw it for myself. No more listening to your colleagues when they come up to the hospital on night shift for a cup of tea, describing you as fearless, no more listening to the rumours about you, that you have ice flowing through your blood, no more listening to 'Blackmore is a liability.'"

"Really?"

"Oh yeah. Someday I'm going to marry a fearless iceberg, a liability. God help me! And…"

"Yeah?" Andy prompted.

"Nah, leave it, honestly," thinking to herself. Someday I'll be Mrs. Blackmore and I'll be proud of the legend that the Iceberg will leave behind when he retires.

Chapter Fourteen

DCS Barlow barked, "Constable Brown, my office, please."

"Yes, sir." June followed Barlow into his office.

"Please, take a seat. Have you met the team yet?"

June nodded as she sat and surveyed the office.

"Okay, here are the rules." Barlow gave the same spiel that he had given the others. "Now, tell me about your relationship with Blackmore."

"It's purely a working relationship, sir."

"Good. I don't need any lovey-dovey stuff here, is that understood?"

"Er, I don't know who you've been speaking to, but you've been misinformed."

"Misinformed about what?"

"About Andy and I." June paused and looked at Barlow. "Why am I here?"

"Because that big eejit needs a minder and you've come highly recommended. Now, go out there, acquaint yourself with all the players in the games nights, then go home. Friday, three in the afternoon, be in the bookshop on New City Road, choose a book and sit at a table."

"What should I do between now and Friday?"

"Do what you want; go shopping, get your hair done, just don't go near Andy and stay away from here. Contact is by phone only."

"Okay." As she was about to open the door, "Sir, where's Andy?"

"I haven't a bloody clue. He's probably away beating someone up, for all I know."

"Sir, Andy is Andy, don't try to change him. He has the makings of a great cop."

Barlow remained silent as June left his office, closing the door.

"Hi June, I'm Sharon," the Detective Constable greeted her as they shook hands.

"Pleased to meet you,"

"It's great having another female in the office."

"Hey McLeod, are you insinuating I'm not all woman?" Amanda joked.

"I take it you've met the guys, June?" Sharon asked, ignoring Amanda's remark.

June nodded.

"That just leaves you to meet Andy, then."

June realised that none of them in the office knew that she had already worked with Andy.

"Just wait until you meet him," Sharon teased.

"Really, why's that?" feigning innocence.

At that moment, the boss opened his office door, killing the conversation. Barlow sensed that he had interrupted something. He placed papers on Chris Harvey's desk before returning to his office and closing the door.

"So, you were saying?" June prompted quietly, with a smile.

"Oh, he's just a big hunk of burning love,"

"He's more than that," interjected Sharon. "And I have the pleasure of wiring him up for his meets."

June looked at her quizzically.

"He's wired up when he meets Anika Salamon, who organises the games nights," Sharon explained. "Listen, sit with Chris, he'll fill you in on who's who."

June went over to Chris and introduced herself. He greeted her and she sat down. For nearly two and a half hours, June was given a mountain of intelligence about the main targets and was shown dozens of photographs.

"And here she is, Anika Salamon," handing June a file. "Take this to your desk, read it and return it to me."

Little did the team know that June already knew most of the suspects, as she had possession of the original documents handed over by Colin Berger.

Tired of sitting alone in his flat and wondering what was happening at the office, Andy decided to go to his local pub.

"Pint of heavy, please, Shona" who was the barmaid for the evening.

Andy picked up his pint and sat at the rear of the pub, his back to the wall, facing the door. This was an inbuilt self-preservation habit of Andy's. His memory was playing like a video over the events down at the Lochside.

I have got to get a grip, he thought, *I have responsibilities now. Catherine, a new house very soon… I must learn to keep my hands to myself.*

The door to the bar opened and in wandered wee Benny. His barstool was at the door, where he sat every day, like a king on his throne.

Everybody knew this, so only a stranger would dare sit there. His attire today consisted of grey boots, ill-fitting denim jeans that were hanging off him, a green sweatshirt, and a grey jacket that had seen better days. Benny's straggling hair hung loosely below his baseball cap, which seemed to be a permanent fixture on his head. 'NY' was emblazoned on the front of the cap.

Andy watched Benny's pint of lager being poured and then placed in front of him; Benny never asked for it, as there was no need. He was in there at the same time every day in the same spot. Money was handed over in silence, Andy observed Benny take the first sip from his glass, then wipe the froth from his overgrown moustache. His unshaven, deeply lined face belied his true age, due to his years of alcohol abuse. Nobody could ever remember Benny having a job, but he was never short of a bob or two for a pint.

Andy's gaze turned to the staff; one was serving at the tables, handing over menus for late lunches or early dinners; one was collecting empty pint glasses from the tables because most people were too lazy to take them to the bar when they were leaving.

Grace was behind the bar, chatting with the customers about whatever subject happened to come up. It could have been politics, football, TV programmes, even trouble with 'the wife.' Grace was everyone's favourite barmaid; a heavy-built, married woman in her mid-forties, with a round face, a ruddy complexion, and short, curly hair. She was not to be messed with, as she had a razor-sharp wit that had been fine-tuned over the years in various licensed establishments. Her barbed tongue could cause grown men to flee her wrath if they misbehaved in 'her' bar, even though she was not the owner of the premises.

Sammy Colquhoun, a thin lad aged eighteen who worked with the council emptying bins, breezed into the premises, and stood at the bar, wearing a football team top, black cords, and trainers. He thought he was the bees' knees. Well, that was until Grace saw his reflection in the gantry mirror as she was putting cash into the till.

"Sammy!" she bellowed, without turning around. "Get yer arse out of here! And get that tap aff. You know you're no allowed club colours in here."

"Bu - but G - Grace," Sammy blurted out. 'I'm goin' to the g - game."

"Listen, Sammy, ah don't care if yer playin', go an' get changed, and another thing, keep yer eyes aff my tits, or I'll come 'roon there an' suffocate you between them." She squeezed her massive breasts together, and Andy watched as Sammy left the bar like a scolded cat.

Meanwhile, two men, who were not regulars in the pub, chatted loudly near to where Andy was sitting. They were righting the wrongs of the earth, ranting and raving about Mrs. Thatcher and her policies, and how on earth could a woman ever become Prime Minister, what was the world coming to? They thought they had the answers to everything. Then the two barroom politicians suddenly became top football managers, ranting about the fortunes and misfortunes of Celtic, Rangers, and Scotland.

Most of the regulars in the bar knew who Andy was and what he did for a living. What he liked about this establishment was that nobody cared he was a cop. They knew Andy for being Andy and that was it.

"Andy!" came a shout from the bar. "We have a spare seat on the bus for Saturday, D'you want it?"

"Sorry, I'll have to pass on that one," Andy replied with a smile on his face. His local happened to be a 'Celtic pub,' from where the local supporters would get picked up on game days and head for Celtic Park. They all knew that Andy had blue blood flowing through his veins and his loyalties lay across the river Clyde on the Southside of the city. It was always a good source of banter, especially on Old Firm days, depending on the result. Unlike in the city, there was never a hint of malice.

Stirred out of people-watching, Andy began to reflect on his days back on the sites, meeting his old mates at the Christmas night out. Life was uncomplicated then, but now it was a different kettle of fish altogether. His thoughts turned to Friday when he was to meet with Anika Salamon again, and then to June, wondering how her first day in the office had gone and hoping she got a warm welcome. He was sure she would have, as they were all a friendly bunch, with one aim; to get convictions.

When Andy returned home, the answering machine on his phone was flashing green; a new message, Andy pressed the play button.

"Andy, it's Alice, can you call me, please? Everything's cleared for your house purchase, just need you and Catherine to sign everything tomorrow."

When the message ended, Andy called Catherine.

"We have papers to sign tomorrow for the house," he informed her.

"Magic! What time?"

"I'm just going to call Alice. Is any time good for you?"

"For this, yes."

"Great! I'll call you back in a few moments." Andy hung up and called Alice.

"Hey, how are you?"

"Honestly, I'm well, Andy," Alice replied, before switching into lawyer mode. "Now, to get to more important matters, all your paperwork is here for signing. Once we get that done, I'll fax the seller's lawyers, the money gets transferred to their account, and you get the keys to your new house."

"So, when would we get the keys?" as this was foreign territory to him.

"Probably within a couple of hours, as soon as the money goes through."

"Geez, that soon?"

"Yep," Alice replied confidently.

"So, what time suits you for tomorrow, Alice?"

"Let me see… Let us say eleven in the morning."

"Brilliant, see you then."

Andy rang Catherine back and informed her what Alice had told him.

"This is all getting so real now, I'm going to have a glass of wine; my stomach is churning."

"Why?"

"Because I never imagined I would be in this situation."

"Well, no rush, I just need you there to sign on the dotted line. I'll get you at ten-fifteen and we'll drive into the city."

"See ya tomorrow!" Catherine blurted out before hanging up.

The next morning, Catherine and Andy walked together down Sauchiehall Street towards its junction with Hope Street.

"Here it is," Andy announced, as he pushed open the door and climbed the stairs to where Alice worked. They called at the reception.

"Hello sir,"

"Hi, we're here to see Alice Blackmore."

"And your name is?"

"If you say Andy and Catherine are here, she'll understand."

"Yes sir, please take a seat."

Andy and Catherine sat together, his hand in hers.

"Hiya guys, c'mon in," Alice looked the part in her business suit, white shirt and heeled black shoes.

"So, this is what a lawyer's office looks like," Andy remarked, impressed.

"Behave you." Alice glanced at Andy; a look not missed by Catherine. "Okay, here are the papers you have to sign. It's only the biggest purchase of your life."

"Geez, thanks," Andy muttered.

"Andy, you sign here and here. Catherine, you sign here and here, beside Andy."

Catherine hesitated for a moment as she looked at the papers.

"Catherine?" Andy prompted.

"Yes, sorry, this is also a first for me."

"I'm just ensuring that if anything happens to me, you'll be secure," Andy reassured her.

"Yes, I know." Catherine signed on the dotted line.

"I'll fax these to the seller's lawyer and in a couple of hours, your keys should be here for you to pick up," Alice informed them.

"Why don't we all go for lunch?" Andy suggested. "And by the time we get back, the keys should be here."

"You two can, I'm working," Alice laughed.

"Suit yourself, It's champagne and caviar for me, courtesy of Mr. B here."

"Darling, I've just bought a house, so it will be a fish supper from the chippy, shared!"

When they returned just after two o'clock, Alice handed them two sets of keys.

"Congratulations, I'm so pleased for you both," as she handed Andy an envelope.

"What's this?"

"Oh, it's just your bill for the services of a lawyer."

"Mates' rates, I hope."

"Well, I do have to earn a living, Andy," Alice stated with a smile.

"Thank you for everything you've done, Alice,"

"You're welcome, and make sure you come to see the kids soon, they miss you both."

"Sure thing," as they left the office and made their way to their new home.

"As we're not married, I'm not carrying you over the threshold, you know that" Andy informed Catherine.

"And I'm not carrying you over, either, so fair's fair,"

Andy put the key into the lock and turned it slowly, savouring the moment of homeownership. Pushing open the door, he stood back, allowing Catherine to be the first to enter. As they surveyed their new house together room by room, they planned what they were going to do to turn this into a very special place for them both to live in for the foreseeable future.

"So, when are you thinking of moving in?"

"Don't you mean, when are we thinking of moving in?"

"Well, I have to make arrangements for that."

"Yeah, no problem,"

Catherine and Andy met Glen, their neighbour, as they were leaving the house and they introduced themselves, before Andy drove Catherine back to her house, just in time for Barry to get dropped off by his carers.

"I have to head back to the flat, see you tomorrow, hopefully."

"Yeah." Catherine smiled. "At least I know now what you're up to now. I am so happy."

Chapter Fifteen

Barlow knew he was taking a massive risk by letting June go into the bookshop on New City Road. She was an experienced police officer, but this was a whole new ball game for her, and one hint of recognition by another officer could ruin the whole inquiry.

June wandered around the bookshop in jeans, white trainers, and a T-shirt. She chose a biography on John F. Kennedy, bought a coffee, and sat down at a small brown lacquered table. She opened the book and started reading. She had made sure that the tables around her were free for Andy's arrival.

When he arrived twenty minutes later, Andy bought a coffee and placed it on a table feet away from June, causing her to groan. He took off his leather jacket and hung it over the back of his chair, looking more like a male model than a cop, Andy again browsed the photography section, this time choosing a book on life in New York City in the sixties, which fascinated him.

"Excuse me," said a woman at his side. "Can I ask you something?"

"Sure," Andy replied.

"I have a close friend who means the world to me," the woman continued, in earshot of June.

"Is her name Catherine, by any chance?"

"Yes. Are you Andy?"

Knowing that he only had minutes to retrieve the situation and get rid of her, Andy, dramatising his anxiety, said; "please listen, I need you to leave for your safety. Something is about to happen here that could be life-threatening, so go home and telephone Catherine, say you saw me. Do you understand?"

"Yes, okay." The woman hurriedly left the premises.

A few minutes later, with Andy back reading his book, Anika arrived. Without looking up, "tea or coffee?"

"Coffee, no milk, no sugar,"

"You know, this is like home for us," Andy remarked. "We always seem to meet here."

"Yeah, it is," Anika agreed. "It's been a while since that first meeting."

Anika took off her jacket, placed it over her lap and put her small clutch bag on the table in front of her. Her eyes scanned the surrounding tables; she was extremely surveillance conscious. June's eyes never left her book, but she closely followed Andy's conversation with Anika.

"There you go," as he laid Anika's coffee on the table.

"Thank you, you're looking very fit." Andy just smiled. "Now, let's get down to business." Andy looked at her, saying nothing. "The report I got on you from the Rooftop was great. Everything I asked you to do was done."

"And how would you know that?"

"Oh, come on, I had you well watched by Marie."

"Marie the barmaid?"

"Yeah, the same Marie you had the lock-in with and took home. The question is, did you screw her?" Anika winked at him.

"No, I did not, Anika."

"Good. Now, getting onto this week; I want you to be my personal, how should I put this… minder, yes, that's the word; minder."

"Meaning what exactly?"

"You'll be at my beck and call twenty-four seven for anything I want, including sex."

"Well, it's been nice knowing you Anika, but I'm out." Andy got to his feet.

"Oh really? I don't think so, now sit down." Anika's tone changed, suddenly sounding more demanding.

"I do," Andy replied, sternly putting on his jacket.

"I fit everything you desire in a woman; mature and constantly horny."

"The answer is no."

"Are you more interested in men maybe? Or younger girls?"

"No and no."

"What is it then? Money?"

"If there's one thing I've learned in life, it's to never mix business with pleasure."

"Why?" Anika paused. "Okay, please sit down."

"Because someone always gets hurt in the end, which is something I would regret."

Anika sat back in her chair, taking a sip from her cup of coffee, and looked at Andy, eyeing his body up and down. She pondered what to do next. Finally, Anika placed her cup of coffee on the saucer.

"What do I have to do to get you into my bed, Andy?"

"Sack me."

"That's not going to happen," she replied.

"There you go then." Andy leaned back in his seat. "So, have you got a job for me this week or not?"

"Yes. Wednesday night at the Golden Thistle, do you know where it is?"

Andy nodded.

"Be there for seven o'clock," Anika told him. "Same money as before."

"Is there a code word?"

"Yes, 'fourteen.'"

"And who's getting my envelope?"

"Marie. She'll be on the bar."

"Okay."

"So that's the business side taken care of, now, what's the deal with you? Wife? Girlfriend? Boyfriend?"

"None, and I'm straight, for your information."

"You're straight and not interested in me, I must be losing my touch." Anika smiled.

"I refer to my previous reasons, Anika, can I ask you something?" Anika nodded. "You know we could all go to jail for a long time if something goes wrong."

"Andy darling, I'd rather die than go to jail," She seemed comfortable in her reply "It'll never happen to me." Anika stood up to leave, she put on her jacket and leaned over the table towards Andy, putting her face close to his. She whispered, "Maybe, I'll dispense with your services after all and have you for myself." She pursed her lips at him. "Take care, baby brickie."

Andy watched as Anika left the bookshop. There was no doubt that she was a very attractive woman and, if the circumstances had been different, there is no way he would have declined her advances.

When he left a few minutes later, June followed him out. Their wires had to be removed and returned to HQ.

Back at the office, DCS Barlow sat behind his desk, facing DCI Donald Jenkins, DI Alan Watt, and DC Sharon McLeod. They listened closely to the recording of the conversation between Blackmore and Salamon, noting down Wednesday, seven o'clock, Golden Thistle. The

Rooftop had been dispensed with for this party A team would be set up to have the meeting watched closely.

"Guys, what are your thoughts on Salamon propositioning Andy?" Barlow asked.

"Well boss, he seemed to handle the situation very well, given the pressure," Jenkins commented in a matter of fact way.

After listening to what the others had to say, Detective Inspector Alan Watt slowly exhaled before saying; "Sir, my understanding is that Blackmore's a lady killer and that he does prefer the more mature women. I believe his current girlfriend is something like eight or ten years older than him. He's young, both in age and service, and he still has that building site mentality, so who knows what he'll do."

"Do you think he could be tempted and put the inquiry at risk?"

The ensuing silence was broken by DC Sharon McLeod. "Sir, I've heard the recordings with Andy speaking to Salamon and I've heard nothing to suggest that he has been flirting with her or giving her a hint that he's interested. Also, he wants more than anyone to bring her to justice as payback for the killing of Susan, and all the rest of it. So I can't see him getting involved with her." "Anything else?" she was asked by the boss.

"I have spoken to June. She is absolutely convinced that there is not a hope in hell that he will go near her. She says he's besotted with Catherine and I trust her judgement; nobody in this job knows Blackmore better than her."

"Thanks, Sharon, well gents?" looking at the other officers.

"I would suggest that we put a watch on Blackmore for a week, see what his movements are, and take it from there," DI Watt suggested.

"Can we spare the manpower?"

"I can arrange it, sir, if you authorise it."

"Okay." Barlow hesitated. "But they will have to be vigilant, as he doesn't miss a trick. Remember what he did to the two retired cops put onto him by Berger."

"Christ, aye," Watt recalled scratching his head.

As they all got up to leave, Barlow told them to sit down again. He had one more thing to say to them; he'd been saving this one 'til the end.

Just then, June Brown returned to the office, armed with a pile of statements she had been getting from potential witnesses.

"June," shouted Barlow.

"Yes sir?"

"Paylova and Blackmore, your thoughts?"

"No chance" was her short sharp reply, as she began to sort out her paperwork.

"You better be right," was Barlow's response.

"I am."

Barlow beckoned DCI Jenkins to close his office door. This was one for senior officers only.

Chapter Sixteen

B arlow's jacket was hanging over the back of a chair; it was unlike him not to hang it up on the wooden coat rack. Leaning on his desk, Barlow placed both his hands on his face and rubbed it slowly before letting out a sigh.

"I got a phone call today from the Crown Office," he announced.

"Good news I hope," DI Alan Watt began; Barlow raised his right hand to silence him. "Sorry, sir." Watt shrunk back into his seat.

"McConnell has been to see the Lord Advocate and discussed the inquiry with him, along with Chloe Agnew. The meeting was held in private." Barlow paused for a few seconds before continuing. "The Lord Advocate, the Right Honourable James Butler QC, apparently listened carefully to them and he has offered his full support to us in this inquiry. The reason they saw him was because of the stature of those involved. The Lord Advocate has instructed that High Court warrants be issued for those where there is enough evidence to justify bringing them before a court. That is the first part." Barlow then shook his head slowly. "Even I couldn't believe what I was hearing over the phone. McConnell requested that Andy to be either removed from the inquiry or put on leave."

"Why the hell would he do that?" demanded DCI Jenkins.

"Andy's brother, Richard Blackmore, has been a major player in the games nights. Enough evidence to put him away for years. Once he is found guilty, of course."

The silence in the office was deafening.

"What did you say to McConnell?"

"I told him that I'm caught between a rock and a hard place, as Andy is the main link to Salamon. If I give him time off or remove him from the inquiry, Salamon might begin to smell a rat."

"So, sir, your thoughts are?" Sharon prompted him.

"The warrant for Richard Blackmore is being brought here as we speak, he's getting locked up today. The last thing we need is him going to Wednesday's party."

Just as DCS Barlow was relaying the information, there was a knock at the door, which DCI Jenkins opened.

"This has just come for the boss,"

"Thanks," taking a sealed envelope from him and closing the door.

Barlow opened the envelope, which contained the warrant for the arrest of Richard Blackmore.

"Donald, take Frank with you for this one," handing the envelope back to Jenkins.

"Sure, no problem," grabbing his jacket and leaving the office immediately, heading for the Blackmore villa in the east end of the city.

As Jenkins and DC Frank Wallace arrived at the address of Richard Blackmore, Jenkins turned the car off the road towards the long driveway leading to the house. Jenkins braked suddenly, bringing the car to a juddering halt just inside the large ornate gates, which had been left open.

"What the hell's going on here?" Jenkins muttered.

"Ah dunno, but something is," They sat in their car, looking at a marked police car and ambulance, its blue light rotating, at the top of the driveway, its reflection bouncing off the large dormer windows either side of the doorway.

"Is that not Andy's car parked up there, sir?"

"It is. I'm getting a bad feeling about this."

"Whose house is this, sir?" having only been told that he was going to execute a warrant.

Jenkins paused. "This is Richard Blackmore's house, Andy's brother. In this envelope is a High Court warrant for his arrest on child abuse charges."

Wallace sat in silence, simply staring out the car window towards the emergency vehicles.

Using the vehicle radio to call force control, Jenkins asked what was happening at the address. Back came the code for a suspected suicide from the force controller. Jenkins considered his options before rolling his vehicle back out onto the road and heading back into Glasgow to the office, arriving there just before eleven o'clock. DCS Barlow was awaiting their arrival.

"Success, was it?" looking at them both.

"No sir, I'm afraid not,"

Barlow frowned. "Oh?"

Jenkins described the scene that had greeted them on their arrival at Richard Blackmore's house and the resulting radio inquiry.

"Have you heard from Andy, sir?"

"No, nothing yet,"

Going into his office and closing the door, Barlow lifted the phone and called an old colleague he knew was working in the East End of the city and therefore likely to be clued up on what was happening.

"It looks like suicide by hanging, but until the post mortem is done we are treating this as a crime scene - just to be on the safe side."

"Has the deceased been identified?" asked Barlow.

"Not officially," his colleague replied.

"What do you mean?"

"Everything points to it being the homeowner, Richard Blackmore. Oh, and Graham, this must be a first; he was dressed in a black suit and wearing full masonic regalia."

"Who found him?" his eyebrow raising.

"Alice Blackmore, his estranged wife, she told the guys at the scene it's her husband. Sadly, she had the kids with her, she had taken them to see their dad earlier tonight."

"I hear his brother was there, Andy Blackmore?"

"Sorry mate, I don't know. I'll try to find out and call you back."

"Thanks, Billy." Barlow put down the phone and sat back, finding it hard to believe that the first warrant issued could not be executed by his team. His mind started ticking over. Was it just a coincidence that, the day the warrant was issued, the deceased committed suicide? Had there been a leak somewhere in the system? Had Blackmore been tipped off that he was about to face justice for his alleged wrongdoings? Or were there other reasons unconnected to the inquiry? Concerning the latter, Andy might be able to assist.

Barlow walked back into the office, where he found DCI Jenkins and DC Wallace waiting for further instructions... if there were any.

"C'mon guys, time to put the lights out and head for home," Barlow closed the door behind him.

Later, in Barlow's empty, pitch-black office, the phone rang.

"Sorry, the person you're trying to call is unavailable right now, please call back later or leave a message after the tone," was the recorded message, followed by a beep.

"Sir, it's Andy, I'll speak to you tomorrow at some point. I think you know the reason by now."

The message ended.

"Good morning, ladies and gentlemen," Barlow addressed a sombre audience at nine o'clock. He surveyed the faces of his team of detectives.

"By the look of you all, you're aware that one of the main suspects appears to have committed suicide sometime in the last twenty-four hours at his home address. His name was Richard Blackmore, and he is the brother of our Andy, who called here last night just after I closed the office, so I'm going to try and get hold of him today. I'll update you thereafter." With that, Barlow turned and went into his office, but not before adding, "DCI Jenkins."

"Yes sir?"

"Get your jacket and car keys, we're going to the city mortuary."

June sat at her desk, stunned by the revelation of Richard Blackmore's death. Sharon McLeod was watching her closely, before rising from her desk and going over to her.

"June, you okay? I would say just by looking at you, you knew nothing about this."

"No, nothing, he never even called me."

"June, don't take this personally. He is probably with his family just now."

"Yeah, you are right Sharon," replied June, shuffling paperwork aimlessly about her desk then running her fingers through her hair and taking a deep breath, trying to regain her composure.

"June you are his best mate in this godforsaken inquiry and this job; he will get in touch with you, just give him time with this one."

June looked up and nodded in agreement. Sharon returned to her desk. June had only known Sharon a few days but appreciated her sympathetic concern for a fellow officer.

As they drove to the mortuary, Barlow confided in Jenkins that they potentially had a major problem on the horizon, and it might be that they would have to accelerate the whole inquiry.

Chapter Seventeen

J enkins parked the car in the small lot of the mortuary and got out, followed by Barlow, who stretched his large frame to relieve the stiffness in his bones. Jenkins waited patiently, before Barlow suddenly made for the back door and pushed it open, leaving Jenkins to scramble after him. Once inside, they passed through the mortuary staffroom to the banks of refrigerators containing the cadavers awaiting collection or pathology.

"Bobby!" Barlow shouted into the empty room. "You still here?"

"Do you think I am a ghost, Graham?" Bobby's Glaswegian voice called back. "How you ever made detective is beyond me." He entered the room from a dark doorway, shaking his head.

Bobby was a veteran of the mortuary. He had been in there as long as Barlow had been a police officer, and their paths had crossed more times than they cared to remember.

"You asked for that one," Jenkins chipped in.

"I suppose I did," Barlow admitted. "Bobby, we're looking for a body."

"Well, I have loads of those," he replied in a deadpan tone.

"Richard Blackmore."

"Yes, came in last night. Never seen someone dressed like he was. I've everything bagged for his missus or the next of kin.

"He's due to be formally identified in fifteen minutes," Bobby informed them. "Two, maybe three coming in."

"Do you know who they are?" Barlow spoke up.

"Yes, hang on." Bobby reached for his clipboard with details of the witnesses.

"Maybe not the phrase to use," Barlow quipped, smiling at Bobby until the gaff dawned on him.

"We you know I never even thought of that!" He shrugged as he consulted the paperwork. "Here you go, Andrew Blackmore, brother. Alice Blackmore, wife, and Catherine Smith, unrelated."

"Thanks, and, em…" Barlow trailed off. "Can we see him?"

"Oh yes you can."

Bobby opened the refrigerator door and slid out the steel tray containing the body. He pulled back the white linen cover soBarlow and

Jenkins could take a close look at the position of the rope, which had not been removed from the deceased.

"Interesting…" Barlow mused. "Thanks, Bobby."

"Nae problemo." Bobby slid the tray back into the fridge.

"Good morning, gentlemen," came a familiar female voice behind Barlow and Jenkins. It was Kim McPherson, a forensic pathologist. "Why are you two in here so early? and Bobby, what have you got for me today?" McPherson's questions were flying fast. "We're in for the suspected suicide," Barlow explained. "Richard Blackmore."

"Well, where is he? Bobby get him out for me would you?"

"This guy is a flippin jack-in-the-box," he mumbled.

Bobby once again removed the tray from the fridge and McPherson examined the deceased.

"Remove the rope," she commanded after taking a few photographs. "I've seen enough. We must show respect to the relatives, and the last thing we want is for them to see that. Now, what else have we got?"

"You only have this one. McGlinchey has five others. Run-of-the-mill stuff."

"Graham, why the hell am I here?" McPherson was staring him down. Clearly nobody had told her of the significance of this death and the history behind it.

Just at that moment, the buzzer in the mortuary sounded, indicating that someone was in the public waiting area. Bobby removed the rope from the neck of the deceased and handed it to McPherson before going upstairs. The public waiting area was a small room which had been painted in cream and brown many times over to hide the years of nicotine stains left by grieving relatives. Dark brown wooden chairs were set against three of the walls, and old timber-framed windows with frosted glass stretched towards the ceiling, obscuring the room from public view.

"Good morning," Bobby greeted the pair of women and the man waiting for him. "How may I help you?" "I'm Alice Blackmore. This is his brother, Andy. We're here to formally identify my husband, Richard Blackmore."

"I'm very sorry for your loss." Bobby's voice was low. "I'll just require a few details from you for the formal identification."

"Certainly." Alice took a seat beside Andy, who was flanked by Catherine.

In the meantime, Barlow had given McPherson a summary of the possible reasons for the suspected suicide.

"So, that's the reason I'm here" McPherson sighed. Bobby returned to the mortuary and prepared the deceased for identification. He seemed uneasy as he handed the details of the witnesses to McPherson, who was one of the most respected forensic pathologists; not only in Scotland, but in the United Kingdom. She took the identification papers from Bobby and glanced over the list;

>Name; Alice Blackmore
>Relationship; Wife
>Occupation; Lawyer
>
>Name; Andrew Blackmore
>Relationship; Brother
>Occupation; Police Officer
>
>Name; Catherine Smith
>Relationship; Unrelated Occupation; Nurse

"Bobby," McPherson said once she was done. "Under normal circumstances, as you know, we would have the deceased identified by each person individually. If it is alright with DCS Barlow and DCI Jenkins, we should allow the family to do a joint identification. I'll speak to them beforehand." McPherson looked at Barlow and Jenkins, who nodded solemnly in agreement.

"Certainly," Bobby replied, wheeling the deceased to the viewing window, which was obscured by a deep red curtain.

"Good morning, my name is Kim McPherson," the pathologist announced upon entering the waiting room. "I'm the pathologist on duty today and I'll be carrying out the post-mortem on Richard. I've decided to dispense with the individual identification procedure on this occasion so that you're able to offer each other support in this difficult time."

To Andy, McPherson's voice started to fade into the distance, her name repeating in his head. McPherson, McPherson, McPherson. He had heard that name before, If only he could access the deep recesses of his mind and remember when.

"Please follow me," McPherson continued.

Alice, Andy, and Catherine followed her downstairs and stopped at the viewing window.

"Are you all prepared?"

"Yes," came a collective reply.

Andy stood between Alice and Catherine, holding their hands. McPherson tapped gently on the glass. The red curtains spread apart, and Andy was reminded of a theatre. Ricky was lying on his back, his body covered by a white linen sheet, his head exposed. The still face of his brother stared at the ceiling, though, as Andy stood frozen in place, it looked like Ricky's eyes turned, ever so slowly, until he was side-eyeing him, challenging his brother even in death. "Is that Richard Blackmore?" McPherson enquired.

"Yes," Alice whispered, staring at her husband's body.

"Yes," Andy murmured, bowing his head and blinking his eyes rapidly.

"Yes," Catherine assented, looking at Andy.

"Would you like a few minutes alone?"

"Please." Andy's throat felt dry but his palms were sweaty.

"Listen, I'll go upstairs. Give you two some privacy," Catherine suggested.

"There's no need for that," Andy assured her.

"Stay if you wish, Catherine," Alice added, though her eyes were still fixed on the lifeless shell of her husband.

"I think you both need time with Ricky." Catherine spoke softly and put a hand on Andy's shoulder before leaving the room.

Andy put an arm around Alice's shoulders as they continued to stare through the observation window. After a few moments of silence, Andy tapped the window and the curtains were drawn closed. The show was over.

"I need to speak to him. Will you come with me?" Alice's eyes were filled with tears.

"Yes, of course." Andy rang the buzzer, attracting the attention of Bobby. "Can we come in for a few moments to be with Richard?"

"Certainly," Bobby answered politely, abandoning his crude Glasgow accent.

Andy led Alice to her husband, his brother.

There was a moment of silence as Bobby left the room and Alice's eyes landed once more on her husband.

170

"Why?" Alice cried suddenly. "Why? Why? Why!" Alice repeated, stomping her feet, as if expecting a reply from Ricky. "You've left two children heartbroken. They will never see their daddy again! How could you do this? To me? To them!" She was breathing heavily at this point and took a moment to calm down. Then, so quiet almost Andy could not hear her, she murmured, "you were selfish to the end, Ricky."

Andy stood silently; his hands folded in front of him as he reflected on his relationship with his brother. He bowed his head, his mind quickly running through his brother's life. Their childhood and the changes as they made different choices in life. Then he and Alice left the room following the mortician.

"Excuse me," once the door was closed, "what's your name?" "Bobby, sir."

"Well thank you, Bobby. From all of us." Andy shook his hand.

"You're welcome, sir." Bobby watched as they left the room and exited the building.

After closing the car doors behind Alice and Catherine, Andy paused at the open driver's door before leaning in. "I'll be back in a few minutes," he promised. Alice and Catherine watched him jog back to the door and re-enter the building.

"Wh-where's he going?" Alice blubbered through her tears.

"I've not a clue." Catherine sighed and took Alice's hand.

"Bobby," Andy called, causing the mortician to spin on his heels. "Where's Ms. McPherson?"

"She's with the police at the moment, and you shouldn't be in here." "Which officers?"

"I take it they are the investigators. DCS Barlow and DCI Jenkins." "Where?"

"In there." Bobby nodded towards the double doors leading to the refrigerators. "But you—" Andy pushed the doors open, ignoring the mortician and leaving him behind.

"Good morning, gentlemen," Andy greeted Barlow and Jenkins, who startled at his entrance. "Ms. McPherson, can I ask why you are doing this post-mortem?"

" I was asked to," she responded matter-of-factly.

"Andy, get out of here!" Barlow snapped.

"Certainly, sir. When I get an answer to my question."

"I was instructed by the Crown Office," McPherson continued, glaring at him. "Is that a suitable answer, Mr. Blackmore?" "Yes, thank you." Andy glanced at Barlow, expecting to see eyes wide with fury. Instead, Barlow was not even looking at him, but was muttering something in Jenkins' ear, Andy frowned. "Sorry to have disturbed you," with that, Andy turned and left the building with a strange feeling in his gut.

"Who the hell does he think he is?" demanded McPherson, glancing between the two policemen.

"He's a head-case is what he is," Barlow explained. "But he's also a police officer. Even with the little service he has, he's shown he has what it takes to get to the top of the tree. Trouble is, he's a walking time-bomb." He shrugged his shoulders.

"Well, Mr. Barlow, if he speaks to me like that again, I'll cut his balls off, and if you can't control your officers, I'll add yours to the collection. Comprendes?" Barlow and Jenkins nodded vigorously. "Right gents, I have work to do. I'll call you later, then send you, my report." McPherson took off her jacket and got ready for work.

As Barlow and Jenkins left the building, they passed Simon McGlinchey, who was heading in for his shift.

"Mornin' gentlemen," McGlinchey addressed them in his typical jovial manner. "Fine day, today."

"As fine as Glasgow gets," Barlow muttered. McGlinchey's smile faltered slightly, but Barlow and Jenkins continued their way, got into their car, and drove off.

McGlinchey entered the cold room and greeted McPherson.

"Good morning, Simon," she replied flatly. She was focused on her work. "I'm here for Blackmore and I would like you to assist."

"It would be my pleasure." "When was the last time you saw a knot like that?" McPherson nodded at the rope, which lay on a nearby table.

"A very long time ago." He examined it meticulously, pondering.

"Who do you know that would tie a knot like that?"

McGlinchey did not need to think about his answer. "A hangman."

"Exactly," McPherson agreed. "This should be an interesting post-mortem."

Chapter Eighteen

A ndy, Alice, and Catherine arrived back at the home of Alice's parents. From the car, Andy gazed at the house and made out two little faces staring at them from a window, awaiting their mother's return, Andy was suddenly transported back to the day his father died. His eyes filled with tears; not for his brother, but for the kids, his niece and nephew, Annie and Alfie.

"Would you like to come in for a tea or coffee?".

"Em, sure. You okay with that, Catherine?"

"Of course."As soon as Alice opened the door and let them inside, Andy's nieces bounded up to him and Catherine.

"Uncle Andy, Aunt Catherine!" Alfie bellowed. "Daddy's an angel in heaven now." Alfie wrapped his arms around Andy.

"Yes, he is," Andy murmured gently, accepting the embrace. "And he will shine on you both forever." The words left a bitter taste in his mouth.

"We're sorry for your loss, Andy," Alice's father croaked from behind the children, Andy shook his hand.

"Thank you. But truthfully, their loss is greater." Andy looked at the children and their mother. "Alice, does mum know yet? Has anyone told her?"

"No, we have to discuss that. How we'll go about it, given the circumstances." As Catherine ushered the children into another room to play, Alice and her parents discussed with Andy the best approach to take with his mother. They decided to speak to her immediately and keep it simple.

At Headquarters, DCS Barlow received a phone call from Kim McPherson.

"What have you got for me?" he prompted.

"He certainly died from hanging, but not from asphyxiation as most do."

"Meaning what exactly?"

"His neck snapped, clean as a whistle. Instant death."

Barlow was quiet, anticipating the worst.

"Now, you want me to say it's a suicide, no doubt about it," McPherson continued. "But I can't. After examining the rope, the way the knot was tied suggests that the person who tied it had experience carrying out hangings, or at the very least had studied this kind of thing."

"Are you saying a third party could have been involved?"

"I am a pathologist. You are the detective, Mr. Barlow"

"Are you going to issue a death certificate for the family?"

"I can do."

"I'll arrange to have the certificate picked up and delivered" "Give me an hour. Oh, and Mr. Barlow, I have taken a range of samples for forensics. They are going to the lab today. Good luck with your inquiry."

"Thank you, Ms. McPherson."

Bobby went to the waiting room in the mortuary to ensure that it was clean and tidy for other relatives who would be arriving soon. The bell rang and, upon answering the door, he was met with a woman dressed all in black; a veiled hat, open-neck blouse, pencil skirt, seamed stockings, and high heels adorning her thin, pale body. Bobby could not see her face clearly through the veil.

"How may I assist you?" leaning down to catch a glimpse of her face. She bowed her head in response.

"A friend of mine has died," the woman moaned insincerely. "May I see him?"

"What's your friend's name?"

"Richard Blackmore." "Please take a seat for a moment." Bobby went through to Kim McPherson and informed her about the woman.

"Is she a relative?" McPherson quirked an eyebrow.

"I didn't ask, to be honest." Bobby grimaced.

Sitting at her desk, McPherson massaged her furrowed brows before conceding to give the woman a view of the deceased; she hated depriving people in mourning from getting closure.

"But get her details," McPherson called after Bobby as he left her office. Bobby nodded and proceeded to prepare the deceased for viewing. Once he was done, he made his way back to the waiting room, where the woman sat patiently, her hat still on, obscuring her face.

"I'll need your personal details and relationship for the record," Bobby informed the woman.

"Certainly. Anika Szymańska, cousin."

Bobby led her to the window to view the deceased. Once the red curtain was pulled back for the second time that day, Anika placed a hand on the glass and swept it back and forth, as if wiping condensation off a mirror or was it to wave goodbye? She nodded to Bobby, turned, and left the viewing room Bobby's gaze followed her until the door swung shut.

He was still standing there, statuesque, when McPherson entered the room a minute later. She did not see him at first, and was startled when she noticed him.

"You, okay?" chuckling. "You seem a bit... bemused."

"It's just that woman. Dressed more for a funeral than a viewing, she was."

"Well, maybe she was just showing her respects." "Maybe so, but something didn't seem right." Bobby walked away, shaking his head.

As McPherson finished dictating her report for the medical typist, she thought about what Barlow had fleetingly told her about Richard Blackmore's alleged crimes and what Bobby had said to her. She wrestled with herself about whether or not to call Barlow about Szymańska's visit. Finally, she gave in.

"Graham," she started once she heard the receiver on the other end pick up. "It's Kim McPherson here, sorry to bother you. Listen, this could be nothing, but Bobby, the mortuary attendant, has had a funny feeling about a visitor today."

"Oh?"

"A woman who identified herself as a cousin of Richard Blackmore came for a viewing after the post-mortem. Bobby thought she seemed out of place. The way she was dressed—it was as if she was about to go to a funeral."

"Did he get her details?"

"Anika Szymańska" There was a pause as the silence continued. "Graham, are you there?"

"Yeah, sorry, I was writing down the name. Thank you for that, we'll check her out."

"Apologies if I've wasted your time."

"No, no, everything should be looked at. I'll check with the family."

Barlow walked into the main office, caught the eye of Donald Jenkins and beckoned him into his office with a nod.

"Close the door and lock it," Barlow ordered. "Listen to this." Barlow related the conversation to Jenkins, who shook his head through all of it.

Andy parked his car outside Lochside Nursing Home, Alice beside him, Catherine in the back. He switched off the engine but did not move to get out, instead resting his arms on the steering wheel. e drew a hand over his weary face and rubbed the sleep from his eyes. Then he stared out of the windscreen at the well-maintained gardens, avoiding the expecting eyes of his sister-in-law and his fiancé. A hand squeezed his shoulder.

"C'mon Andy, let's do this," Alice murmured.

Andy nodded. "Ready, Catherine?"

"Yes."Andy, Alice, and Catherine made their way to the office of Sister Valerie Cross, who oversaw the nursing home.

"Hello, Sister," Andy greeted her.

"Hello Andy!" Valerie Cross replied, her voice sickeningly sweet. "Big visitation party today." She wiggled her eyebrows.

"Valerie, we have some unfortunate news."

Andy explained why they were there—to deliver the news of Ricky's passing to his mother. He did not go into detail about Ricky's death.

"I'm so sorry." Valerie's eyebrows were now still; a pair of dead, bushy caterpillars. "Your mother is in the lounge."

Sister Cross led them to the lounge, where Andy's mum sat blankly staring at a television set, which was turned much too quiet for her to hear. In as jovial a manner as he could muster, "Hiya, mum."

She turned her blank stare to her son. "Hello."

"Mum, it's me, Andy." Andy knelt in front of her and took her fragile hands into his own. "Yes, I know! Do you think I'm stupid?" She leaned to one side and tried to peer at the television. "What are you doing here?"

"Mum," he started, trying to catch her distant eyes. "There's something I have to tell you. It's about Richard."

"Oh, hello dear, how are you?" after noticing Alice, who was standing behind Andy with Catherine.

"I'm fine, mum." Alice gulped, trying to hold back the tears.

"Mum," Andy continued, "Ricky died."

"Oh, dear. That's a shame."

Catherine glanced at Alice and gave a slight shake of her head, as if to say, she has not got a clue who Richard is.

"Mum, do you understand what I've said to you?" "Yes, yes," she replied, waving a hand at him as she continued watching the TV.

"Mum, do you remember Richard?"

"Of course I do. He lived near us." Andy's heart sank.

Andy turned to Alice and Catherine and shook his head. Catherine stepped forward and grabbed Andy's hand, pulling him away.

"See you soon, Mum," Alice choked out before giving her mother-in-law a gentle hug. "Is that alright? We have a lot to do."

"Yes dear, that will be nice."

Before Andy reached the exit, he stopped and spoke with Sister Valerie Cross if, in her opinion, his mother was able to comprehend anything she was told. She said that, given the advanced stages of his mother's dementia, it was doubtful. But she would ask the staff to keep a watch for any signs of acknowledgement of what he had told her, Andy drove back to his flat with Alice and Catherine.

At the police station, DCS Barlow was speaking with DCI Jenkins.

"We have a problem now, Donald," Barlow announced, "with Annika going to the mortuary." Jenkins nodded in agreement. "We didn't need this right now, not before the next Games Night for Christ's sake!"

"That's not all," Jenkins pointed out. "We have the funeral to contend with and the safety of Andy. If Salamon shows up, his cover will be blown right out of the water."

"Christ, you're right." Barlow silently pondered his next move while Jenkins watched him. "Donald, bring in DI Watt and DS Wallace. Oh, and Chris as well."

Barlow watched as each of them took a seat. "Gentlemen, we have a potential problem that could blow this inquiry apart. Anika Salamon, using the name Anika Szymańska, visited the mortuary to see Richard Blackmore today, stating she was his cousin." He looked around the room. "We have reliable information that a Games Night is going to take place on Wednesday night. Now, depending on when the funeral of Andy's brother takes place, Andy's whole involvement in this inquiry could be put in jeopardy, as well as the inquiry itself. We have to assume that she'll be going to the funeral, where she'll see Andy. This is the part where I would appreciate your thoughts."

"What are our options?" DS Watt, leaned back in his chair and folded his arms.

"Not a lot," DI Wallace chimed in, rubbing his chin.

"I'm thinking of calling McConnell," continued Barlow, "and making him aware of the situation. Secondly, I would like to raid the party on Wednesday and detain everyone there, especially Salamon, Andy must be arrested along with everyone else, otherwise people might get suspicious. Is everyone in agreement, or do you have any other suggestions?"

"I'll support your decision," DCI Jenkins called out.

"I'm with you, sir," DS Wallace added.

"DI Watt?" Barlow prompted. "You seem deep in thought."

"I just hope we have enough evidence to start bringing them in."

Barlow nodded and turned to the remaining colleague who had not spoken. "Chris?"

"Well, sir, with the intelligence we have gathered, which Amanda is logging daily, Andy's wire suggests that only he and Marie are aware of the venue for the next party. Everyone else attending will get told by someone else through a chain of phone calls. This whole set-up is quite brilliant."

"In what way?"

"It's simple but smart. Everyone going to the Games Night is protected by each other, using a pager system. Guest A has Guest B's number, but not the other way around. Guest B has Guest C's number, and so on. So on a Games night Anika starts with one number and then each one pages the other, so no one knows who belongs to what pager. My guess is only Anika has all the pager numbers of the participants, and she is the one that kicks off the chain reaction a couple of hours before showtime."

All eyes were now on Barlow as he sat pondering his colleagues' input.

"Okay, let me speak to McConnell." "Thanks, everyone." He dismissed the officers and they left his office.

Barlow dialled the number to McConnell and listened to the continuous ring.

Come on, pick it up! "McConnell here," he answered, panting. "S-sorry, I had to… run upstairs."

"It's Barlow, sir. I must speak to you."

Chapter Nineteen

A ndy was pacing the length of his living room when his phone started ringing. He picked it up instantly.

"Andy?" DCI Barlow's voice echoed through the receiver.

"Yes?" "We have your brother's death certificate here at the office, and the Procurator Fiscal has released his body. You can make funeral arrangements."

"Thank you, sir."

"I'm going to send DI Jenkins and DS Wallace with the certificate. They have to speak to you alone."

"How come?"

"They will explain everything when they get there. Will you be with your sister-in-law or at your flat?"

"What would you suggest, sir?"

"Preferably at your flat."

"Okay. I'll need an hour or so as Alice and Catherine are here and need to leave shortly."

"Sure." Barlow hung up.

Andy informed Alice and Catherine that the death certificate had been issued and that he was getting a visit from his senior officers.

A short time later the doorbell rang.

"Come in," waving in DCI Jenkins and DS Wallace.

As they entered the living room, the officers shook hands with Andy and offered their condolences.

"Take a seat, gents." Andy gestured at the sofa. "Would you like anything to drink?"

"No Andy, thanks for the offer though."

Andy introduced Alice and Catherine to his colleagues, before Wallace produced the envelope containing Ricky's death certificate and handed it over to Andy.

"Thank you." Andy accepted the envelope. It felt heavy. "Barlow said you had something to speak with me about." They flashed glances at Alice and Catherine.

Catherine promptly stood up and announced, "we'll go through to the bedroom, let you guys have a chat."

"Thanks, Catherine."

When Catherine and Alice left the room, Jenkins turned his attention to Andy.

"Will you let us know when your brother's funeral is? We're planning to raid the Games Night on Wednesday night."

Jenkins explained that everyone, including Andy, would be arrested as part of the raid.

"Alice must never find out about this," Andy muttered, burying his head in his hands. Then, looking at the officers, "who knows how deeply involved Ricky was in all this?"

"Based on their statements, it seems they know as much as anyone else I'm so sorry, Andy, it has nothing to do with you, mate!" DS Wallace assured him.

Andy nodded. "Okay, then. Wednesday is on." "Great, I'll let Barlow know,"

"Thank you, Andy."

Andy saw both officers out of the door and closed it behind them. "Catherine, Alice, you can come out now."

"Okay," Catherine called, before coming out of the room with Alice. She looked out of the window and watched as the officers drove off.

"How much did you hear?" noting that the bedroom door had been left open.

"To be honest, everything." "Hell." He eyed Alice, who sat down on the sofa, her expression blank.

"I'm sorry, Andy," she murmured. "But I'm glad you told me about that woman, now that I know how wicked she is. I know that you want to see this through, but I'm worried about you going to the party on Wednesday, in case she finds out who you really are."

"I'll cross that bridge on Wednesday, and thank you for your support today.That goes for you too Catherine."

Catherine wrapped her arms around the man she loved and placed her head on his shoulder.

"C'mon, I'll take you both home," Andy murmured.

The following morning, Andy and Alice went to the undertakers to arrange Ricky's funeral. They introduced themselves to the funeral director, Ms Walsh, who showed them into her office. Ms Walsh was a small, slim woman in her late forties, dressed appropriately for her grim job. She had little make-up on, and her dark brown hair was swept into a tight ponytail.

"Now," Ms Walsh squawked "I assume by your coming here that you would like to make funeral arrangements for a loved one?"

"Yes," Alice replied. She dressed in all black, and was wringing a small white handkerchief in her hands.

"May I ask who the deceased is, please?"

"My husband."

"Do you have a death certificate?"

Andy reached into the inside pocket of his suit jacket and handed over the envelope. He watched her closely as she whipped out the certificate with ease and unfolded it. There was no response from Ms Walsh as she lifted her pen and started noting down the necessary details.

"Would you happen to have your husband's birth certificate?"

Alice, ever diligent, reached into her handbag and handed over a second envelope to Ms Walsh, who made additional notes before returning them to Alice.

"That's everything I need, thank you.Now all we have to do is make the necessary arrangements. What did you have in mind?"

Over the next hour, the details of the funeral were meticulously arranged to Alice's wishes. A short service was to be held in the parlour for family only. No flowers were to be permitted, except for a family wreath. Closed coffin, no viewing.

"Is there to be a purvey?"

"No," Alice replied firmly. "The family will meet at home and that shall be it."

"Please follow me." She led them into another area of the parlour; a wide room with low ceilings made up of rows upon rows of coffins in all shapes and colours. "Here we have a selection of coffins." She gestured at the coffins with a hand, like a car dealer pointing to the latest models. "Is there anything here that would meet your requirements?"

Alice looked to Andy for guidance on this one.

"Something presentable. Dark timber, brass handles?" he suggested.

"Certainly. I would recommend this one." Ms Walsh indicated a coffin.

"Is that okay with you, Alice?" She nodded.

"Finally, is this to be a burial or a cremation?"

"Cremation." "Morning or afternoon?"

"Afternoon."

"Right, then all I have to do is make a few telephone calls and I'll be with you in a few minutes.".

Soon Ms Walsh returned to confirm. "A short service is arranged for Friday at one o'clock and the body would be cremated at two o'clock. If there's anything else, please let me know."

"Certainly." Alice shook hands with Ms Walsh as they parted.

"Thank you," Andy added, also shaking her hand. "Oh, and Ms Walsh? If anyone comes here using the name Szymańska, wanting to see Ricky, can you call this number please?" He handed her a slip of paper. She nodded, eyebrows furrowed.

At Alice's request, they went to her villa. They sat in the car for a while, staring at what was once a family home full of joy and laughter. It was the place Alice had celebrated the birth of her children, and where they had grown up. Of course, it had all been a lie, and once the truth came out, the house had morphed into a scene of crime and death.

"I don't want my parents involved in all this malarkey with the Lodge," she spoke up eventually.

"I understand." Andy placed a reassuring hand on hers, but a pang of guilt withdrew it quickly.

That evening, two representatives from the Masonic Lodge arrived at Alice's house.

"I'm James Houston and this is Charles Conway," announced a balding, stout man. "We're friends of Richard. I believe you've been expecting us?"

"Yes, please come in" Alice waved them inside, a small grimace revealed her tension. She led them into the lounge, where Andy was lounging on the sofa.

"Gentlemen, this is Andrew Blackmore, my brother-in-law."

"Pleased to meet you both," Andy stood up and shook their hands, trying desperately, for Alice's sake, to sound sincere.

They all sat down.

"As you're both aware, Richard is— was a member of our Lodge, of which I'm the current Master," Houston started. "Charles here is the Almoner. We are here to offer our deepest sympathies and offer any financial assistance. We would also like to honour Richard with a full masonic funeral." Houston and Charles raised their eyebrows in unison.

"Please, go on," Andy groaned through gritted teeth.

Alice sensed a fuse was about to blow.

"We would take care of everything, of course taking your wishes into consideration. Following the funeral, you would all be invited back to the Lodge for a meal and drinks, all at our expense." Houston smirked, and Andy had to dig his fingernails into his palms to keep from throwing himself at the man. He thought of Catherine, and that disapproving glare she gave him when he lost control. "Given Richard's stature, I expect that members of the Grand Lodge of Scotland will be present, or at the very least represented. I wouldn't be surprised if the Grand Master himself attended."

Andy nodded to Alice, who was watching him closely.

"What part do you play in all this, Mr. Conway?" she asked interrogatively; her lawyer instincts were kicking in.

"I must keep in contact with you and ensure that you and your children are cared for in this sad time, as well as in the future," he explained. "But that's just part of my duties. If there are any financial issues with respect to the funeral, I'm here to assist with that as well."

"Thank you." Alice bowed her head. "Andy, over to you."

Houston turned to Andy and clasped his hands on a knee. "How can we assist you, Brother Blackmore?"

Andy felt the fuse inside light, and he had to summon all his energy to remain calm.

"First of all," he started, shivering slightly at the ice cold anger that spilled down his spine, "cut out the Brother Blackmore shit."

Houston hmmmphed, taken aback by the response. "We just assumed —"

"Don't assume anything," Andy growled. "Alice, may I?"

She nodded.

"Now gentlemen, let me be clear about this." Andy paused. "Alice and I were at the undertaker's today, and we arranged everything. The service at the funeral directors will be private, for family and close friends only. We'll welcome members of the Lodge to the cremation, but I want you to get one thing straight... your services are not required."

"Well," Houston uttered, shuffling in his seat to address Alice, "if those are your wishes, Mrs Blackmore, then we shall honour them."

"This is what Andy and I, both want. We discussed it before your arrival. But there is no disrespect intended towards his friends in the Lodge."

"Tell me something," Andy demanded, "I know he was a member of the local Lodge, but was he also a member of the Grand Lodge of Scotland?"

"Yes, he was," Houston confirmed, glancing at Conway. "Why do you ask?"

"He just seemed to spend a lot of time at the Lodge."

"He was well-known in many Brother Lodges, locally and further afield."

"It's nice to know he was respected in that circle."

"This will come as a surprise that his family hasn't consented to a Masonic Funeral."

"I'm afraid our decision is final."

"Can I ask when the funeral will be?"

"Two o'clock, Friday, at the Crematorium."

"Thank you." Houston and Conway rose to leave the house.

"It has been nice meeting you gents," Alice commented. Begrudgingly Andy stood and shook hands with the men a second time.

Alice followed them into the hallway and thanked them for their visit before she showed them out.

"Well, this is going to be interesting," she remarked, turning to Andy once the door shut behind her. "Thanks for your support."

"You're welcome. I'll be heading down the road myself now."

"Do you have to?"

"Yes, after I take you back to your parent's house and your magical children."

All throughout his trip home — dropping off Alice, trading niceties with her parents, and parking outside his own home — Wednesday night plagued his thoughts.

Chapter Twenty

A ndy was back in the city he loved and, despite the crowds on Argyle Street, he felt alone. Glasgow was being smothered in grey rain, and Andy reluctantly ducked into a a department store to purchase a new white shirt for his brother's funeral. He was browsing the racks with a scowl when a female voice spoke behind him. "Hello, Andy." He spun around and saw Anika Salamon.

"Oh, hello." Andy smiled. "Fancy meeting you here." "What are you doing in here?" "I like to wander around the city centre from time to time when I'm not working." Andy knew it was a terrible lie, but it was the only thing he could come up with on the spot. "Such is the life of a brickie. What about you?"

"I'm in for a new blouse." "A friend of mine passed away and his funeral is on Friday."

"I'm sorry to hear that." Andy struggled to keep his tone even. "Were you close?"

"Yes, and a bit more than that, for a while," she confessed, Andy's mouth went dry. "Do you fancy a coffee?"

"I thought we were keeping this arrangement professional?"

"I'm asking you for a coffee, not to climb into bed with me. I'm in mourning after all." Andy glanced around the store and caught two men watching him from a distance.

"Sure, why not?" "Good. They have a new cafeteria on the top floor."

"Lead the way."

"And here was me thinking you were going to get me something nice to wear, for your eyes only." "I thought you said you were in mourning," Andy teased.

"You're the first to ever reject me, but I respect you for that, believe it or not." She sounded sincere. They made their way to the top floor and Andy, on Anika's instruction, got them a table far from the occupied ones.

Andy watched the escalator, knowing that one of them was under surveillance. Whose side were they on, his or hers? Anika, for one, seemed oblivious to the prying eyes. Which probably made them hers.

Andy thanked Anika when she came back and handed him his black coffee.She sat down and slowly stirred her coffee, staring into Andy's eyes in a manner which unnerved him.

"Tell me about you, Andy," Anika demanded.

"Why?" he responded softly, easing back into the game he had been playing with her, meeting her gaze. "You know everything you need to know about me. I'm an unmarried bricklayer brought up in Glasgow. Not exactly exciting, is it?"

"Oh, on the contrary. There's something dark and mysterious about you I'm trying to work out." Anika rested her elbows on the table, her back to one of their surveyors, who appeared at the top of the escalator and walked to the counter and bought a coffee. "It shouldn't take me long."

The other man also purchased one. They sat at separate tables; one of them was reading a paper while sipping his coffee, and the other was seemingly staring out the window, though when Andy looked over he found the man's eyes staring straight at him in the reflection, Andy turned back to Anika, who produced a make-up case from her small handbag and started dabbing powder on her face.

"Do I look better now?" She smiled.

"You always look good, Anika." "You know, tonight is your last shift with me."

"Why's that?" He tried to sound disappointed, but acting had never been his strong suit, Andy had never been asked to be anything other than himself.

"Andy, when I want something, I usually get it, and you said you don't mix business with pleasure."

"Correct. It's a bad mix."

"So, I propose a promotion. From now on, you shall be my driver, minder, and…" she paused and smiled coyly, "companion."

"Really?"

"You can start now. See the guys behind me with a keen interest in us? Go tell them I'm going to try on some see-through underwear, and if they wish to join me, I would love that." "Eh?" Andy was nonplussed.

"They're cops, Andy. It's amazing what you can see in the mirror of a compact case."

"Are you sure?" Andy feigned surprise, and scratched his head to seem nervous

"Very. Get rid of them." Andy stood up and casually strolled over to the guy with the newspaper. Leaning forward, he whispered into the man's ear, "you and your mate have been burned, get out of here."

The phrase sent a clear message to the undercover officer that he was speaking to a fellow policeman.

Andy returned to his seat. "They declined your offer," Andy informed Anika as the two officers left. She laughed. It was a loud and boisterous laugh.

"And what about you?"

"Sadly, so will I, as I must be going. I'm sorry for the loss of your friend. I hope the funeral goes well."

"He was quite well-known, so I expect a large turnout. It should be fun watching the people from the Games Nights interact with the others who were in business with him."

"Earlier you said you were more than friends. Meaning what? Did you live together?"

"Oh God no. He was married. Had a wife and two vile children."

Andy observed how sad Anika looked as she stared down at the table, swirling her coffee with a spoon and letting out a deep sigh, Andy could see that she had tears in her eyes. A sign of weakness? Surely not. A performance then? I'm not the only one playing a game.

"He must have been special to you." Andy's voice was soft and quiet.

"Yes, he was." "It's good to talk about these things, sometimes." Andy was trying to glean more information. Anika dipped a hand into her bag and pulled out a small tissue, with which she dabbed her eyes.

"You remind me of him a bit," Anika remarked. "His name was Richard. He was a chemist, and he was introduced to the Games Nights by a friend." She paused. "Richard attended a few parties, at first a watcher hesitant to get involved with the girls." Anika seemed to drift into a daydream, Andy stayed silent, fearing the worst. "Anyway, you don't want to hear all about this." Anika waved her hand, dismissing the story.

"Please, continue," Andy blurted. Then, for fear of seeming too eager, "I'm here for you." Andy leaned forward and took hold of her hand, giving it a little squeeze. Anika reached out and placed her other hand on his, slowly moving hers around. If Andy did not know any better, he would have found the gesture tender, Andy knew that she was an expert in seduction. This was likely all part of her game. Or is she genuinely grieving a lost friend?

Anika looked up at Andy as if she was about to say something, but then drew back, Andy could almost see the cogs turning in her head; she was considering how much to reveal. Finally, in a quiet voice, she began to reveal everything.

"At one of the Games Nights he had been drinking and was slouched back in a chair, watching what was happening. I had been watching him for a while, when I noticed he was sexually aroused. I was attracted to him, so I approached him and straddled him on the chair." Anika said this as if it were the most natural thing in the world to do. "It wasn't long before our clothes were on the floor, and it wasn't long after that I gave him my number. We were lovers for a couple of years, until Sandra came along. She and her man Brian were into anything that moved, no matter what age."

Andy was dumbfounded but had to control his emotions.

Anika continued, "Sandra introduced Richard to a beautiful young girl, about fourteen, that Brian was besotted with. She was one of the girls from a care home. Soon after, Richard was just as entranced, then, Richard began to change. He quickly forgot about me. Became cold. Drank more and more."

"What happened to her?"

"Last I heard, she'd managed to escape the games nights. Hopefully, she put the money from Richard and Brian to good use." Anika shook her head sadly. "Brian and Sandra died in a tragic accident, and now Richard is gone too. As far as I know, he was a gambler and an alcoholic. Last time I saw him, only a couple of nights ago, he told me a few... things." Anika stared at the table, unblinking.

"What things?" Andy whispered.

"That his brother was a cop, and he was having an affair with his wife." When Anika stopped talking, Andy feared that he had been discovered. "I should have seen his suicide coming," she continued. "Just the way he was acting..."

"What was he like when you saw him a few nights ago?" Only as soon as the words came out did Andy fear his question was suspicious, but Anika did not seem to notice.

"He called me crying. His wife had left him and taken the kids, and he said he wanted to see me. I drove to his place, and he told me all about his wife and brother having an affair. She was in love with him and vice versa. We had a few drinks and I stayed overnight with him. It was some house. Big fancy place."

Andy nodded. "Listen, time is wearing on," Andy pointed out, glancing at his watch. Anika nodded and they got to their feet.

"Are you still on for tonight at seven, as arranged?" Anika quirked an eyebrow.

"Yeah, no problem." "Good. I need you on the doors. Big night tonight." Anika began to walk away, before she returned to plant a kiss on Andy's forehead. "Thank you for listening, Andy. No man has ever done that for me."

Anika made her way to the escalator. For the first time, he saw what she really looked like; a woman in her forties with blonde hair, blue eyes, high cheekbones, a perfect complexion, and a figure that seemed to belong to a much younger woman. He could see why Richard was attracted to her; too bad her morals could not match her looks.

Andy stared into his almost empty coffee cup, his heart aching; not for himself or even his deceased brother, but for Alice and the kids. He made no secret of the fact that he loved those kids to bits, and while he was deeply in love with Catherine, he knew in his heart that there was a special place for Alice there, and there always would be.

A man approached Andy's table. He had long hair and a beard and was wearing jeans and a black leather jacket zipped open over a T-shirt. He whispered into Andy's ear, "when you're driving home, you're going to be stopped by a marked police car. Get into it." With that, the man walked to the escalator and disappeared.

Andy finished his cold coffee before leaving the cafeteria and making his way to get fitted out for the funeral.

Part Three

Free at Last

Chapter Twenty-One

A ndy strolled down Argyle Street toward the Trongate, passing by fishmongers and a bridal shop before reaching a small, unassuming doorway that led into the tailor shop. He climbed the narrow staircase to the first floor."Good day," exclaimed a young, female assistant.

"Hello. I would like a suit," Andy replied.

"Certainly!" The assistant beckoned to a man with a measuring tape around his neck.

"How may I help you?" the tailor, was a small, heavily built, balding man.

"I need a new suit."

"For a wedding, is it?" Andy decided to avoid the question.

"Something like that." Andy looked at the suits on the rails, bearing hefty price tags.

"Seventeen and a half collar, yes?"

"Yeah, bang on." Andy looked at the tailor, impressed.

"Is it a formal suit you're looking for, sir?" Andy nodded. The tailor handed Andy a jacket and trousers.

"Try that on."

"You're not going to measure me?"

The tailor smiled and dropped the formalities. "Just try it on."

Andy went to the changing rooms and tried on the suit he had chosen; it fit like a glove. He returned to the tailor, who ran his hand over Andy's shoulders, checking the length of the sleeves, then stood back and checked the length of his trousers. He stood in front of Andy and smiled.

"Perfect." The tailor clapped once, loud.

"How the hell did you do that?"

"It's like everything in life, you just get better as the years go by, just like you will." Andy found himself unnerved by the comment. "Now, sir, would you like a dark or light tie?"

"Dark."

"There you go, sir." He handed Andy a black tie checked with thin, navy stripes. "Perfect." The tailor took the purchases to the counter, where the assistant hung them in a black bag.

"Thank you for everything," shaking the tailor's hand.

"You're most welcome. Best wishes to you and your family for Friday."

As Andy was leaving the store, the hairs on his neck stood on end and he felt a cold shiver run through his body.

Andy wondered, why did that man seem so familiar? How did he know about Friday? Come to think of it, how the hell did Anika know where the funeral service was to be held? How did she know Richard died in the first place?

At four o'clock that afternoon, DCS Barlow addressed the mass of police officers in the Force Headquarters gymnasium, the only room large enough to hold all the police personnel from every Division in Glasgow. Barlow spoke from a raised stage overlooking the seated officers. Among the officers was Ashley Bell, a senior social worker who had a team of three workers with her.

"I'm sure you all want to know why you've been asked to report here, but let me first introduce my team." Barlow gestured at the people seated behind him on the stage. "There is one person missing from this line-up, DCI Jenkins." He paused briefly. "He is on duty now but shall be with us as soon as possible. With us today we have David McConnell and Chloe Agnew. They are both from the Crown Office in Edinburgh."

The officers in the gymnasium began to shuffle uneasily. "What's going on here?" one of them murmured, though Barlow could hear him.

"In answer to your question, Inspector, you will all be drip-fed what is going on here. At the back of the room a buffet has been prepared. Please help yourselves. Toilets are to the left of the exit door. Beyond that, you're not allowed out of here until we say so. All communication with the outside world is now prohibited." Senior officers exchanged furtive glances. This type of operation was unheard of.

It was not long beforeAndy saw blue lights flashing in his rearview mirror, indicating to him to pull over on Dumbarton Road. A traffic officer, donned in a white-topped cap, approached the driver's door, closely watched by Andy through his offside mirror. The officer rapped his knuckles on Andy's window, which he lowered.

"Mr. Blackmore, step out of the vehicle and follow me, please." As he got into the back of the police car, Andy reasoned he must have seemed like a driver nicked for speeding to passing motorists .

"Hello Andy," DCI Jenkins greeted him as he got into the car.

"Hi boss," Andy replied, taking a seat next to him in the rear seat.

"I heard what happened with Anika today."

"I thought you would have by now, sir."

"Gimme your warrant card, please"

"Eh?"

"Hand it over!" Jenkins demanded, holding out his right hand, palm up,

Andy was about to lash out with a snide remark when an image flashed in his mind; Barlow at the morgue, his head turned away from Andy, like a father tired of his son's antics. He remembered the sinking feeling in his gut. So, Andy complied without another word and Jenkins put the card in his pocket. "Good lad. Now, any changes to tonight's arrangements?"

"No sir. Seven o'clock, Golden Thistle. The password is 'fourteen'."

"Entry price?"

"One hundred pounds."

"The reason I want your warrant card is because you're going to be arrested along with everyone else. The boss and I'll take you away for an interview."

Andy nodded. "Listen, please make sure the barmaid, Marie, is okay."

"Why?"

"She is as much a victim as the kids, and, well, let's just say that without her and Kerry, we would not be this far forward in the investigation."

"Alright, alright. I'll see to it personally." Jenkins sighed.

"Thank you." Andy left the Traffic Department car.

Andy arrived that evening at the Golden Thistle to find the premises locked up with no lights on. Something is not right here. A taxi drew up and a red-haired woman in a long coat stepped out. It was not until she had paid the driver and turned around that Andy recognised her. "Anika? What the hell have you done to your hair?"

"Don't you just love it?" She sauntered up to Andy and unlocked the door to the Thistle. "Wait until you see the rest."

She winked before pushing the door open, leading him inside. She went about turning lights on and overturning bar stools, Andy helped. When they were done, Anika turned to Andy and unzipped her coat.

"What are your thoughts?" She wore a red Basque, with suspenders holding up her black stockings, completed by a pair of black high heels.

"Jesus, you're mad."

"Thanks." Anika laughed. "But remember, I'm your boss."

"Yes ma'am." Andy gave her a mock salute. "Hell, that red hair makes you look so sexy." Catherine's face flashed in his head.

"It's because I am sexy, as you will find out soon enough."

Andy could not help but stare, watching her every move; her long legs striking the ground as she strutted away, and every strand of hair that shifted as she did.

Next to arrive was Marie. She greeted them both.

"Hi Marie," Andy responded hoarsely. His heart sank as he looked at her, knowing what was to happen that night. Would she be okay?

"Hello Marie," Anika echoed, not bothering to glance her way as she continued preparing the premises, Andy and Marie helped her as best they could. Eventually, Anika approached them with two envelopes in hand. "Andy, your last pay, and Marie, here is your pay for tonight, you lovely lady."

"Is this Andy's last night with us?" Marie piped up.

"It is," she confirmed, "as a bouncer." Anika smirked. "He'll be my new driver and companion, and even my minder. I mean look at those muscles babe."

Marie looked at Andy, as if to ask, what are you doing?

"Marie, tell me, woman to woman, is Andy boy here good in bed?" "Of course he is," the concern in her eyes instantly replaced by amusement. She had played this role for a long time. "I taught him everything he knows." "Thanks for that, Marie," Andy joked, before walking away from the bar.

"It's true and you know it!" she called after him. Anika just looked at them, wondering what that was all about.

Andy went to the bathroom and changed into his all-black bouncer outfit, which consisted of a puffer jacket, black shirt, black trousers, and shoes polished to perfection . He then took his place at the main entrance, having pushed them back against the wall.

The opening of the doors was like a signal to the vehicles which had begun lining up over the last half hour. The teenage girls and boys climbed out of the cars; Andy counted ten of them entering the building as their chauffeurs left. The cars were scheduled to return at about four in the morning. Unbeknownst to Andy, these vehicles were soon to be stopped by a fleet of officers who would detain the drivers.

Andy welcomed the teenage guests with a strained smile, fighting every urge to shake the children by their shoulders and scream at them to run. After paying and depositing their coats, the teenagers made their way to the free bar. Soon after, the customers began arriving. By ten o'clock, there were at least a hundred people in the hall, with music blaring out of the speakers as adults danced together. The children were left to lounge by the bar or on the couches, merely on display until some depraved person chose them. It was not long before the adults had drunk enough to gather the courage to approach the younger guests. One by one, they were picked off by both men and women and engaged in open sexual acts while others watched. Some of the children were picked by lone degenerates, while others were adopted by groups of people.

Andy's mind wandered to the fact that this would be over soon... definitely not soon enough.

"Fourteen," a man at the door barked, breaking Andy out of his thoughts.

"H-how many do you have with you, sir?" Andy stammered.

"Ten, including myself."

"Head through to the cloakroom. Anika will take your money."

As Anika charged the man one thousand pounds, Andy watched unmarked police vehicles discretely begin to surround the premises. Everything had been meticulously planned by DCS Barlow, right down to not informing the officers what they were about to raid. They thought they were raiding a regular pub. McConnell and Agnew were both with Jenkins, taking observations on proceedings from a nearby vehicle. The social workers, except for Ashley Bell, did not know why they were there.

"Ashley, what's going on?" Robert, one of the social workers, spoke up.

"Sorry Rob, I can't say." Ashley was nervously tapping the steering wheel of her car. Marked police carriers, with sixteen officers in each, parked in the surrounding streets, close enough to be at the Golden Thistle within a minute. "Won't be long now."

"Until what?"

At ten-thirty precisely, a codeword rang out on every officer's radio. The raid was about to begin. Moans turned to screams as officers stormed the building, turning on the lights and yelling at the crowd of people to get on the ground. All the exits were promptly blocked by uniformed officers, and dozens of pairs of handcuffs flashed under the bright lights as officers began the arrests, Andy was the first to be detained by two officers, having been the first person in their line of fire.

They were not aware of his identity, and shoved him ruthlessly toward the vehicle containing Jenkins, McConnell and Agnew, as per instructions. Barlow was out on the roadway, watching his operation unfold.

Inside the hall, the screams continued as men and women grabbed their belongings and tried to flee the scene. But the officers at the exits grabbed them swiftly, pinning them to the floor and cuffing them. The detained whined as they were hauled to their feet, protesting their innocence as they were led to awaiting police vehicles. They would have to be driven to different police offices all around the city centre; such was the size of the operation.

The social workers came next, escorting the children from the premises to the waiting unmarked police vans specially commissioned for this raid. They would all be dealt with as victims and witnesses.

Within twenty minutes, DCS Barlow was at the scene inspecting the vacant hall; all of the party guests had been detained for further inquiry. Uniformed police officers remained in position at the main door. "Where's Anika?" when Barlow got back into the car.

"She'll be in a van somewhere." Barlow ran a hand over his face, yawning deeply.

"I didn't see her coming out."

"She'll be somewhere, Andy. Calm down."

"Mm." Andy jingled his cuffs. , "These are quite tight." "Oh, I forgot about them." Barlow chuckled.

"Get out of the car and I'll take them off," laughing and shaking his head. As he released Andy from the handcuffs, he handed him his warrant card. "Better put that on 'big man' in case you get arrested."

"Thanks." Andy put the lanyard around his neck. Upon feeling the rough fabric around his neck, he realised how naked he had felt without it. He really was a lifetime away from his life as a brickie.

Andy glanced out of the window and saw Marie, handcuffed, being led out of the Golden Thistle by two officers, Andy flung his door open and ran over to them. She glared at him, mouth puckered and eyes alight with betrayal.

"Let her go!" Andy snapped.

"And who are you?" one officer demanded.

"I'm the man who will get DCS Barlow on your case if you do not release her now."

"Sure, calm down," rolling his eyes before inspecting Andy's warrant card. He glanced over at Barlow in the vehicle, who gave him a curt nod, before releasing Marie from her handcuffs.

As soon as she was free, Andy took her aside.

"Have you seen Anika?" he whispered.

"No." She winced, rubbing her wrists.

"I never saw her leave" "Me neither."

Andy and Marie made their way back inside and looked around the empty hall. Where there had been blaring music before there was now only an eerie silence. Discarded clothing lay on the floor and across tables, and copious amounts of alcohol lay untouched in bottles and glasses, some of which had been upended, dripping into puddles on the floor, Andy made his way to the cloakroom to find that the cash box was gone. Did Anika escape?

Pushing open the door to the gents' toilet, Andy called to see if anyone was hiding in the cubicles. There was no reply. He walked in cautiously, seeing that one cubicle door was closed. He thought he could see the tip of a white shoe poking out from underneath the door, Andy steadied his breathing and wiped a bead of sweat from his forehead. I should have brought backup. He approached the door slowly before suddenly kicking it open. The cubicle was empty, as were the others, and what he thought had been a white shoe was just a square of toilet paper.

Then he made his way towards the ladies toilet, making his presence known as before. gain, he was met by silence. This time, all six cubicle doors were closed One by one, he began to kick open the doors. Each one was unlocked and empty, except the last, which, when he struck it with his boot, did not budge, Andy put an eye to the crack between the door and the frame and saw a big eye staring straight back at him. His heart leapt in his throat, but as the other eye withdrew and Anika's head came into view, he calmed down. But he still kept his guard up, Andy tapped on the door. "Anika, open the door, please."

"Why? It's over for me, Andy."

"Please op—" "Who are you?" she shrieked suddenly, startling Andy.

"Anika, I'll explain everything. Just open the door." He struggled to keep his voice even, sympathetic.

From behind the locked door, Anika shuffled about, but made no move to let Andy in.

"Do you remember when I told you I would never go to jail?" she croaked, sounding defeated.

"Yes, I remember." "I meant it. I'm only going to ask you one more time. Who are you?"

"My full name is Andrew Blackmore. I'm Richard's brother. I'm a police officer and… I'm here to arrest you." Andy waited for a reply.

"Well that is not going to happen." She chuckled dryly before unlocking the door. She left it closed, Andy approached the cubicle door and hesitated, not knowing exactly what he would find on the other side. It was silent save for the drip, drip, drip of a faucet.

Andy swung the door open to reveal a dishevelled Anika sitting on the toilet pan, the cashbox at her feet. Her long coat was open, tears were streaming down her cheeks, trailing mascara, and her hair was in wild tangles. Her bleary eyes fixed on the warrant card hanging from his neck. Anika smiled. "Good job. Here give this to Marie." She kicked the cashbox over to Andy. "I don't need it where I'm going." That was when Andy saw the boning knife in her hand.

"Can I ask you one last favour, Andy?"

Andy gulped and nodded, not wanting to make any sudden movements.

"Walk out the door and don't look back."

"I'll stay with you," Andy slowly approached her, wanting to keep her talking until he could take the knife. "Nobody deserves to die alone, like Ricky."

"I'll tell him you said hi." She grinned as she drew the knife across her throat and painted the floor with her life.

As Andy returned to the main hall, Marie appeared from a back room. "I can't find her anywhere." She threw up her hands in defeat.

"Me neither," he muttered, handing the cashbox to Marie without looking at her. He felt distant from his body, like he was running on autopilot. "Go."

"Thank you," stroking Andy's cheek and turning his face to meet her eyes. He nodded at her before she turned and ran.

Andy slowly made his way downstairs and stood at the corner of the pub. He saw Jenkins standing by a side door and approached him. "DCI Jenkins could you come with me, please?" Andy led him to the ladies toilet. Anika Salamon's body was slumped on the toilet seat, her blood draining from her body out of her carotid artery. Her eyes were open, staring at Andy, her arms hanging limply by her side. The knife used to end her chaotic life lay on the tiled floor.

"That is all I need," before closing the cubicle door.

Standing on the pavement outside the Golden Thistle, Andy looked up at the stars. "Time I head home to Bankvale," he mused.

"Andy," Jenkins called, ambling over to him.

"Yes, sir?"

"How did you know Salamon was in that cubicle?"

"Instinct. Just instinct"

Jenkins stared at Andy; if he strongly suspected Andy was there with her at the end, he would never be able to prove it.

"And Marie, where is she?" "Haven't a clue, sir." Andy shrugged.

"Are you sure about that?"

"Absolutely."

"The cash box then?" Jenkins raised his eyebrows. "There must be about, what, ten or twelve grand in that box?" "Let's just say—" he paused. "Let's just say that cashbox will save you a small fortune that would have been taken out of the tout fund, and it will give someone a new start, far away from here."

Jenkins looked at his feet and shook his head, his hands clenched deep in his trouser pockets.

"That is one hell of an expensive tout, Andy."

"But worth every penny, don't you agree?"

"Tell me something." Jenkins lowered his tone. "How long have you known her?"

"Since I was eighteen, sir."

Jenkins shook his head again and smiled before saying, "I'm leaving Anika where she is, for now. Scenes of crime officers and a photographer will need to attend, but, by the look of it, this has suicide written all over it, Andy, thank you for everything you have done under the most trying of circumstances. Now, go back to your family and take care of them. We will see you when your family business is over, and then we will get your side of all this sorted."

Andy watched two uniformed police officers enter the Thistle, where they would position themselves at the entrance to the ladies' toilets to protect the scene.

"Sure thing, no problem." Andy started walking away, before he turned around. "Oh, and sir?" he called. "Good luck." "What with?"

"Telling the boss that Anika's dead."

As soon as Jenkins got back in the car, Barlow remarked that he had taken a long time. "Swapping life stories with Andy Blackmore are we?"

"You just don't want to know this one."

Andy dragged his feet to his car, exhaustion wearing at his limbs, when a figure seemed to materialise out of the darkness next to him, Andy startled and put a hand to his chest.

"You okay?"

"Where did you come from?" Andy laughed shakily.

"I was in one of the unmarked cars along with Sharon. Did they get Anika?"

"Yeah, they did, but she's dead. Killed herself in a cubicle in the ladies toilet."

June did not flinch, instead grabbing him by the shoulder and turning him to look deep into his eyes. He nodded. She smiled and patted his cheek before walking away. Nobody knew him better in the job than she did.

Andy surveyed the scene all around him; the last of the police vehicles, the unmarked cars, the vans, and the personnel carriers were slowly but surely leaving the scene, carrying the accused and the victims.

The Games Nights were finally over.

Andy got back to his empty flat in the early hours of the morning. He dimmed the small light in the living room, poured a large brandy, and flopped down on his beloved old couch. Catherine was working the nightshift. As his head fell back against the couch cushions, he closed his eyes. Immediately, the evenings' events flashed in his mind and he began to relive Anika's last moments. He could hear her voice clearly, smell the stench of urine, and taste the iron in her blood pooling on the floor.

He could still see her drawing the razor-sharp knife across her neck, the blood spurting like a fountain, her eyes never leaving his as her breathing became shallow and laboured until her chest heaved one last, deep breath. Her blood flowed down over her body and dripped into the toilet, turning the clear water red. Her arms hung loosely at each side of her lifeless body, the blood-soaked knife falling from her grasp to clank against the floor.

If she had lived, she would have spent years in prison. Maybe fifteen years. It would never have been enough; she had condemned countless children to a life plagued by memories of abuse.

Was it wrong of me to play judge, jury and executioner? I suppose Anika played the part of the executioner... But no, I tried to save her! And if I had saved her? Would her suffering in prison at all make up for all the pain and sorrow she caused me? My family? June? Will I ever tell June what I did, or didn't do? I can't, not as long as we wear the badge.

Andy finished his brandy and went to bed, his bouncer uniform condemned to the bin and his conscience muddled.

Chapter Twenty-Two

DCS Barlow was sitting in his office with David McConnell and Chloe Agnew when there came a knock at the door.

"Come in, Donald," Barlow called without looking up, drawing another glass from his desk drawer and pouring Jenkins a whisky. "Here's to what has been a successful operation." Barlow raised his glass and the others followed suit."The death of Salamon is very unfortunate. I've sent a car to her house to have it secured until we can search it." Barlow looked at his watch. "It's late. I suggest we call a press conference for one o'clock today. Thoughts?" "It would certainly kill speculation," Jenkins admitted. "The rumour mill will be in full swing after all." "Everyone agree?" They nodded. "I'll arrange it through our press officer." He turned to McConnell and Agnew. "Do you want to do the statement or shall I?"

"It's all yours," smiling at Barlow.

Barlow returned the gesture, though behind that smile was a nagging anxiety; the knowledge that he would have to put this all together rapidly.

As McConnell and Agnew stood to leave, McConnell put his briefcase back down on the chair he had just vacated and scratched his chin.

"Something on your mind?" Barlow guessed.

"You know, Graham…" He trailed off, lost in thought, not noticing Barlow grimace at the sound of his first name. "The death of Salamon is not going to be easily explained away. People will be asking a lot of questions. Why was she not immediately detained? Where was she? Why was she not found? They'll remark that surely police officers had gone into the toilets to search for hiding suspects. Yet she was somehow not found until, bold boy Blackmore conveniently stumbled upon her dead body." Barlow detected more than a hint of bitterness in the man's voice. But before Barlow could respond, McConnell stormed out.

"Graham, Donald," Agnew exclaimed nodding at them and chuckling awkwardly. "We'll see you both later today. Goodnight, or should I say, good morning." She followed McConnell and closed the door behind her.

Barlow and Jenkins sat in silence for a while, staring into their whisky glasses and pondering McConnell's words.

"You know he's right, Graham."

"I know. What are your thoughts on her death?" Barlow swallowed the remains of his whisky and forcefully set his glass down on the desk.

Jenkins took a deep breath, swirling what whisky he had left in his glass. "See, to be honest with you, I would rather not think about what happened in that toilet." He paused. "I think the only person that knows the truth is Blackmore, and we both know what he's like." Jenkins finished his whisky. "Listen, there's one more thing you should know. Marie, the barmaid… She's gone, and so is the cashbox with all the money from the party."

"How do you know that?"

"Blackmore said he saved you a fortune from the tout fund."

Barlow groaned and instinctively reached for the whisky bottle. "One for the road?"

Later that morning, while the people of Glasgow got ready for work and children got ready for school, unaware of the harrowing events of the previous evening, the shocking news came over the radio.

"We are getting reports of a police raid on a party last night at licensed premises just outside of Glasgow city centre. It is believed that dozens of people were taken into custody and that children, and other young people, were taken away by police and social workers. We shall update you on this report whenever we can."

One student, who was packing her rucksack in her student flat at the University of St Andrews, punched the air with delight, knowing exactly what the newsreader was referring to. "Free at last!" She opened a small diary and brushed a finger over the telephone number of the one person she trusted. After her classes, she would make the call she had waited so long to make.

Catherine, who was about to finish another night shift, heard the news on the ward radio at the same time. She sat down at her desk for a few minutes, proud of Andy for exposing all those involved. She knew he would likely be asleep by now, but she had to resist the urge to call him.

By ten o'clock, Barlow was back at his desk typing his statement for the press. The night shift CID officers were still on duty, interviewing suspects who had voluntarily remained in the office — anxious to clear their names.

"What do we have?" Detective Inspector James White.

"Forty-five in custody, including a few females, for numerous sexual offences against children."

"Occupations?"

The officer looked down and shuffled his feet on the linoleum. He cleared his throat. "Two senior police officers, a counsellor, a social worker, and a host of other dignitaries retired from public service."

"Are the officers ours?" Barlow feared the worst.

"No sir, from an outside force." Barlow looked around the office. The night shift officers were exhausted.

"We have to get these guys home for a kip and let the early shift carry on as best as they can."

"Yes, sir."

"Has their Chief Constable been notified of their incarceration?"

"I believe so, sir."

"Great."

"Thanks for everything, Graham. Your guys have done an amazing job."

A few hours later, people began to assemble in the dedicated press room, and it was not long before the room was jam-packed; word about the raid had already spread far and wide, as expected. Journalists streamed in, their accreditation checked by Larry Docherty, the Force press officer, though nearly all of them were familiar to him. Notepads were at the ready and pencils were sharpened as the assembled awaited a statement. Camera crews from both national and local TV stations stood at the rear of the room, and freelance press photographers sat on the floor, waiting for the people who would occupy the long table at the front of the room where the statements would be delivered. Everyone assumed it would be done by Larry Docherty himself. . "Right Larry, we're ready when you are," shouted one of the journalists.

"I'm not doing this one today, sorry," Larry replied jokingly. There was a rapport between him and the press; a symbiosis. He needed them as much as they needed him to get the news out into the public.

"Who is, then?"

"The Senior Investigating Officer. You have the main man today, DCS Barlow, instead of this old lag." He pointed at himself and the crowd chuckled.

As the clock ticked past one, there were a few mumbles from the journalists who had deadlines to meet. Ten minutes later, three people entered the room via a side door. As they sat down at the table, they put their nameplates in front of themselves. Barlow, the Senior Investigating Officer, rose to his feet.

"Good afternoon ladies and gentlemen of the press. I'm Detective Chief Superintendent Graham Barlow. To my right is Mr. David McConnell and to my left is Ms Chloe Agnew, both senior advocates from the Crown Office in Edinburgh." The journalists took note of their unusual presence. "First of all, let me apologise for being a little late in starting the conference. That was my fault, as I had to deal with something before coming down to see you all.

"At ten-thirty last night, a police operation took place outside Glasgow city centre. Information had been received that children from care homes around the city were being used for sexual activities." Barlow paused and looked around the room as journalists scribbled frantically. "A protracted inquiry into the allegations was carried out and the premises was identified, resulting in last night's raid. Numerous people have been detained and children were rescued by social workers. Several people will appear in court tomorrow to be charged with sexual offences against children.

"I would now like to thank the dedicated team of police officers involved in this inquiry. What they have recorded in writing has been harrowing, to say the least.

"Now, if we do this in an orderly fashion, I'm prepared to answer any questions you may have. I'm sure you will understand that some questions cannot be answered for legal and operational reasons, as this is a live inquiry." Barlow nodded at Larry to select members of the press.

"David, go ahead please,"

"David Johnstone," he introduced himself. "Mr. Barlow, how long has this been going on for and who are the people behind this? How many were arrested in last night's raid?"

"At this time, we are unsure exactly how long this has been going on for, but we suspect that, due to the secrecy surrounding it all, it has been going on for a long time. Secondly, we have a lead as to the people responsible and, finally, we have forty-five in custody. They will all appear in court tomorrow."

"Billy, you're next."

"Thanks. Do you think the Social Work Department and the police have been lax in their approach to this whole inquiry, and can you tell us who has been charged?"

"I'm not going to venture into who did what and when." Barlow's eyes narrowed. "As soon as we found out about this, a team was put together and the inquiry began. If that is lax, then you're entitled to your opinion. You should know that I cannot reveal the names of the accused. Next question."

Lisa Shaw was next to speak. "Can you tell us if the accused are connected in any way? Related for instance? And there is a rumour that a coffin was seen being carried out from the venue last night. Are you able to confirm this?"

Barlow looked at McConnell for approval and got the nod.

"I have no information that any of the accused are related. As for the second part of your question, I believe that there was a sudden death on the premises last night, but I was not present when that happened."

"Man or woman?"

"I believe it was a female."

"Can you tell us anything about her?"

"I'm sorry, but I can't reveal that at the moment until the next of kin has been informed. After that, we'll send out another press release."

A hand was raised at the back of the room, catching Barlow's attention.

"Okay, last question to you." "Thank you." He identified himself as David Diamond, a freelance investigative journalist.

"And your question is…?" Barlow prompted.

Everyone in the room knew that Diamond was like a dog with a bone, and if he had information on this, then what was about to come out was likely to be a cracker. Diamond spoke in a manner befitting his private school education.

"Chief Superintendent, considering last night's events and the details you provided, would you say that the attendants are likely to be people from high-profile professions? Also, I understand a young officer provided key information months ago, if it had been acted upon more quickly some kids may have been saved sooner? And finally, will you be reopening the inquiry into the alleged accident that killed four people at Lochside, one of whom was a retired senior police officer?"

DCS Barlow, noted down the questions as they were being asked, "David, I'll try to answer your questions each in turn. As to the nature of the attendants employment, I have no details currently. As to the police officer you're referring to, I'm not aware that he spoke to senior officers about this in the past, and I will investigate that personally. If there has been any neglect of duty, at any level, then it shall be dealt with and so shall the people involved. Finally, as to your final question, I'm aware of the incident and I believe this was a tragic accident that was dealt with by the Traffic Department. I'm happy to speak with you in a few days if you have any evidence to the contrary."

"One last question," Diamond, wagged a finger in the air. "Why are two of Scotland's finest senior advocates here with you today?"

Barlow looked at McConnell, who rose to his feet as Barlow sat down.

"We knew that there would be immense public interest in this case when it became public," McConnell explained. "We were here from the start, along with the Senior Investigating Officer, to ensure that the whole inquiry ran smoothly, and to offer legal advice. I hope that answers your question."

"Yes, sir, thank you." Diamond scribbled something in a notepad. "And here was me, thinking it was to prevent another cover-up." He giggled. This drew a glare from McConnell and Agnew and was met by a deathly silence from the crowd.

Larry Docherty finished up the proceedings as Barlow, McConnell, and Agnew made their way out of the room back to Barlow's office. As a sea of anxious journalists and reporters pushed their way out of the room, eager to be the first ones to hand their stories to their editors, David Diamond stood stock still, smiling at Larry.

"That was a cheap shot, David," Larry remarked.

"Maybe so, but it's true and they know it." Diamond patted Larry on the shoulder before leaving the room. Larry watched Diamond saunter down the corridor with his hands in his pockets, happy that he had rattled a few cages.

In Barlow's office, the officers discussed David Diamond's comments.

"We have to secure convictions or Diamond is going to be all over us like a rash," McConnell yammered. "If there is sufficient evidence against those in custody, we should start there and get the public onside immediately."

"I'll see to see what state the police reports are in, and what the evidence is like, and if there's corroboration," added Barlow.

"Great," replied McConnell as Barlow left the room.

Later, DCI Jenkins received a phone call "Hello, this is Angela from the city mortuary. I just wanted to let you know that the death certificate concerning Anika Marina Salamon is now ready."

"Excellent, I'll have it picked up within a couple of hours." Jenkins put down the phone and called Barlow to tell him the news.

"Does that include the police officers?"

"All of them"

"Wow. I suppose I have to do the police report for this one?"

"I suppose you do, Mr. Barlow," he answered with a cheeky grin.

Meanwhile, McConnell and Agnew were busy ploughing through the statements that had been prepared for the Procurators Fiscal.

"Okay, I think we have enough to keep them in custody pending a trial," McConnell sighed heavily.

Barlow phoned the duty officer in the main holding office. "How many are locked up now?"

"Ten. The others are scattered around various offices. I just put the last one to bed."

"Can you phone around the other offices and find out how many we have in total for court?

"Sure."

"In total, around all the offices, there are forty-five in custody for tomorrow," Barlow announced to the office.

"What about the rest that were taken in?"

"At the moment, they are being treated as witnesses and allowed to go home."

"Now that's a result," declared McConnell. He turned to Agnew. "Chloe, I think you and I are in for a very long day tomorrow."

"Aye, and for a very long night putting all of this together."

Chapter Twenty-Three

A ndy mumbled a tired greeting into the telephone.

"Hey Mr. B." Catherine's voice was sweet and loud. "Fantastic result last night. Are you all ready for tomorrow?"

"As ready as I'll ever be. Will you be there with me?" He rubbed his eyes, struggling to wake up.

"Of course." "Things have been mental, as you know, and I forgot that next Friday is my last day in the flat before we move into our new house."

"Oh my god, that's true!" "There is so much I need to tell you about yesterday."

"I'll be there for you, that's a promise. I love you so much."

"I'm going to see Alice and the kids today. Make sure everything is finalised. I'll pick you up at your place in the morning. Have a nice, quiet night shift."

"Okay, love you."

"And you know what, Catherine? Someday soon, I want to marry you."

"Good." She hung up.

As Andy was getting ready to leave the flat, the phone rang again.

"Hello?"

"Thank you, thank you, thank you!" It was a woman's voice, a familiar one.

"Er, thanks for what?"

"For not letting me down. Susan would be so proud of everything you have done."

"Kerry?"

"Yes, Andy, it's me. I kept your phone number, waiting for this day to arrive."

"How's university?" "It's wonderful. My inspiration is still Susan. She always will be."

"It's great to hear from you again, Kerry, but I have to go. It's my brother's funeral."

"Oh Andy, I'm so sorry. What was his name?"

"Ricky."

"Really? I once knew someone called Ricky."

"I know."

"What?" Kerry sounded startled.

"Anika told me everything."

"Oh no, please no." "Listen to me. What happened was not your fault. You were a victim and now you're a survivor."

"Thank you, Andy. I wish you all the best."

"You too." Andy ended the call.

Putting down the phone, Andy pulled on his jacket and lifted his car keys from the table, the sound of Kerry's voice still ringing in his head, Andy decided to call her back.

"There's something you need to know," he started, "something which is not yet public." He paused. "Remember Anika Salamon?"

"Yes, she was the one that got me into my… situation."

"She's dead."

There was a long silence. "Why are you telling me this?"

"To give you closure, Kerry. To let you enjoy your life freely. That's what Susan would have wanted for you."

"I hope that bitch Anika rots in hell." Kerry spat the words with venom.

Andy paused, not knowing what to say to that. "If you ever need me, you know how to reach me."

"Thank you, Andy. For everything."

Andy left his flat, got into his car, and made his way to Alice's parents' house.

"Andy! Come on in," Alice exclaimed, wrapping her arms around him. "Did you see that report on the TV about the raid on the pub last night?"

"Yeah, I saw it. Is everything ready for the funeral tomorrow? I just came to check if you were okay."

"I'm fine, but—" Alice was cut off by the living room door crashing open.

"Uncle Andy!" yelled Annie and Alfie, jumping on him. He laughed, until a bony knee struck his groin and he winced.

"Careful kids," Alice cautioned. "We don't want Uncle Andy injured beyond repair."

"How are my favourite niece and nephew in the world?" Andy spoke through gritted teeth.

"We're good," Annie replied.

"Have you had Fish and Chips since I was last here?"

"No, we're not allowed them." Alfie sulked.

Andy played with the kids, rolling around on the floor with them as they laughed loudly.

"Right you, stop winding them up, and you can put them to bed later, now that you've gotten them hyper."

"Okay, who wants to play police?" "We do!" shouted Alfie.

"To the bedrooms, quick march!"

As he tucked them up tightly in their beds, Andy told them that he loved them very much.

"We love you too, Uncle Andy," they choroused.

They cannot possibly comprehend what is happening. But someday they'll grow up and start asking questions about their dad.

As he got up and turned around, Andy found Alice standing in the door, her arms folded and her head leaning against the doorpost. He didn't know how long she had been watching them. They would have some memories of him and Andy knew all he could do to be there for them and Alice.

"Do you know what?" Alice whispered.

"What?"

"I wish…" Alice's voice drifted off into the distance.

"What?"

"Nothing, it doesn't matter." She turned and made her way back to the living room, Andy following. They joined her parents and sat down. Everything had been checked and double-checked for the funeral, so there was nothing left to do.

"Andy," Alice started again. "I want Catherine in the family car with us. It'll be you and me, Mum and Dad, and Catherine."

"What about the kids?"

"A friend will collect them from nursery and school."

"Have you decided about the minister?"

"I've asked the minister from the local church to conduct the service."

"Sounds fine Alice."

"What's bothering you Andy? You look worried."

"Mum." Andy looked at Alice and her parents.

"There's one seat left in the family car do you want her there?" Alice tried to meet Andy's eyes, but he was staring down at his intertwined fingers now, thinking in silence; she could see he was struggling with it. "If she was my mother, I'd want her there, no matter her state of mind."

"But Ricky was your husband, so the final decision should be yours. What do you think he would have wanted?"

"Honestly, Andy, I don't think he'd give a damn who was there." Alice's mum gave a little gasp, and her father grabbed his wife's hand.

"Decision made then. Let Mum stay where she is."

"Are you sure?"

"Positive. See you at the funeral parlour tomorrow then?"Alice nodded."Goodnight everyone. See you tomorrow."

Alice showed him to the door."Thank you."

"For what?"

"For being the best uncle to the kids, and a great brother-in-law."

"See you tomorrow." Andy kissed her cheek. Alice watched as Andy got into his car.

Chapter Twenty-Four

A n inmate yelled from one of the cells. "Turnkey, when we movin'?"

"You'll know when the van gets here," the duty officer responded.

"Any rolls 'n' sausage?"

"Aye, they're on their way in. Gie us a minute."

"Well dae us a favour and flush the lavvy. This place is mingin'!"

"Naw, ye can sniff it for a while yet." For those who had been caught during the night's raid and were now kept in custody, this was a side of life they were certainly not used to, and it terrified them. They knew that, if they went to prison and the other inmates found out what they were in for, they would be fair game for serious assaults or sexual abuse.

With the prisoners fed and watered, the turnkeys at every office would be shouting at the inmates to pick up their bedding and stand by their doors.

As the cells were unlocked, prisoners filed out one by one, piling their mattresses and throwing their blankets into a large container for conveyance to the laundrette. The female prisoners were kept apart from the men.

With handcuffs applied, the prisoners were filed onto the buses heading for the Sheriff Court. Those who were wise kept their mouths firmly shut. Given the number of prisoners who were linked to the Games Night inquiry, they were separated from the other prisoners, including the two senior police officers.

David McConnell and Chloe Agnew were at the Procurator Fiscal Office to oversee proceedings, fearing that bias could lead to a case collapse and accusations of a cover-up, especially from the national press.

Following a meeting between the advocates and the Procurators Fiscal, a decision was taken that every accused would be indicted and appear in private before a sheriff. A separate court would be set aside for the proceedings, given the number of accused.

The press corps was hovering in the main foyer of the Sheriff Court, expecting the accused to make their appearance in the dock, where their identities would be revealed and the charges against them made public.

David Diamond hovered in the background; he knew more about this case than anyone else there, as he was concealing copies of explosive evidence given to him by Andy Blackmore. The Sheriff Court and the High Court of Justiciary felt like home to Diamond. That was where he would contact his informants, who always fed him more information than the police or the Crown Office.It was where Diamond had made his living as an investigative journalist, and it was where a small band of police officers gave him the leads that led to his television programmes, bringing numerous awards for his investigative journalism. Many times had he proven that a criminal was guilty as charged, despite their protestations. Once, Diamond had given evidence of a miscarriage of justice, which definitely went up the noses of the police and the justiciary. Diamond was loved and hated by both the police and criminals of the city, but, more than anything, he was respected.

"Good morning, Mr. Barlow," Diamond purred, leaning against a marble pillar, arms folded. He casually watched the lawyers scurrying around, their black gowns flowing as they sped from court to court, their assistants trailing behind them carrying mountains of case files.

"Good morning, Mr. Diamond," Barlow replied politely. Barlow knew Diamond from way back when he was a young journalist making his way around various newspapers. Barlow did not dislike Diamond as a person; it was his methods in obtaining information that he was not a fan of .

"Big day for you and your team," Diamond remarked.

"I've had bigger."

"Really? With two of your own appearing in front of a Sheriff for child abuse? I doubt it." At no time did his gaze divert from the activity around him.

"How the hell—" Before Barlow could finish his sentence, Diamond pushed himself off the wall and greeted a defence lawyer he had not seen for a few years.

When he returned a few minutes later, Diamond apologised for his absence."

"As I was saying before we were rudely interrupted by the Queen's Counsel," Diamond started, laughing "we need to talk."

"I doubt it somehow."

"It's your call." Diamond shrugged.

"And what do you mean by that?"

"The evidence I have would secure convictions against everyone you have in custody. I can offer private viewings of the tapes I have in my possession."

"You're bluffing." Barlow was not entirely convinced of his own statement.

"You're a tough one to crack Barlow. Usually my informants bite right away." Diamond clapped Barlow on the shoulder and laughed. "Tell you what, I'll give you twenty-four hours. Speak to Andy Blackmore. He'll confirm what I have. On second thought, make it forty-eight hours. After all, it is his brother's funeral today." Diamond turned and, without saying another word, walked away with his hands in his pockets.

Barlow watched Diamond amble down the corridor. He now had a massive decision to make; get in bed with an investigative journalist or risk losing everything. What would that do for his career, if the Crown Office found out that he had known of the existence of evidence proving the guilt of the accused and done nothing about it?

If there was one thing Barlow wanted, it was one more promotion. Assistant Chief Constable Barlow. It had a nice ring to it, and it would give him a sizeable pension. He put his hand in his pocket and found a card that had been slipped in unbeknownst to him.

> David Diamond
> Investigative Journalist
> Tel. 888 2469
> Ext. 1873

Across the city, Alice and Andy were about to say goodbye to Ricky for the last time. The local funeral parlour was packed with family members on Alice and Ricky's side, Andy saw a lot of familiar faces he had hoped to avoid for longer. Alice's parents were by her side, and Catherine was by Andy's, despite running on little sleep after her night shift.

The service, which was conducted by a local minister, was short; a few kind words of solace and a couple of prayers, then it was out into the daylight where they were faced with a large black hearse, the coffin lying in full public view through the clear windows. Ricky's final journey was to the crematorium, some twenty minutes away.

Alice and her parents entered the family car first in the back seat. The long, black Mercedes was polished to such a level that it could have been used as a shaving mirror. Catherine and Andy sat apart on two individual seats, with their backs to the driver. The vehicles gently pulled away from the parlour, barely reaching twenty miles per hour en-route to the crematorium.

There was one spare seat in the vehicle, which should have been occupied by Ricky and Andy's mother, Andy's heart was aching with the knowledge that she was not present for her own son's funeral, but he reasoned that, even if she had been there, she would not have been entirely present anyway.

At one fifteen, the hearse containing the remains of Richard Blackmore passed through the open gates of the crematorium, Andy was curious to see which direction the hearse would take; if there was any justice in death, Ricky's remains would go to the west chapel, not to the east where their father's funeral had taken place.

It was a plain grey rotund building. The Garden of Remembrance was at the rear. With small marble stones which had been beautifully engraved with the names of the departed. Beyond that lay the peaceful, tree-lined gardens which fanned out towards the River Clyde. When in full bloom, the trees offered the dead protection from the elements, their entwined branches resembling a leafy archway through which sunlight streamed like heavenly rays. Each day the Book of Remembrance, locked away in an oak cabinet, would be procured for viewing on the anniversary of the death of a loved one.

The cortège slowly made its way towards the west chapel, climbing the gentle incline until it came to a halt. The female undertaker, seated in the front seat of the hearse, stepped from the vehicle. She was dressed immaculately in black trousers, a matching waistcoat, and a claw hammer jacket bearing a red velvet collar. She donned atop hat, leaving only her groomed ponytail visible, and she held a black cane in a gloved hand.

The undertaker walked a few paces in front of the vehicle, up to the chapel doors. She turned and faced the hearse, giving a short, respectful bow, observed by a large group of mourners who had gathered for the service. Then she turned to face the chapel.

Alice watched as the driver of the family car got out and opened the rear door, Andy assisted Catherine out of the vehicle, followed by Alice's parents, and, finally, Alice herself, Andy felt her hand squeeze his as she stood beside him. Her eyes glazed over when she stared at the hearse as Andy guided her into the chapel, a place he had come to know too well over the years. He knew that he would be back again soon with his mother if she kept deteriorating at the rate she was currently.

Glancing at the size of the crowd, Andy was not sure that they would all fit into the chapel. He laid eyes on a group of mourners who were peering at him, and Andy knew he was becoming the focus of attention. These were Ricky's closest allies from the lodge, and several were senior police officers and dignitaries. Even in mourning, Andy mustered the bravado to nod and smile at them. He wanted to send the message that he would be coming for them next.

Two marble steps led into the vestibule, where the undertaker's representatives handed out hymn books to the congregation. The walk down towards a man in black felt long and sluggish, like Andy's shoes were sinking into mud. Behind the man lay the dais where the coffin would be laid to rest, and behind that loomed a large, dark cross.

Andy and Catherine took a seat on the front pew to the left of the alter, and Alice and her parents joined them. Cousins and other relatives sat behind them.

The congregation filtered in, packing the seats in the chapel to full capacity. Those that could not get a seat stood around the perimeter. A spindly woman took a seat at the chapel organ and began to play. As requested by the family, not one piece of masonic regalia or insignia was visible, but the brotherhood were hard to miss nonetheless.

The undertaker, now standing at the top of the aisle, raised her hands. Everyone stood in unison and the volume of the chapel organ increased Andy felt a chill run down his back and his feet felt as if they were sinking further and further into the floor. The coffin was carried into the chapel by six pallbearers and laid to rest on the dais. They bowed their heads as a mark of respect before making their way out of the chapel. Glancing around, Andy saw that many eyes were upon him, but the last thing he would become was intimidated.

Chapter Twenty-Five

J ust after the commencement of the service, the door at the back of the chapel opened. A few heads turned to see who the latecomer was; a young woman slipped in, ducking her head under the gaze of the crowd as she took a spot in a back corner behind a sconce. She listened to the minister wax lyrical about Andy's less than an angelic brother.

"Richard, or Ricky, as most knew him, was a dedicated family man," the minister began. "He recently provided a home for his mother, building a small flat that was attached to the rear of his house, so that he could offer her twenty-four-hour care as a debilitating ailment struck her. His brother has always been someone Ricky could turn to in times of strife, and he was so proud when Andrew achieved his ambition of joining the police service." The minister looked down at the family pew. "There is no doubt that the love of Ricky's life was his wife Alice, who gave him their children, Annie and Alfie, the apples of his eyes. He built a successful chain of chemists, which was dedicated to Alice and his children." The minister paused as he looked at his notes. "The turnout here today is a testament to the high esteem in which Ricky was held by his brothers in the Lodge and by society in general. Now it is time to say goodbye, to a much-loved son, brother, husband and father."

The minister raised his right hand and everyone's eyes turned to the dais. "We now commit the body of our brother to your arms. Ashes to ashes, dust to dust, in the sure and certain hope of the Resurrection to the eternal life through the Lord, Jesus Christ."

As the curtains closed on the dais, Catherine gripped Andy's hand tightly. Alice sobbed, knowing Annie and Alfie would never see their father again. The young woman at the back of the chapel let tears roll down her face.

"We will finish with the 23rd Psalm," the minister continued, the organ player striking the opening chords. As the congregation sang, the minister left the pulpit and made his way to the family and offered his condolences. When the song ended, he returned to the pulpit.

"Ladies and gentlemen," he announced. "Ricky's family have decided to keep the reception at their house to family only, which we all have to respect. For our brother travellers, tea shall be served at the lodge." As the organist began to play an unfamiliar tune, the family made their way to the vestibule, where they would meet the mourners, Andy hated this bit with a passion, so he excused himself.

Standing outside the chapel, Catherine and Andy observed the young latecomer walking down the driveway.

"I hope someone gives her a lift," Andy commented. "It's a long walk back to the nearest bus stop."

"Do you know her?" Catherine enquired.

"No, I don't think so." Just then, a mourner came over and asked, "Mr. Blackmore, may I have a word, please?"

Andy looked up at a tall, well-built, balding stranger. He looked to be in his mid-to-late fifties. The way he addressed Andy, and the stance that he adopted, indicated that this was either a serving or retired police officer.

"Sure." Andy shrugged, trying to seem indifferent, though he was curious as to who the man was; his face was familiar to him.

"Follow me, please." The man limped away slowly.

"Tell Alice I'll be back soon," Andy asked Catherine as he squeezed her hand.

He followed the stranger into the garden of remembrance, where they stood, side by side, facing the breeze from the River Clyde.

"Mr. Blackmore, you have caused a lot of grief in your short career in the police service."

"Oh really?" Andy arched an eyebrow. "In what way?"

"You know very well in what way. Your career is over, Constable Blackmore."

Andy stared at the ripples on the River Clyde before turning back to the man. "Let me tell you something, asshole. If you were part of the Games Nights and you're a cop, then it is your career that is over. Then again, no matter what career you have, your days in it could be numbered. You have no idea what I have secreted away, just waiting for the right moment." Andy paused. "Do you want to know something else? In case you missed the significance of today, this is my brother's funeral. Tell me, do you have a family?"

"Yes…"

"See, if I was you, I'd walk away now." The breeze blew Andy's dark hair back from his face as he screwed up his eyes against the wind. "Or your wife will be arranging your funeral before today is out."

"Are you threatening me, Blackmore?"

"Absolutely not, I never threaten anyone." He paused for a few seconds. "I only make promises." Andy's voice was calm but menacing. As he turned and walked away, the man followed closely.

"Andy, hurry up, our car has to leave!" Catherine called out as he approached her.

"Be right there!" "Nice lady," the man commented, stopping Andy in his tracks. An impossible image flashed in his mind; Susan smiling at him, tears streaming from her eyes, her face disappearing from view over the edge of a cliff, Andy turned around and shoved his face in the man's so that their pupils were mere millimetres apart.

"If you or anyone goes near her, I will personally kill you." Andy spat the words, and the man flinched as spittle landed on his cheek, Andy walked briskly back to the car before stopping to look back at the man, who had not moved a muscle. "Oh, I forgot to say!" Andy clapped his hands together and smiled broadly "It was a pleasure to meet you."

Once Andy got in the car, Alice asked him if everything was alright and who the man was that he had been speaking to, Andy told her that it was an old colleague of Ricky's who was offering his condolences to the family. Catherine took one look at Andy and knew that he was lying; he made almost no eye contact with Alice during the conversation, instead looking out of the window and at the man. Catherine saw a quiet fury in the man's eyes, but underneath that she saw fear. She got a bad feeling in the pit of her stomach.

Alice took her relatives back to her house for the wake. As was the case with so many families, this was one of the few times all of the relatives got together, until the next funeral. When, after a few hours, all the guests had departed, Alice, Andy, and Catherine sat together in the lounge.

"You know what?" Andy remarked. "We're sitting here with not a car between us. I left mine at the funeral parlour."

"And mine's at my flat," Catherine commented.

"Mine's at Mum and Dad's," Alice added. "I propose that, due to our lack of transportation, I phone my parents and ask them to look after Annie and Alfie tonight so we can indulge in a few drinks."

"Geez, I won't last long." Catherine laughed. "I was on night shift last night and I've still not been to bed yet."

"Oh, that's too bad. You'll miss all the stories I have to tell about young Andy." Alice winked, Andy said that he would get a taxi to the funeral parlour and drive back to the villa.

Elsewhere in the city, David McConnell and Chloe Agnew were eating lunch while double-checking all the paperwork in their possession before Procurators Fiscal presented their cases in front of several Sheriffs.

Christmas had arrived early for the defence lawyers; in addition to their usual clients, who provided a regular source of income, the police raid on the party had opened a whole new source of clients. Like their counterparts in the prosecution service, they too had working lunches; visiting new clients in the cells, as the traditional confidential interview rooms were filled to bursting. There was no way they were going to get to see everyone in the interview rooms before the courts reconvened at two fifteen that afternoon.

At two fifteen, on the dot, everyone stood as the Sheriffs entered their courts and climbed the few stairs up to their chairs, overlooking the Procurators Fiscal and the Defence lawyers. The courts were closed to the public, as all the accused were appearing in private.

"Right, let's get going," one Sheriff announced.

One by one, the accused from the Games Nights were brought before the Sheriffs and remanded in custody for seven days, pending further inquiry. At one point, the door to the court opened and a female accused was escorted to the box. Mr. Hoffman, the Procurator Fiscal, read out the charges against her, all of which involved the sexual abuse of a child under the age of sixteen years over a period of two years.

"How does your client plead?" Sheriff Duncan asked the Defence lawyer, Diane McGurk.

"Sheriff, this one I've not come across before." "Explain." The sheriff peered at her over his spectacles.

"Well Milord, I'm instructed to say to you that, if you're prepared to allow her to go home to her children, she'll plead guilty to the charges, but, if not, it's a plea of not guilty."

"Ms McGurk, it's quite simple. Your client can either plead guilty or not to the charges, or make no plea or declaration. Can I suggest that you advise your client one way or another, as there are many people downstairs desperate to meet me before I go home?"

McGurk turned to her client and they exchanged a select few mumbled but heated words.

"Milord, my client is prepared to plead guilty to charges one to four, and not guilty to the more serious fifth charge."

Sheriff Duncan flashed a look at the Procurator Fiscal, who nodded his agreement to dropping charge five to get the pleas of guilty to the other four.

"Ms McGurk, I appreciate your client's decision to plead guilty at this early stage of the proceedings, meaning that we do not need to put the witnesses through the turmoil of giving evidence against her." As he shuffled the papers in his hands, the Sheriff continued. "I have to be seen to be fair and equal. If this were a man standing before me, jail would be my decision. So, being fair and equal, your client shall be remanded in custody for seven days, pending a Social Enquiry Report."

"Oh, my children," the woman sobbed. She was promptly led back to the cells by two female police officers.

As Ms McGurk went back to the law library where the defence lawyers were gathered, she asked if they had faired any better with their clients, but the unanimous answer was "no." Everyone who had appeared before a Sheriff that day had been remanded in custody.

The final accused appeared before a Sheriff at seven o'clock that evening. As he studied the charges against the accused, the Sheriff's eyes drifted to the personal details and the accused's occupation. Throwing the papers down on the bench in front of him, the Sheriff leaned back in his large green leather chair.

"Well, Ms McGurk?" "As you can see, Milord, the charges are almost identical to those who have gone before you today. My client has instructed me to make no plea or declaration to all charges and requests bail."

"And why should your client be treated differently from all the others?"

"Milord, given my client's occupation, he believes his life could be in danger in prison." McGurk watched as the sheriff leaned forward, the palms of his hands on the bench.

"I'm trying to weigh up what would be said if your client was released on bail and if he would be in more danger when mixing with the public. I'm sure that the prison service can ensure his safety by isolating him from the main population. Therefore, I'm remanding your client in custody for seven days, and, looking at the charges when he appears before me again, I shall be remitting his case to the High Court, just to let you know." Two police officers stepped forward, taking hold of their colleague's arms and leading him downstairs to the cells.

As the first of the accused was led to the prison bus, the court officers noticed that a crowd had gathered out on the street. A bottle came flying over the high gates, smashing into smithereens on the concrete a few feet from the vehicle. Shouts of pervs and paedos filled the evening air.

Eight police officers, who had been dispatched earlier from the Divisional Headquarters, lined the pavement, watching the last of the accused being ushered onto the bus. With the engine running, the heavy gates were opened to a crescendo of jeers and boos. A marked police car led the way, blue lights flashing, as the prison bus sped out of the car park onto the main road, bottles crashing off both sides of the vehicle. Despite the unruly behaviour of the crowd, the police knew that they had to handle this protest wearing kid gloves. Accordingly, no arrests were made.

The bus disappeared into the night, carrying its cargo of new prisoners. The danger that faced them was the other inmates awaiting their arrival, who — despite their own shortcomings — had little tolerance for child abusers. It would be worse for the police officers; their occupation and rank would not save them in there, and nothing would save them if they were recognised by prisoners that they had incarcerated. Prison for a police officer would prove to be hell on Earth; a living nightmare far from their families, manicured gardens, and expensive cars. That life was a million miles away from where they were now, sitting on the wooden benches of the reception area before being shown to their new home.

A 'trusty' stood at the side of the prison warders, booking the prisoners in. The trusty was usually an inmate who had worked his way up to that exalted position. Meanwhile, the prisoner warder lifted the property bag, which he had received from the court staff, and dumped the contents onto his desk.

"Take these," the warder commanded the prisoners, who accepted dark trousers and a pink shirt from the trusty. Gone were the fine clothes that the accused had arrived in. Following this was an intimate search to ensure that they were not entering the prison system with contraband.

A short time later the Prison Governor arrived.

"Good evening, sir, late night for you, isn't it?"

"Yes, I decided to stay on a while, what with the number of prisoners we're receiving. I take it we have room for everyone?"

"We'll manage, sir."

"Don't we always?" The Governor picked up an envelope that contained the property of one of the police officers. There was no doubt that the Governor had received advanced notification of his new guests, and the last thing he needed was aggravation in the general population. "Thanks, Jamie, well done today," looking at the trusty. "You can go back to your area now." The Governor waited until the trusty was well out of earshot before saying to the warder, "Solitary confinement for these two prisoners."

"Yes, Governor." The Governor walked away, watched by two Senior Police Officers who were nervously observing their new surroundings.

Andy had taken a taxi to the funeral parlour to retrieve his car, then drove back to Alice's house. When he returned, all Andy could hear was the sound of Catherine and Alice's chatter in the lounge. He was pleased that they were getting on. When he entered, they turned to look at him.

"I've been away for twenty-five minutes and look at the state you two are in." He laughed.

"Let's go home," Catherine slurred, the worse for wear from drink and tiredness. To Andy, she was still as beautiful as ever.

Alice hugged Catherine, then wrapped her arms tightly around Andy.

"Tell the kids I'll see them very soon."

"Yes, I will," Alice mumbled, very inebriated. "Listen... my kids love you to bits, and Catherine too! Sooo, I do not want either of you to be strangers here. Please don't let that happen."

"No chance," Andy assured her. "Are you wanting a lift to your parents' house, Alice?"

"Don't worry about me, Andy. You see to Catherine."

"Your place or mine Catherine?" once they were driving down the long driveway. When he received no answer, Andy repeated his question to no avail. He turned and saw Catherine's head resting against the passenger door window as she slept, Andy smiled.

At seven-thirty that evening, DCS Barlow looked around Anika Salamon's home as the force support unit searched each room methodically. Scanning the lounge, Barlow wondered what kinds of atrocities had transpired in this very room. . Barlow switched on the TV and saw, at first to his confusion and then to his horror, a pixelated version of himself from behind, standing in this room. In the background he could also see his officers moving around the house. Barlow startled, looking behind him for the camera. He could not spot anything. But then, in a corner of the ceiling, he noticed what looked like an intruder alarm sensor. He bent over, picked up a discarded receipt, crumpled it up, and threw it at the sensor. Quickly, he turned back to the TV in time to see the receipt hit the lens dead on, obscuring the view of the room for a fraction of a second. "My God," he whispered underneath his breath. Immediately, he began frantically pulling open drawers and upending boxes all over the home until he found what we were looking for; dozens of video cases containing hundreds of cassettes neatly filed in chronological order. Barlow procured one of the cassettes and popped it into the player hooked up to the TV. After nervously fumbling with the remote, the tape started playing on the TV. He watched a man cavorting naked on a bed with two young teenage girls. He knew the man.

Sergeant Jones entered the lounge, his eyes darting from the TV screen to Barlow. Jones gulped but did not say anything.

"Yes?" Barlow prompted him.

"Sir, this is the last room we have to search."

"Make sure to take the video recorder, and every single video in that drawer." He pointed at the cabinet in which the had found the tapes. Sergeant Jones nodded, promptly getting a few officers to help him box up the videos.

Standing out on the gravel driveway, Barlow watched as box after box of potential evidence was taken from the house. Any one of his officers could have overseen this operation, but Barlow wanted to be there himself for the final hurdle. It was closure.

"Sergeant!" Barlow hollered. "How many vans have you loaded?"

"Two so far. One for the loft and one for the rooms."

"Is the search finished?"

"Yes, as soon as the lounge is done."

"Right, tell all your officers to head for your office. The drivers of the vans will come to mine." Barlow shook his head. "Sergeant, you have no idea what you and your team may have recovered tonight. My thanks to them all."

Back at headquarters, Barlow personally oversaw the unloading of the boxes, which were placed in a secure room. As the final box from the lounge was laid on the floor, Barlow locked the door and put the key in his pocket. Looking at his watch, he saw that it was almost midnight. Switching off the office lights, he realised this was another night he would not get to see his wife, as she would likely be in bed by now.

Being married to a Senior Investigating Officer was not easy, but she was used to it and he knew she would always be there for him.

Driving home, Barlow had a gut feeling that the search of the Salamon home would prove to be explosive. He considered his next move; Whoever was to view the hours of videotapes? Should it be the current team or officers, who he knew could cope with such matters, or should it be a new team? The welfare of his team was uppermost in his mind. Also, there was the issue of David Diamond and his revelation; he had to speak to Andy about that.

Upon arrival at his house, Barlow crept upstairs and slipped into bed. His night's sleep would have to be short, as he had to go in at seven in the morning.

"You, okay?" Jean mumbled as she rolled over to rest her head on his chest.

"Fine," Barlow replied, wrapping his arms around his wife and planting a gentle kiss on her forehead.

Chapter Twenty-Six

A t half-past five in the morning, Graham Barlow quickly switched off his alarm clock before it woke his wife. After showering and eating, he headed for the force headquarters. In the underground car park, DCS Barlow stopped at the security kiosk.

"Good morning, sir," the security guard greeted him. "How are you today?"

"Could be better," Barlow replied from his vehicle.

"You're in early this morning."

"Aye, in to see Assistant Chief Constable Gilmour."

"Good luck."

"How do you mean?"

"Some new guy's in now. Ralph McGrory, ACC Crime. That's his car over there."

"Thanks for letting me know. Have a good day."

Sitting at his desk, Barlow waited for the phone to ring as his officers trooped in, one by one. When he finally looked up, he saw that everyone was present.

"Guys, we may have a problem," Barlow announced, referring to McGrory becoming ACC Crime. Then he saw Andy, who had his head in his hands. "You okay, Andy?"

"Yes, sir, I'm fine." "Andy, you have bereavement leave available to you."

"Yes, I know, but I would rather be here, thank you."

"Okay… well we're here to finish the job we started," Barlow continued. "We have a duty to those kids to see this through. When we became police officers we swore an oath, which included serving without fear or favour, and no matter how long we are in this job, that goes from day one to the last." He paused. "Following the search of Anika Salamon's home, hundreds of videos and photographs were recovered." He folded his arms. "For all I know, most of them could be old recordings of Coronation Street, but I doubt it, having seen a few minutes from one tape."

"Aye, you wish." DI Watt laughed briefly, stopping when he received a glare from Barlow.

"Anyway, there are two things I can do here. I could assign the viewing of the tapes to a whole new team or keep it in house. But I would need you to volunteer."

"I'm in," DI Watt blurted.

"So am I," added DS Wallace.

"Count me in," DC McLeod followed quickly.

DC O'Donnell looked uncomfortable. "Sir, as a father of two kids, this inquiry has been hard for me. This might be too much."

"I'm in the same boat as Lindsay," DC McLean agreed.

"I respect your honesty," Barlow replied. "Andy?"

"Sir, you know this whole inquiry has been a nightmare for me, given my past relationship with Susan." Some of the officers shuffled their feet, trying to mask their surprise; it was a side of Andy many of them had never heard before. He sounded neither confident nor angry, just defeated. This inquiry had left a lot of them feeling like that. "I need closure on a lot of things, so I'm in."

Barlow nodded. "Amanda, do you still want to remain as the loggist?" "Yes, sir. We're a team, so let's finish this together." "Chris?"

"Oh, I suppose so," with a laugh. "But I will—"

There was a rap at the door.

"Andy, see who's there, please," Barlow requested.

Opening the door, Andy came face-to-face with ACC McGrory.

"Can I help you, sir?" Andy enquired.

"I'm here to see DCS Barlow," McGrory replied.

"I'll tell him you called."

"Let me in!" McGrory snapped. "Do you know who I am?"

"I know who you are, but I'm sorry, sir." Andy had to hold back the comments floating in his head. "On the orders of the Crown Office, no one, except for the inquiry team, is permitted access to this room." With that, Andy closed the door in the face of the new Assistant Chief Constable. As Andy turned around the whole team was looking at him. "What you lot looking at? I didn't make the rules!" he pleaded with outstretched arms as they all started laughing.

Within minutes, the phone in Barlow's office rang. He answered it as his team watched.

"S-sir, hmm, yes I understand that… the officer who answered the door did as instructed. Yes, sir, I knew I had an early morning meeting at seven o'clock, but that was not with you." Barlow winced as the phone on the other end of the line was slammed down. He knew that this inquiry had to be wound up soon, as his budget was likely to be whipped out from under his feet. His saving grace was that he had the Crown Office Advocates on his side.

"Right," Barlow barked, clapping his hands as he got up and faced his audience. "Here are the teams. Watt with Blackmore, and Wallace with McLeod. First, we need to get through a mountain of videos, see what we have got and, if worst comes to worst, get people identified, both potential witnesses and suspects." He paused before continuing. "On second thought, start with the photographs." Barlow shook his head, a wry smile on his face. "The reason we're starting with the photos is that, simply put, I don't have any televisions or video players in here." Everyone had a good laugh at that. "Even I'm allowed a cock-up now and again." Barlow chuckled.

Andy had taken to Barlow the first time he met him; he just seemed like one of the boys, and in many ways had been a valuable mentor.

They divided the photographs them into the following categories; those where only the children were identifiable, those where only the adult was identifiable, those where both the child and adult were identifiable, and those where neither could be identified, Andy was trying to remember the name of a man he recognised when there was a knock at the door. DC McLean answered it.

"DCS Barlow, please,"

"Who's asking?"

"Superintendent Fiona Gallagher." Barlow stood nearby, watching his officers go through the photographs one by one. He noticed that one photograph had been set aside by Andy, but he said nothing.

"Sir," McLean called out. "Superintendent Fiona Gallagher is here for you."

"Right, tell the boys to conceal everything in the cupboard. Gallagher is Special Branch."

Once the photos had been tucked away, Barlow opened the office door and said, "Fiona, it's been a while!"

"Too long." Gallagher smiled.

"Fancy a coffee in the cafeteria?"

"Boss, I remember what it was like to be your pupil. I can tell when you're busy with an investigation."

"I suppose you do." "You were the crème de la crème, Fiona."

"Can I come in for a quick, private chat?"

"Are you not going to introduce us?" Barlow looked at the man next to her.

"Oh, yes. Detective Sergeant Greer, this is Detective Chief Superintendent Barlow."

"Nice to meet you, son," Barlow said, shaking his hand. "But I'm afraid you'll have to go off for a tea now. Fiona, get in here."

Entering the office, Gallagher looked around. All she saw were detective officers going through witness statements at their desks.

"Sit down, Fiona." Barlow lowered himself into his chair. "So tell me, why are you here?"

"Boss…" Gallagher paused. "We know that you searched Salamon's house. We know that you have removed boxes of potential evidence. This is hard for me. Honestly it is. You were my mentor for years. You helped get me to where I am today, but my instructions are to seize everything you have from the house of Anika Salamon."

"I hear you got married, Fiona."

"Y-yes," she stammered, caught off guard by the sudden change in subject. "A long time ago."

"Any kids?"

"Two, can you believe it?"

"What ages are they?"

"Christine is thirteen and Harry is ten."

"And what do you know about this inquiry?"

"Not a lot, just that it's to do with child abuse and I'm to seize everything you have."

Nodding, Barlow leaned forward and gave Superintendent Gallagher a look that she had seen a hundred times before when they had worked together.

"What would you do if someone sexually abused your daughter, Fiona?" Barlow murmured. "What if it was your son?" He paused. "You know, if there was one person I would want on this inquiry, it would be you. You're a brilliant detective. That's what got you where you are." She looked down, ashamed at the praise that preceded what felt like her inevitable betrayal of her past mentor. "So, what would you do?" Gallagher said nothing. "Who was it that sent you here?"

Superintendent Gallagher stared out of the office window. Below her the city was coming to life again; people going about their business, shops opening, down-and-outs gathering their belongings to wander around the city.

"McGrory," she finally replied.

Barlow nodded. "Did you find anything of interest here?"

"Despite a thorough search... nothing." "In a week, you're going to get confidential information, causing you to return here."

"Okay." "Right then, see you next week" Barlow saw her out of the office.

With Gallagher gone, the trawl through the photographs resumed.

"Do you know who this is?" showing him the photograph, he had set aside.

Watt looked at it. "I haven't a clue."

"Give me a look," Chris Harvey chimed in. "Oh yeah, that's... Jesus, what's his name?" He closed his eyes, concentrating, before triumphantly saying "Danny Brown! That's who it is. Danny Brown, the chairman of the Police and Fire Committee." "He was at my brother's funeral. He took me aside from everyone and told me my career was over and that he would personally see to it. Well, it looks like his career is over now, that's for sure." He stared at the photograph of a naked Brown with two young teenage girls in a compromising position.

After nearly twelve hours, the last of the photographs was laid on its respective pile, Andy lifted the photo of Danny Brown and placed it on top of the 'identifiable suspect' stack.

"Guys, I've secured two televisions and video recorders," Barlow announced. "We'll start the viewing first thing in the morning. It'll be done behind closed doors, naturally."

"What's worrying you, Graham?"

"To be honest, McGrory's unhealthy interest in everything we are doing is causing me some concern. I'm praying that there is nothing concerning him on the tapes, but I'm getting a bad feeling about it."

"Christ, that's all we need,"

"What is it, Donald?"

"Remember the fatal accident at the Loch?"

"Berger's, you mean?"

"Aye, Berger's. It's all coming back to me now. McGrory was a close pal of Berger."

Barlow sighed. "That's just what I was hoping not to hear."

"How are the team bearing up to all this?" "I think the guys with kids are struggling a bit."

"We should keep an eye on them, in that case." Jenkins yawned. "It's home time for me."

As Jenkins started his car, he noticed two figures entering the building.

"Shit," he swore, remembering that he had left his house keys on his desk. He quickly swung his car around and parked outside on the double yellow lines. He asked the commissionaire to watch out for the traffic department officers, who were always hounding the area.

Jenkins took the lift to the office, where he found the two same men standing in the hallway.

"May I help you, gentlemen?"

"We're looking for Mr. Barlow."

"Really? At this time of the night?" The men looked at each other. "Gentlemen, I take it you have some sort of identification on you, like your warrant cards?" Reaching into the back pockets of their trousers, both men begrudgingly produced their warrant cards for inspection.

"Detective Inspector Galloway and Detective Sergeant Mulholland," Jenkins read aloud, looking at their identification, "Now, on whose orders are you working?" He paused. "Wait, let me guess. ACC McGrory."

"Sir, we were told to speak to Mr. Barlow," Galloway replied.

"By who?"

"We can't discuss that."

Jenkins sighed. "Once again, Barlow is not here, so I suggest you leave."

"Yes, sir." The men walked away.

"Graham," Jean Barlow called to her husband from the hallway, "Donald's on the phone for you." When Barlow picked up, Jenkins told him about Galloway and Mulholland.

"Do you know them?"

"Not personally, but someone will be getting a phone call in the morning. Thank you telling me Donald. Goodnight."

Barlow went over to the sideboard in his home, opened a door, and took out a crystal glass, followed by a bottle of Cardhu whisky. He proceeded to pour a large malt for himself before sitting down in his armchair, wondering why so many senior figures were so interested in his inquiry. That question was to be answered in the morning when the videotapes would reveal their secrets.

Chapter Twenty-Seven

A t seven-thirty the following morning, Watt and Andy Blackmore inserted the first of their stack of videos into the grey Sony video recorder. The television screen flickered to life. Likewise, Wallace and McLeod began their viewing.

In his office, Barlow rang Fiona Gallagher. "Good morning, Fiona. Can you tell me why DI Galloway and DS Mulholland were here last night asking for me? Considering I had only left the office minutes earlier, that would suggest we are being watched by your lot."

"Honestly, I don't know anything about it. They're not part of my team."

"They may not be part of your team, but you're their gaffer, Fiona."

"Leave it with me. I'll get back to you later." She sounded concerned.

An hour after commencing their viewing of the tapes, the four officers needed a break; so overpowering was the content of the footage from the party nights. Watt walked into Barlow's office, where he was sitting with Jenkins.

"Can you both come with me, please?" he paused "There's something you have to see."

When they entered the viewing room, Watt closed the door behind them and pressed the 'play' button on the video recorder. They watched the graphic scenes with revulsion and horror, Andy knew the names of a few of the girls, as he had been watching them as they came and went from the children's home.

As the recording continued, various adults were identified by Andy; Brian and Sandra Berger, and Sheena Gough. All were deceased, so they would evade justice, but the weight of the law was about to come down heavily on many others.

"If there's anything further you think I should see, just give me a shout," sighing. It did not seem to matter how many times he watched the tapes, or how many days had passed since he had started looking into the Games Nights — sometimes he still could not believe the nature of the case they were investigating.

Those who were in the main office watched Barlow head to his room. His whole demeanour had changed; he looked like a man with the weight of the world on his shoulders. Jenkins followed him into his office.

Slouching back in his chair, Barlow ran his hands through his hair while Jenkins took a seat opposite him and rested his arms on the desk. Neither spoke for a while, but both were deep in thought.

"What now?"

"I suppose I have to call the Chief and ask to see him."

"I don't envy you in this one."

Just as Barlow reached for the phone on his desk, it started to ring. He shared a look with Jenkins before picking up the receiver.

"Sir, it's Fiona Gallagher. Can we talk somewhere later today, away from the offices?"

"Sure. Are you going to be at your desk all day?"

"Yes."

"Well, something's come up here that needs my attention. I'll call you later."

"Okay, thank you." She ended the call.

Barlow listened to the line go dead, then called the Chief Constable's office. A secretary informed him that the chief was just about to leave the office to attend a meeting with ACC McGrory.

"Can you inform him that it's a matter of urgency?"

"Hold on, please." "DCS Barlow, Chief Constable Hale here. What's so urgent it can't wait?"

"Sir, can you come to the office being used for the abuse inquiry, please? There is something you have to see for yourself."

"This better be good, Barlow. Give me five minutes."

"Oh, and sir? Come alone."

"Alright." Hale detected a note of concern in Barlow's voice.

When the Chief arrived, Barlow led him into the viewing room. Nobody spoke a word as the Chief Constable watched the events on the tape.

"How long does this go on for?"

"Quite a length of time, sir, involving several participants," Watt replied.

"Who's seen this?"

"All of us in here, sir and there are other tapes which we have viewed and logged the activities of the participants."

"Oh, and the Crown Office are aware of the existence of the tapes, sir," Barlow added.

"How did that happen?" Hale demanded.

"Because I contacted them."

"You had no right!" The Chief was almost shaking with anger.

"Sir, we have been working with two senior advocates since the start of this inquiry."

"You have?" Hale exclaimed, knowing nothing of the set up

"Have you not been getting updates?"

"No. Bring me up to speed, please. Your office."

An hour later, as the Chief Constable was about to leave, David McConnell and Chloe Agnew arrived. Barlow carried out introductions.

"Come to my office when you've finished here, please," Hale said to the advocates. "I'm going to get hold of the Deputy Chief Constable."

Chief Constable Hale knocked on the door of his Deputy. "Come in."

"Sir," quickly getting to his feet.

"Peter, sit down. We have to talk."

It didn't take them a long time to decide; Harrison first called Barlow and asked for him and Jenkins to come to his office, then McGrory.

As McGrory entered the Deputy Chief Constable's office, he was confronted by a furious Chief Constable.

"Close the door," growled Hale, trying to remain calm. He held out his right hand. "Mr. McGrory, please hand over your warrant card. You're suspended indefinitely, with immediate effect."

"What?" McGrory exclaimed, the colour draining from his face.

"Your warrant card. Now!" Hale was irate.

Taking off his warrant card from around his neck, McGrory handed it over to the boss.

"I... I don't understand." "Oh, I think you do," you're being suspended pending further criminal inquiries into the abuse of females under the age of sixteen."

There was a knock at the door as Barlow and Jenkins arrived.

"Please escort Mr. McGrory from the building, gentlemen."

"Yes, sir," Barlow replied.

"Can I at least get my jacket?" requested an ashen McGrory.

Barlow looked at the Chief, who nodded.

"I'm going to need your car park authorisation, too." McGrory handed it over in silence.

As the lift descended to the basement car park, McGrory could not help but add one last, snide remark.

"You know this will go nowhere, gentlemen. A total waste of public money and police time."

"Good luck sir,"

McGrory closed his car door and drove out onto the busy city street, wondering how he was going to explain to his wife that he was suspended.

"Bingo!" Andy exclaimed at the TV.

"Who've you got now?"

"Danny Brown with a young boy and girl."

"You want this one, huh Andy?"

"Yes… but it's the boss's decision who gets what." The words felt strange coming out of Andy's mouth. Not bad, just unfamiliar.

At noon, Watt rubbed his eyes, "Okay guys, let's switch off the machines, we need a break."

Barlow saw them leaving the office, "Where are you all going?"

"Down to a café, if that's okay with you, sir?" Watt replied.

"Yeah, sure. Take as much time as you need."

"Thanks, we'll be back in an hour."

Later that afternoon, Barlow called Fiona Gallagher and arranged to meet her at their old haunt, the Café de Paris at three o'clock. They sat in a quiet corner, steam rising from their two coffees.

"Boss," Gallagher started, addressing him in her usual manner, "I know exactly what your inquiry is about now. Your team has provoked a lot of angst among some serious people."

"I'm aware, but we have a duty to those kids, and you know I don't care whose feathers I ruffle."

"The thing is… Galloway and Mulholland were sent to break into your office last night. Fortunately, or unfortunately, depending on how you look at it, your Jenkins forgot his house keys and went back to the office to get them, so they had to call the job off after he challenged them and had them identify themselves. Now, it doesn't take a rocket scientist to work out on whose instructions they were acting."

"How do you know this?" Barlow sipped his coffee, looking at her over the rim of the mug.

"Let's just say I had a word with those concerned. Their remit was to get all the tapes and make them disappear, and, before you ask, they have written out their statements to that effect."

Barlow carefully put the cup on the desk.

Gallagher laughed. "Boss, please take care. This is not over." She got to her feet. "Thanks for the coffee."

When she left, Barlow reflected on her comment, tapping his finger on the table rhythmically, as he often did when deep in thought.

At four o'clock, Watt went into Barlow's office.

"What can I do for you?" looking up from his desk.

"Andy and I want to go after Daniel Brown, sir."

"When?"

"Immediately, if possible. We have a feeling he might do a runner, now that McGrory's been suspended."

"Can we get him into court in the morning?"

"Going with what's on the video, that should be doable."

"I see no reason why not to go get him then."

"Thank you," eyes wide and bright. He turned to go when another idea occurred to him. "Sir, when everyone else has been remanded in custody, why was McGrory allowed to walk today?"

"Don't worry. We're going to get him for everything, including conspiracy to pervert the course of justice." Watt looked at him quizzically. "Watch this space," Barlow looked down at papers on his desk.

Chapter Twenty-Eight

A t six o'clock in the evening, Watt and Andy made their way out of the city to the plush suburbs on the south side, Andy was quiet, realising that he had not seen Catherine for days. Friday was fast approaching, and they were supposed to be moving into their new house. He had done nothing about it since receiving the keys. More than the panic of moving, he missed her. He had gotten used to waking up beside her every morning.

"Andy, this one is yours," as they arrived at their destination. "Just remember to stay calm. No throwaway lines."

"Yes, sir," taking in the large, newly-built brick villa. "Wow, nice house." Semi-circular stairs led up to an oak front door with curved, frosted glass side panels. A large red Jaguar sat in the driveway at the entrance to a double garage. Personal number plates reading DB 42 were fixed to the front and rear of the vehicle.

The doorbell chime sounded in the hallway and within seconds the door swung open. Daniel Brown, who had confronted Andy at his brother's funeral, stood before him. Brown's eyes narrowed when he saw Blackmore. He was wearing his business suit, with a sky-blue shirt and dark tie. He held the evening newspaper.

"Daniel Brown? I'm ADC Blackmore and this is Detective Inspector Watt."

"I know who you are," he snapped.

"Yes, I remember we spoke in the Remembrance Garden at my brother's funeral." Andy paused.

"I hope you remember what I said to you," Brown growled.

"Oh yes, I remember," Andy replied calmly. "May we come in, sir? We need to speak to you."

"What about?"

"Let's just say I don't think you will want your wife to overhear this conversation."

Brown looked taken aback by this. "Come into the lounge. You have five minutes. I'm going out shortly."

"You certainly are," Andy quipped, earning a sideways glance from Watt.

Once they were sat in a grand lounge complete with leather armchairs and bookshelves lining the walls, Andy cleared his voice and began

"Sir, you have been implicated in some serious sexual offences which we wish to interview you about. You have a couple of options. I can either arrest you right now and detain you for up to six hours, or you can come with us voluntarily. Your choice."

Just then, a woman strolled in and started at the sight of Andy and Watt. "Who are these men, Daniel?"

"They're police officers, dear. Gentlemen, this is my wife, Frances."

Frances Brown was a small, plump woman with permed grey hair. She wore a cream blouse, brown cardigan, tweed skirt, and a pair of well-worn slippers, Andy's heart went out to her; her world was about to come crashing down.

"Is something wrong?". "Is this to do with you being Chairman of the Police and Fire Committee?"

"No dear. They're making some spurious allegations against me, but it will all be sorted soon."

"What kind of allegations?"

"I'll tell you when I get home later."

"Oh, do you have to go with them? Can they not do it here?"

"No, Mrs Brown," Andy interjected. "I'm sorry, but this has to be done at the office."

"Well, don't be late." Frances Brown kissed her husband on the cheek and rubbed his shoulders with the palms of her hands. "And put your jacket on, it could get cold."

"Blackmore," Danny muttered once his wife left the room, "I made you a promise at the crematorium and I mean to keep it. So, you better have evidence, and that goes for you too Inspector."

"Have you made up your mind then?"

"Will you be coming with us voluntarily?"

"Yes, but I want my lawyer present."

"Certainly."

When they arrived at the office, Andy got out of the car first.

"This way, Mr. Brown." Andy led him into the building and to the interview room.

"Gentlemen, let's not mess around," Danny Brown was confident, sitting down with a huff. "You have no evidence against me."

"I've contacted your lawyer as requested," Watt informed him, ignoring his comment.

"When will he get here?"

"Because you're here voluntarily, he has declined to attend. But should your circumstances change, he would like to be informed. Then he'll come and see you. Mr. Brown, you're about to be interviewed about having unlawful sexual intercourse with females under the age of sixteen years, in addition to indecent assaults on males at various premises over four years. You are not obliged to say anything but anything you do say shall be taken down in writing and may be given in evidence. Do you understand?"

"Yes of course I do! Do you think I'm stupid?"

"What do you know about the games nights, as they were known?"

"Nothing."

"Mr. Brown, with the permission of DI Watt, I'm going to tell you some things which may change your answer. I don't want to be here all night interviewing you." Andy looked at Watt, who nodded his approval. "We have numerous videotapes recorded at the games nights. You feature prominently in at least one, and I'm sure you're going to feature in a lot more before we get through them all." Andy and Watt watched Brown closely; like McGrory before him, his face drained of all colour as beads of sweat started to form on his brow. "So," Andy continued, "how would you like to make a voluntary statement about everything, from start to finish?"

"If I do that, I want my lawyer here."

"I'll try to get him," Watt replied.

"Why is a person in my position not being interviewed by senior officers?" Brown demanded when Watt returned. "I take it, Blackmore, that you know all about your brother and the goings-on in his life? If not, let's get that all out."

"I'm well aware of what he was up to, but he is not here to give us his side of the story. You are." Watt was impressed with Andy for not losing his cool; he thought the mention of Ricky would surely have set him off. He was playing a blinder tonight.

When Danny Brown's lawyer, Mr. Cameron, arrived, he asked to have a word in private with Watt.

"This is DC Blackmore's inquiry."

"Mr. Blackmore, if you would," the lawyer paused making a sweeping gesture at the door, Andy followed him out into the hallway.

"So, what do you have?"

"More than enough evidence for unlawful sexual intercourse and indecent assaults."

"Really?"

"He's on video and we still have more to trawl through."

"Good thing your honest reputation precedes you. What do you want?"

"A voluntary statement."

"Will he be released?"

"Nope. Court first thing in the morning and as I'm sure you know; everyone so far has been detained in custody."

Cameron puffed out his cheeks as he ran his fingers through his hair. This small, rotund man had a fearsome reputation as a defence lawyer who always gave officers in the witness box a hard time. Even now he seemed ready to go to battle for his client. He was wearing a smart suit and, in one hand, held a brown, bulging briefcase.

"What age are the girls?"

"Between thirteen and fourteen, from care homes. The boys are about the same age."

"Boys?" Andy nodded. "I've been in this game a long time. I can read police officers like a book, and I know you're telling me the truth." Cameron sighed. "I'll advise my client accordingly."

"Thank you."

When Watt and Andy stepped outside to let Cameron speak with Brown, Watt whispered, "Cameron will tell Brown to say nothing." Andy shook his head and smiled just as the door opened.

"My client is prepared to make a full statement, gentlemen," Cameron informed them.

Because Andy and Watt were privy to certain information, they were not permitted to take the statement themselves, so a Detective Sergeant and a Detective Constable who were not connected to the inquiry were brought in to take the statement. It took several hours, from just before eight in the evening to almost midnight.

The completed statement was read back to Brown, who then signed the bottom of each page to prevent allegations of material being added following the conclusion of the proceedings, Andy had prepared a holding charge on the instructions of the Advocate while Watt oversaw the wording of the charge.

"Mr. Brown, up till now you have been here voluntarily, but you are now under arrest," Andy announced. Brown was again cautioned at common law before being charged with unlawful sexual intercourse with a thirteen-year-old female. Brown did not reply as he was searched and stripped of all personal property. He was left with only his shirt, trousers, socks, and shoes, which were placed outside his cell door. Even his black leather belt had been removed and put into his property bag.

"Wait," Brown uttered. "I need somebody to tell my wife I'm going to court tomorrow."

"I can see to that," came the duty officer.

"I would like Mr. Watt and Mr. Blackmore to do it if that's alright. I know they will treat her with respect."

"What do you want me to tell her?" Andy spoke up.

"Everything."

"Are you sure?"

"Yes, everything please," a forlorn Brown quietly bowed his head.

The final indignity for Brown was having the cell door slam shut behind him and hearing the other inmates instantly start at his arrival.

"Hey pal, whit are ye in for?" one of them shouted.

His life as a businessman, councillor, and Chairman of the Police and Fire Committee was over.

As Mr. Cameron picked up his briefcase, he looked at Andy and Watt.

"I think you will be getting a few pleas of guilty on this one gents, and Blackmore, for one so young in service you appear to have a great future ahead of you in this job. Well, at least until you cross me in court."

"Thank you, sir. I'll make sure I'm not too hard on you," Andy replied with a smile, earning a wry smile from Cameron as he walked away.

"I'm sure our paths will cross again Mr. Blackmore," he commented halfway down the hallway, his voice echoing up to Andy and filling him with a keen sense of anxiety he was not accustomed to.

Once Cameron left, Watt and Andy went back to the office. They were both shattered, as it had been a very long day. They still had to break the news of Mr. Brown's arrest to his wife before the night was over.

"Well Andy, I must commend you on your demeanour tonight and the way that you have handled everything," as they drove back to

Brown's house. "Now, there's one last job for you. Breaking the news to Mrs. Brown."

As Andy was doing this, he treated her in a manner he would have wanted his mother to be treated. There was no easy way to tell someone that their spouse of over thirty years had betrayed them in such an unbelievable fashion. Mrs. Brown was left with the task of telling her two daughters and son that their father was in jail and the reasons why he was there.

"We'll see ourselves out, Mrs Brown, I'm so sorry we had to bring you this news." She just nodded.

As the officers opened their car doors to leave, they a piercing scream burst from the living room and filled the night air, followed by uncontrollable sobbing. The world that Mrs Brown and her family had known was no more. Up until now, they were a respected family, but in the future, they would be known only for the horrible legacy Danny had left them with.

Chapter Twenty-Nine

A t the morning meeting, the first question from Barlow was, "Where's Andy?"

"Sir, he didn't finish until after three this morning, so I told him to come in at midday," Watt explained.

"Well, Watt, you're much older than him and you're here," Barlow teased with a smile.

"Listen," Watt continued, "while we're all here and Andy's not, I want to say that he was brilliant last night. How he dealt with Daniel Brown, the way he handled his lawyer, and the empathy he showed Mrs Brown when breaking the news to her, all of it was commendable."

"That's good to hear. Bodes well for the future."

Just then, the office door opened, and Andy walked in.

"I thought you were coming in later," Barlow remarked.

"I figured we have work to do. I couldn't get to sleep anyway. I don't think I will be able to 'til we finish this thing"

"Right, then go with Watt and get some tapes done. But I want both of you out of here by one."

"Jesus Andy, have you looking in the mirror this morning," Sharon remarked "When are you moving to your new house?"

"Tomorrow morning."

"Good luck!"

"Cheers."

As the tapes started to play, Andy and Watt tried to remain stoic at the sights of abuse and the equally terrible sounds of ecstatic shouting and wild laugher as the abusers' made demands from their young victims.

"Kerry baby, over here," an out of view man called, Andy's heart skipped a beat, and he sucked in a breath. He knew that name. Worse yet, he knew that voice. He could feel Watt's eyes on him as a scantily clad Kerry Ferguson entered the frame and sauntered across the room in the video, smiling, eyes empty.

"Yeah, just like that," the voice spoke again. There was no doubt in Andy's mind; it was his brother who had called her over, Andy prayed that the camera would not reveal Ricky, as he would have to identify him to Watt. No doubt they would feature in one of the tapes, especially Kerry, as she had been much in demand while in care.

Andy and Watt finished their shift early that afternoon and were about to leave when there was a knock at the office door. As always, nobody was permitted access, so Chris Harvey opened the door.

"May I come in?" Chief Constable Hale asked. His Deputy was also with him.

"I'll ask the boss," Chris replied.

Moments later, Barlow approached the door.

"We need to speak, Detective Chief Superintendent."

"Sure, come on in, sir. You too Mr. Harrison."

Everyone in the room got to their feet in the presence of the Chief and his Deputy. Rather than go into Barlow's office, they stood in the middle of the main office floor.

"Please sit down." "No need to stand on ceremony for me."

The Chief Constable looked at each of the officers in turn as he carefully considered his words. With everyone's attention focused on him, Hale sombrely began to speak.

"A short time ago, I received a phone call from Chief Superintendent Hall in Y Division. His officers received a call to go to the home of Assistant Chief Constable Ralph McGrory about half-past seven this morning. Mr. McGrory was found dead in his bed. The police casualty surgeon believes that he died of a heart attack. A post-mortem will be carried out in the next few days. Mr. McGrory was, in days gone by, an excellent police officer, belying his private life, which none of us was aware of, other than those he was involved with." Andy could not help but scoff. Hale paused, eyeing Andy, before he continued. "I do not doubt that he will feature in this inquiry as time goes by, so I'm therefore offering you my full support to get to the truth of everything that went on at the games nights. I do not know what Mrs McGrory knows or how much he told her, but I'll find out shortly when Mr.. Harrison and I visit her. Thank you all for your attention." He looked at Barlow. "Detective Chief Superintendent, a few minutes of your time, then I'll let you and your team get on with their work."

Barlow showed Hale and Harrison into his office and closed the door.

"See you guys on Monday," Andy called as he left the office. When he arrived home, he called Catherine.

"Hello?"

"My name is Andrew Blackmore and I haven't seen my girlfriend, who I love very much, for several days due to a shit working life, and I don't know if she remembers me."

"She has vague memories of you." Catherine laughed.

"That's great to hear, because she's the only person I trust, and I need to speak with her urgently."

"Barry's here, so should I come to your place?" "Yeah, great."

When Catherine arrived at Andy's, they sat together on the couch.

"Okay, here we go," Andy started. "First of all, what I'm going to tell you is to get this out of my system. Secondly, it is confidential. You really shouldn't know this, and it can never be discussed." Catherine just looked down at Andy, whose head rested on her lap as he stared at the ceiling. She gently stroked his hair.

Over the next hour, Andy offloaded everything he knew about Richard and those he was connected to.

"Oh Andy, what a mess. What can I do to help?"

"You're doing it now. You know how difficult it is for me to share — and what I want is for us to be able to share and to support one another."

Catherine pulled Andy close and kissed him on the cheek.

Andy, sat up, "now then, I have a pile of boxes to pack and a van to collect in the morning for the big move into our new place."

"Will you be okay here on your own?" preparing to leave.

Standing up he answered, "oh aye, I'll be just dandy."

Andy winked and pulled her into his arms.

A short time later, memories came flooding back as Andy packed up his spare belongings; The time he had spent there with Susan and Catherine respectively. Joining the police. Homesickness. Parties with friends. This had been a good home, but now he was about to start on a new adventure with Catherine by his side. A few hours later, Andy's flat was looking bare; everything he owned was packed away.

Early the next morning he collected a box van from a rental agency and drove it back to his flat, luckily finding a parking space where he did not have to carry the laden boxes too far from his flat.

Once he was back in his living room, surveying the scene and dreading the task at hand, there was a knock at his door. *A visitor is the last thing I need,* he thought as he answered the door.

"Hey big man," June exclaimed, all smiles as she pulled him into a hug. "We hope that you have a huge takeaway for us, as we're giving up our day off to help you move." June laughed "You definitely meant to arrange it for this weekend, didn't you?" June swatted at his shoulder.

"We?" Andy murmured, rubbing his eyes.

As he looked out onto the landing, he noticed a group of familiar faces from his shift.

"Why are you all doing this?"

"It's tradition, Andy! We all muck in at times like this." "Right, the sooner this gets done, the sooner the carry-out gets consumed," replied Andy gleefully, earning a cheer from his colleagues. His friends.

A few hours later, all his worldly goods were moved into the new house, dozens of boxes scattered around the various rooms when Catherine and Barry arrived with a bottle of champagne.

"What the hell?" she shrieked looking at Andy's shift en-masse with a huge smile on her face. "June?"

"Catherine, when one of us move house we all move house. It's a team effort."

"Looks like I am going to marry his whole shift, as if he is not enough to contend with." Catherine laughed and then shrieked as the cork exploded from the champagne bottle, which Barry was holding, looking sheepish.

Andy and his shift all stood together with Catherine and Barry, raising their glasses in a toast. Faces turned on him expectantly. In a matter of seconds, all the weight of the past months began to fade.

"Here is to the future, we shall always be one, forever."

Epilogue

As the final boxes of evidence were sealed with heavy-duty duct tape, Barlow gathered his team for one last time in the main office. Two bottles of whisky were on the table, along with a tumbler for everyone. There was a knock at the door, which Chris Harvey answered. A young police officer handed him a tray of sandwiches and cakes that Barlow had ordered from the canteen.

The team was at their desks, which they had occupied for almost a year, and at this moment in time there was a finality about the whole process. Barlow got to his feet, a large whisky in his right hand. He looked into the glass, as if to summon some courage, or inspiration.

"Ladies and gentlemen," he began. "In all my years of police service, this has been one of the most difficult and distressing inquiries. Being the so-called boss on this one has been difficult, especially as the father of two teenage children. I cannot begin to imagine what those kids have been through. The damage could be irreparable. What has been a big letdown personally is that I believed in this job. That we are here to guard, watch and patrol; to protect life and property… but we failed those kids. To have senior police officers and others in positions of trust involved in this scandal has been eye-opening, to put it lightly. This little team has been one of the best I have ever worked with, and I'll tell you why. You guys have had to go out there and listen to those kids telling their stories about the abuse they faced. You have had to view the tapes with all the horrors contained in them and you have my total admiration. I have investigated some horrendous murders, but this has been above and beyond what any human being should have to deal with. I'm glad that Mr. McConnell and Ms Agnew have been able to join us today, as they have been an important part of this team. Their expert knowledge of the law was invaluable."

Barlow paused and looked into his glass.

"To my DCI and friend, Donald Jenkins, and my DI, Alan Watt, thank you both for your support from day one. DS Frank Wallace, thank you for overseeing the daily running of the inquiry. I know that being a Sergeant is probably one of the hardest ranks in this job. Lindsay, Grant, and Sharon, I do not even know where to start thanking you guys for all the hard work you have put into this inquiry. For pushing my budget to its limits with your overtime claims…" Barlow winked at the officers and raised his tumbler in a toast. "Thank you. Big Chris, the legend, the intel man. Do you think I go about here with my eyes and ears shut? The commissionaire told me about the day Chris took possession of the envelope containing information on Salamon. He said it was like something out of a Bond movie, with a leather-clad, helmeted biker delivering the information. Then I was accused of running a betting syndicate up here, as Chris told a senior officer that the envelope contained betting tips for that day's horse racing. Well, there was only ever gonna be one winner in this race and that was us. Amanda, the only non-police officer in the room, you have honestly been amazing. I'll always treasure your support of the guys in this team and for everything you have done."

A firm knock at the door interrupted Barlow just as he was getting into the full flow of things. Chris opened the door to Chief Constable Hale and Deputy Chief Constable Harrison. Their eyes immediately focused on the refreshments and small buffet. Drinking on duty was a disciplinary matter and everyone there knew they would be in bother for it.

"Mr. Barlow," came from Hale in a commanding tone. "I trust all your officers are off duty?"

"Yes, sir. We finished about an hour ago."

"Well, if you have two more glasses, Mr. Harrison and I have also finished for the day."

Barlow looked around. "Sorry sir, I only have a couple of mugs left."

"Mr. Barlow," interrupted Chief Constable Hale. "If you are referring to Mr. Harrison and I, your career is over, you do realise that?" A few ooohs and ahhhs reverberated around the room, followed by laughter; with Hale and Harrison joining the company, Barlow continued.

"The only person I haven't mentioned in this inquiry yet is Andy Blackmore. As you all know, Andy was instrumental in bringing this whole inquiry to the fore. He was the link to almost everything we did, Andy, you can be proud of what you have done for the kids." He locked eyes with Andy, who smiled at him. Barlow was stunned for a moment. He did not think he had seen Andy smile like that before; it was neither a gloating smile nor a cocky one. It was strained, but it was genuine. Barlow could not help but return the gesture. Then, he looked at each officer in the room with that same grin. "Thank you everyone. This inquiry is now officially closed." There was a moment's silence before a round of applause broke out.

Andy would always believe that this was just the tip of the iceberg, and, in the coming years, more atrocities would surface. A separate inquiry was held, which investigated the actions of the staff at the children's homes; many staff resignations were accepted as a way of reducing the impact on the public inquiry. Daniel Brown appeared before the High Court in Edinburgh on numerous charges relating to the sexual abuse of males and females. He was sentenced to ten years' imprisonment. His wife divorced him, and his business and reputation were left in tatters. Others who were identified from the videos received sentences of between two- and five years' imprisonment.

A few weeks later Andy received a personal letter with an update:

Dear Andy,

I just wanted you to know what happened to everyone involved, just so you have some closure.

Graham Barlow got his wish and was promoted to Assistant Chief Constable (Crime) and moved to Force Headquarters. He oversaw many serious crime inquiries before his retirement.

Jenkins, Watt, and Wallace all moved up one rank; Jenkins was promoted to Detective Superintendent, Watt to Detective Chief Inspector, and Wallace to Detective Inspector. They were all transferred to various Divisions within the force.

Detective Constable Lindsay O'Donnell returned to his division, as did Detective Constable Grant McLean.

Detective Constable Sharon McLeod's contribution to the inquiry was noted at the highest level and she was promoted to Detective

*Sergeant; the first in a series of promotions for
her in the coming years.*

*Amanda Carson's contribution was noted for her
detailed accuracy, and she was spirited away to
the Crown Office where she worked alongside
Chloe Agnew.*

*Kerry Ferguson graduated from St Andrews
University with a first-class Honours degree and
went on to become a successful schoolteacher. As
Susan had been an inspiration to her, she became
an inspiration to a new generation of pupils.*

*Marie, who mysteriously disappeared from the
Golden Thistle, was never seen again in The
Rooftop Bar. She moved abroad very soon after
the raid. Everyone lost touch with her but we have
a sneaking suspicion where she was relaxing.*

*Hope you are very happy with Catherine and
Barry; and that you have a long contented
married life.*

A friend.

Andy and Catherine set up home together after Barry moved into his
one-bedroom, sheltered housing property. Catherine sold her flat after
she and Andy got married, Andy decided that, though he had friends
from the east-end going back many years, Barry was to be his best man
at their wedding. He kept his promise to June; her name was first on the
guest list, followed by the rest of his shift.

Alice sold her family home and moved into a modest bungalow, and
gave Andy his share from the sale of his mother's house that his brother
would have denied him. Despite everything she had been through, she
got her career as a successful lawyer back on track. Annie and Alfie
stayed at the same primary school to give them some continuity. Andy
and Catherine continued to see them as often as possible. Andy's mother,

lived out the remaining years of her life in the nursing home, before dying peacefully in her sleep.

Over the next few years, Catherine advanced at the hospital to the role of Ward Sister and beyond, while Andy passed his promotion exams and was promoted to Sergeant in the city centre. His career slowly began to take shape. His first day seemed like a lifetime ago, yet he still had a burning ambition to return to Bankvale someday; no longer serving as a novice officer, but to run the place. This was the beginning of life as a Sergeant, and the end of Constable Andy Blackmore.

Ranking of Police Officers

CC	Chief Constable
ACC	Assistant Chief Constable
ADC	Acting Detective Constable
DCS	Detective Chief Inspector
DI	Detective Inspector
DS	Detective Sergeant
DC	Detective Constable
Div. Com	Divisional Commander
Intel	Intelligence.
Insp	Inspector
Sgt	Sergeant
SIO	Senior Investigating Officer

Glaswegian

Aboot -	About
Ah've -	I have
Aff -	Off
Dunno -	Do not know
Faintin -	Fainting
Fer -	For
Naw -	No
No -	Not (no going to do it)
Telt -	Told
Tout -	A person who secretly provides information to the police or a police officer
Whit dae -	What do
Worthy -	A person possessed of good qualities.
Wummin -	Woman
Ya -	You

Japanese Phrases

Karategi -   Formal Japanese name for the suit used in
              competition or practice

Dojo -   The room or the hall where martial arts are practised

Sensei -   A teacher

Kata -   A system of training exercises in karate or other
              martial arts

About the Author

Born in the northeast of Scotland Simpson moved to Glasgow in the late 1950s spending his formative years in the East-end of Glasgow. His working life was spent in the civil service, forming life-long friendships with those in the Emergency Services. It was those friendships and a love of writing that led him to create this series while he enjoys the quiet life he returned to in the northeast of Scotland.

Other Works by this Author

Available Novels

Andy Blackmore Series:
An Officer's Tale
The Secondment

&

The Publisher

New Releases

&

Coming Soon

From this Author

Please Visit

JasamiPublishingandProductions-CIC.org

Simpson Munro

Printed in Great Britain
by Amazon